Embellishment

A Fake-Dating, Best-Friends Hockey Romance
Romance
Ella Haines

LIBRA LIBROS LLC

Contents

Warning: This book contains content such as swearing, a deceased father due to drunk driving, a resulting PTSD-like relationship with alcohol, and **steamy sexy times**. *If* you have triggers – please see the Author's Note page or Content Warning at the end for more details.

This is a work of fiction. Names, characters, places, and incidents are the product of the author's imagination. Any resemblance to actual persons, living or dead, events, or locales is entirely coincidental. It warrants repeating: this is a work of fiction. Made up. Fabricated. Not real. Suspend your disbelief and just enjoy the ride. Some things may be inaccurate. Police procedurals. Medical processes. The mental wanderings of a fictional character. I try to be as accurate as I can during the time of writing: I research, I collaborate, and reach out to professionals. But at the end of the day, this is fiction, so sometimes I need to draw a line and keep getting words on a page.

Just go with it and enjoy the story in the spirit it was intended. Two flawed people falling in love.

First edition June 2024

Cover designed by Get Covers

Edited by Des at Imagination Pen Editorial

Proofread by Markups by Mackenzie

ISBN 978-1-956865-55-4 (Paperback)

ISBN 978-1-956865-49-3 (Ebook)

Published by Libra Libros LLC

Springfield Cyclones: Roster & Coaches

Team Roster

Teemu Werner, #45, Goalie
Brian Thompson, #30, Goalie
Henrick Langstrom, #5, Defenseman
Patrick Conley, #6, Defenseman
Ilya Sergechev, #33, Defenseman **(C)**
David Kasselbeck, #29, Defenseman
Benjamin Wilder, #21, Defenseman
Max Van der Beek, #25, Defenseman
Dale Cartwright, #27, Defenseman
Paul Owens, #22, Defenseman
Bobby Davidson, #17, Right Wing **(A)**
Ian Novac, #19, Left Wing
Ty Daniels, #37, Center
Jason Miller, #99, Right Wing
Mitchell Collins, #2, Left Wing
Tommy Kolbeck, #77, Center
Pavel Savic, #87, Right Wing
Christian Rudiger, #46, Left Wing
Jonathan Chamberlain, #88, Center
Vladimir Savic, #18, Right Wing
Derrick Bergeron, #42, Left Wing
Evan Frazier, #49, Center

Duke Grammar, #53, Goalie

Coaches

John Montgomery, Head Coach
Dennis Savuk, Assistant Coach
Casey Spencer, Assistant Coach
Scott Zachar, Assistant Coach

Author's Note About Content Warnings

See list of content/trigger warnings here on my site at www.EllaHaines.com/Triggers

The list is also found at the end of the book through the table of contents

WARNING: will possibly contain plot spoilers by nature of disclosing – proceed as you are comfortable

About

Secret Crushes, Sizzling Chemistry, and a Fake Romance That Feels All Too Real

***

Thea Sharppe doesn't believe in giving up on her goals, no matter how daunting they may seem. With top brand endorsements under her belt and leading the Ice Crew, she's set her sights on becoming the first female Rinkside Reporter for the Springfield Cyclones. But there's one more challenge on her checklist: capturing the attention of Ian Novak, the team's star forward, whom her late father believed was her perfect match. However, when Ian appears more focused on outdoing Bobby Davidson—Thea's best friend on the team—Thea devises a fake dating scheme to provoke Ian's competitive nature. Despite Bobby's initial reluctance, he knows Thea's determination all too well and finally agrees.

***

Bobby is every hockey fan's 'old reliable'. They want him on the ice in overtime, but they don't necessarily draft him first in their fantasy leagues. He's charming, yet humble; intelligent, yet unassuming; and successful, yet approachable. Above all, he's Thea's rock and will do anything to make her happy—even if it means ripping his own heart to shreds while winning her the attention of the self-centered Ian Novak.

***

As the lines blur between reality and pretense, Thea stands at a crossroads where each path demands a sacrifice of a part of her identity.

Will she honor her father's dream for her, or break free from predetermined expectations to follow her heart?

CHAPTER ONE

March 24, Wednesday afternoon
Thea

Why couldn't he just *see* her?!

Naked, preferably.

But clothed would work too.

Anything, really.

Ian Novak just needed to freaking notice her in a non-platonic, I-need-to-ask-her-out-now kind of way.

Thea Sharppe leaned against the cold railing at the edge of the ice rink, her breath fogging as she watched the Springfield Cyclones wrap up their practice. Her heart raced with anticipation; she could feel the energy in the air, electric and alive.

It was the final month of the regular season before playoffs.

The hum of the Zamboni warming up behind her signaled that the team's practice was coming to an end. Soon it would be her turn on the ice to practice her dance routine as a member of the Cyclones Ice Crew: The Chill Chasers. The hum of laughter and conversation behind her, coming from her teammates, droned on intelligibly as she watched the hockey team work through their final drills.

She watched Ian's harsh movements as he churned across the ice, his dark hair glistening with sweat, flattened under his helmet. She imagined the flexing of muscles in his legs as he pushed off from one skate to another. Her stomach fluttered, and she fantasized what it would be like to be the reason for the intensity that lived in his dark, brown eyes.

She blew out a scoff that made the plexiglass in front of her steam up.

Yeah, right.

Ian was focused on nothing but hockey, hockey, and more hockey.

Well, that...and competing with Bobby Davidson.

That brought a smile to her face.

Bobby and Thea became friends two and a half years ago—not long after her dad had died in a car accident. He was her *best* friend in the whole wide world...and he absolutely *hated* that Thea had a thing for Ian. Bobby thought Ian was a first-degree schmuck.

It didn't matter how many times Thea teased and tried to explain the allure of bad boys, and the popular fantasy of being 'The One' who could reach out and fix one.

Bobby would dive into how much of a dick Ian was, asking how she could possibly think there was a good guy in there somewhere.

It was a familiar dance. Thea would ask for examples of how terrible Ian truly was. Bobby would give them. And then Thea would point out that all of Ian's dickishness was aimed at Bobby, no one else, and how it seemed to be a personal problem. Then, it would end with Bobby telling her she was being a complete fool for harboring a crush on 'Ian the ice-hole' before huffing and retreating back into whatever book he was currently reading.

Bobby was clearly biased and just missing something about Ian—there had to be *something* special in him, just waiting to be coaxed out.

Otherwise, why would her father have made a note in his journal about Ian being her soulmate? Her dad had worked and interviewed *hundreds* of incredible athletes in his career. And never once had he tried to set her up with any of them—sometimes to her disgruntlement—until Ian. So why would her dad have wanted Thea and Ian to date if Ian was truly as irredeemable as Bobby promised? He wouldn't have. Period. Her dad *knew* her better than anyone—and if he said Ian was the guy for her...then he was. Simple.

Bobby was clearly letting their rivalry color his opinion.

He needed to put down the escapism books and mingle more. Find someone. Get laid. Then he'd remember what it felt like to long for someone and not even be noticed. At this point, he'd probably been celibate for so long that he forgot what it was like to have butterflies around the person who made his heart wiggle.

At least, she assumed it was that. She'd certainly never heard him talk about any women in his life…Thea made a note to get a date scheduled for Bobby on her mental to-do list. Not like a his-future-wife quality date, but like, maybe someone who also liked to read.

The thought made her stomach tighten.

Meh. Maybe not.

The coach issued a few sharp whistles and like a school of freaking fish, the men changed direction on the ice and players were swapped out. The lines were all jumbled and Thea tried to make sense of it.

Why in the world was he having Tommy on the first line with Ty and Ian? Where the hell was Bobby?

She scanned the ice furiously for her best friend. Her eyes skid to a stop, and her breath froze.

On the bench?

Bobby was on the bench!?

He was *always* first line!

What the fuck, Coach?

Thea gritted her teeth as she watched the men cycle through their drill. Two sharp whistles later and the second forward line switched out. Thea watched Bobby explode over the boards, sprinting from his spot on the bench, his signature intensity shown in every harsh thrust of his skates.

Unlike Ian's punishing skating technique, there was a smoothness to Bobby's that always made her think he'd do well on the Chill Chasers with her and the rest of the Ice Crew.

Another opinion of Thea's that irritated him to no end.

Especially because he tended to be a *wee* bit too violent on the ice.

Was that why he was bumped down to the second line?

Sure, Bobby had been in a bit more fights this year, but the team had a good streak going, and if the bruisers on the team weren't going to make a statement, *someone* had to. It wasn't anything new; that sort of attitude and dedication is what earned him the A on his sweater.

Bobby had stepped up and made sure his team wasn't being pummeled. It wasn't common to see a winger on the first line take on the enforcer role...and yet, he had done it to protect his team. Because that's what an alternate captain did; they took on roles that they wouldn't normally assume to get the job done.

And now he was being punished for it?

That was bullshit!

Her heart pumped loudly in her ears, and she rolled her head to elicit a loud crack from the tension crawling up her neck. Thea chewed on her thumbnail as she watched the drill unfold, her frustration with Coach Montgomery's treatment of Bobby rising like lava in her chest.

Lila, her roommate and fellow Chill Chaser, stepped up beside her. "Guess our practice is starting late?"

"So, it would seem," Thea muttered back, refusing to take her eyes off the drill in front of her. Even the Zamboni had shut off at this point. Practice would be done when it was done, schedule be damned.

Three short whistles and the forward lines rotated again. Thea watched as Bobby sprinted off the ice and the third line erupted out.

"Damn, the defense has to be dragging."

"Mmm," Thea hummed in agreement, replaying the most recent games in her head. The defense had been looking a little gassed out there during the third periods lately.

"Is this their punishment for the OT loss last week?"

Lila, bless her heart, enjoyed hockey for the sake of it. It was what it was, and it was entertaining. That was enough.

Thanks to her dad, Thea was a *little* more analytical. Which was why she was an absolute shoe-in for the on-ice reporter job that was opening up. She could pass the torch as Captain of the Chill Chasers and start living up to the legacy that her father expected of her. Thea's interview last week was as smooth as Zamboni-cleaned ice, and now she was just waiting for the offer to drop. There was no way that they'd pass her up...she hoped.

"This drill's design seems centered on building not just physical endurance, but mental acuity," Thea mused, her gaze fixed on moving players. "By emphasizing continuous shifts in defensive positioning and quick transitions from defense to offense, it's targeting not only the players' physical stamina but also their ability to read the offense and anticipate." Thea shifted her weight slightly, her mind already processing the possible implications of this particular drill. "It actually pairs well with the upcoming matchups—all of whom have fast and fierce forward lines..." Thea spit out a piece of her nail that she'd torn off and tucked her hands into her sweatshirt to prevent more nervous nibbling. "Doesn't explain Bobby being bumped—however slight it may seem—though..."

Lila shot her a curious glance, but Thea remained focused on the tactical intricacies of the drill.

Several rotations later and the first line was changed—now Ian was bumped to second and Bobby had moved up to the first line.

Thea couldn't stop her small grin.

'Atta boy.

Though...too bad for Ian.

Maybe he'd want a sympathetic shoulder to cry on after practice.

If only he knew she existed. Sure, he flirted with the best of them. But that was it. Flirting.

She needed the opportunity to prove to him what a fucking bombshell-catch she was, damnit!

Was that so hard?

The fantasy of taming the notorious bad boy with a secret heart of gold had her mind drifting as she watched the coach gather the men around him at center ice. The Zamboni roared to life just as the coach gave a piercing final whistle, signaling the end of practice. The men dispersed. Ian coasted over to the home bench and exited the rink.

Guess she wouldn't be getting a flyby smile as he exited the tunnel today.

Thea sighed, disappointment settling in her chest. Lila gave a chuckle and a pat to Thea's back before moving to sit on a side bench and put on her skates.

As other members of the Ice Crew popped open the Zamboni gate, Thea stepped back and watched as the Zamboni started making its loops around the ice.

Maybe if she posed naked on the Zamboni, Ian would notice her...

She dropped her daydream as she watched Bobby coast over to the opening in front of her and step off the ice. His smooth transition to and from the rubber flooring never ceased to amaze her.

Sure, she played hockey in college and could changeover with the best of them, but damn, Bobby made it look as easy as breathing.

There was an extra oomph of fluidity about him that she just couldn't explain.

"Hey, Thea-Bea," Bobby gave her a grin, the sweat dripping down his forehead, his helmet in his gloved hands.

"Bobbyo." She greeted back with a smile, her heartwarming at the sight of Bobby's bright eyes and gentle grin. "Looking a little slow out there today, Grandpa. Pull a hamstring again?" She nodded her head to his padded legs.

"Slow my ass. I was lightning. Though, I won't deny the hamstring was a little tender yesterday. Did you catch the last game?" Bobby leaned against the wall beside her, pulling off his gloves and lifting up his practice jersey to wipe at the sweat on his forehead. Thea was met with a wall of washboard abs and quickly looked away.

Some of his teammates continued down the tunnel shortcut past them, barking out tired greetings. She smiled back, giving them nods, and turned back to Bobby who was now working on balancing his helmet and gloves on the top of his stick, his face focused. His dark hair stuck to his forehead and his angular jaw was framed by his thick but well-groomed facial hair.

"You think I would miss it? I had five bucks that you were going to be called for boarding at some point and yet...you didn't. Not sure what you paid the refs to overlook that..." Thea teased, shaking off the weird feeling she got whenever she noticed that Bobby was actually attractive.

"If the commissioner could hear you now. Tsk, tsk. Plus, if I told you, I'd have to kill you. And I rather like you, so let's not." Bobby chuckled.

"Blind as mice. All of them." Thea rolled her eyes.

"Hey, who's side are you on?"

She scoffed but didn't answer.

Movement by the Zamboni entrance had them both turning, and Thea's heart gave a stutter. Ian had apparently changed his mind and decided that the Zamboni tunnel was the way he wanted to go to get back to the locker rooms.

Ian hopped off the ice, his steps choppy, and his gaze flickered between Thea and Bobby as they lounged against the wall. The rest of the Ice Crew was gathered across the way, idly chatting as they waited for the Zamboni to make its way slowly around the rink.

A smirk played on Ian's lips as he approached, interrupting them.

"Hey, Bobby," Ian said, his tone laced with a competitive edge. "Tell Thea about the view down on the second line. It's a lot easier to get into stupid-as-shit fights on a lower line when you don't have as many people depending on you, yeah?"

Bobby's body stiffened but his face remained carefully blank. "It's not like the second line is much different than the first—you're barking up the wrong tree with the trash talk. Plus, I haven't committed nearly as many fouls as you."

"Bullshit. Stats have you at *least* twelve minutes more than me in the season."

Thea's head ticked back and forth between the men.

Or should she call them *children*?

"Just because the refs are watching me closer," Bobby said, a small wrinkle formed between his eyebrows as he frowned at Ian.

"It's not hard to *not* be an idiot. Make better timing choices, dude. All of us are thinking it—you're letting the team down with your fucking fights. Be better."

Thea bit her lip and tried to not to let her emotion show.

The competitive streak between Ian and Bobby was non-fucking-stop. She tried to view the interaction as a good learning experience for her. If she was going to be the on-ice talent for the Cyclones' own broadcasting channel, then she needed to let the dynamics play out and keep her opinions to herself.

That is, until she saw Bobby's hand fist...

Okay, intervention time.

"Ian, to be fair, you seem to have a way of knowing exactly when the refs aren't looking. It's like a sixth sense."

"Ah, flattery will get you everywhere, Sharppe," Ian said, turning to Thea. His gaze lingered a moment longer than necessary before adding, "Especially when you're discussing hockey and all my extensive skills."

She rolled her eyes playfully, hamming it up. "Is it flattery if it's honest?"

Bobby stiffened further beside her, but she'd be damned if she didn't take advantage of this rare moment of flirting with Ian. Maybe *this* would be the time that she wooed him with her brilliance and caught his attention...

Ian nodded his head over to Bobby but kept his eyes on her. "Why do you even put up with him? He's a mopey-ass hermit. I can't imagine the conversations are riveting. What does he do for fun? Collect quarters?"

Thea chuckled and reached out to push at Ian's arm, turning up her inner flirt.

"Hey, he has one from 1922 that is in mint condition!"

Bobby glowered and crossed his arms.

Ian gave her a grin that could melt the ice. "So, you're just as wild as he is?"

She didn't collect quarters! That was *so* not the message she was trying to send.

She corrected quickly—like the broadcaster she was born to be.

"Oh God, no. I think I drive Bobby nuts with my extroverted-ness. I think I'm his pet project. He's never met a girl who won't ooh and ahh over his library before, and the fact that I won't sleep with him is a bonus—no pressure."

Ian's dark eyes darted between the two. "I've wondered... everyone always says you aren't a couple—just friends."

He said it as a statement, but there was definitely a question there.

Bobby opened his mouth, but Thea jumped in. "God, no. *Totally* not a couple. We're not each other's types."

Ian gave them an assessing look. Thea could practically sense Bobby vibrating with the need to stop this conversation and get away.

Too bad.

He was the glue that was holding this little session together. As long as he didn't talk, Ian would remain a captive audience.

"Besides, I have way different standards for my men, and we'd be a relationship disaster, ya' know? Can you imagine Olivia Pope dating Huck?"

As Thea finished her comparison, the tension in the air thickened, growing palpable between Ian and Bobby. Bobby's eyes narrowed slightly, a flicker of annoyance passing over his features at Thea's attempt at flirting. *Shit*. She probably shouldn't have compared him to Huck...

Bobby's jaw tightened imperceptibly as he fought to keep his emotions in check. He pushed off from the wall, stepping closer to where Thea and Ian were standing.

"Well, I suppose that settles it then," Ian remarked with a hint of sarcasm. "Just Miss Pope and her little lapdog."

Fuck.

Thea forced a smile, masking the unease bubbling beneath the surface. "Maybe that wasn't the best compar—"

With a curt nod, Ian turned to stride down the tunnel, his demeanor suddenly distant. "Well, I should get going. Have a good...whatever it is you two do together..."

Thea turned woodenly and watched him go, a knot of disappointment forming in her stomach. She had hoped for more from this encounter, but it seemed that tensions between Ian and Bobby were too high for anything meaningful to transpire, especially with her shitty attempt to dispel any jealousy from Ian about Bobby.

As Ian disappeared down the hallway, Thea heaved a sigh and turned to Bobby, her expression softening. "Thanks for not making things worse back there."

Bobby shrugged. "What are lap dogs for?"

Thea gave him a shove and took a close look at his face. "You know you're not Huck. I was just trying to explain to him that you and I are not each other's types. At all."

Bobby's expression shifted to one of curiosity, his brow furrowing slightly as he paused before responding, a hint of restraint evident. "Sure. I get it."

"You're not mad? You look...something."

"I look how I always look, Thea-Bea. I get it. You wanted me to keep the peace. I kept the peace. We all know how he gets when he feels like he's the target of a joke, and you wanted your moment. I get it."

Thea nodded, a sense of gratitude washing over her. Despite their personality differences, Bobby always had her back. "You're seriously not mad about my shitty comparison?"

Bobby gave her a soft chuck on the chin. "Hey, in my book group, I compare you to judgy Elizabeth Bennet all the time. We're even. There are worse things to be compared to than Huck."

The psychopath?

"Like what?"

"Heathcliff."

Heath Cliff? Who the hell was that?

Thea gave him a puzzled look, her forehead wrinkling, but Bobby was back to spinning his stick with a frown on his face.

"Bobby?"

With a short shake of his head, Bobby brushed off whatever dark thoughts were plaguing him and gave her a weak smile. "Gotta get going, Bea. Have a good practice." Without waiting for her response, Bobby made his way toward the locker room, leaving Thea alone in the dimly lit corridor. As she watched him go, she couldn't shake the thought that she had hurt his feelings. They had never been an item; not even close. But somehow...she got the vibe that her quick refusal to the idea somehow bothered him.

But as much as she wanted to dive into unpacking that, the Zamboni roared onto the gate and came back down the tunnel.

Time for her own practice.

She'd think about Bobby's somewhat less-smooth walk back to the locker room later.

CHAPTER TWO

March 24, Wednesday night
Thea

"Bobby! Open up! I brought a peace offering!" Thea kicked at the door of Bobby's upscale loft. The team owned some fancy buildings near the arena that they had converted to swanky apartments for the players. If a player didn't want to deal with the hassle of home ownership, the apartments were the next best thing. And they were the absolute shit.

It was like living in a dorm with all your best buddies, except with all the modern luxuries, including a private terrace.

Combine that with the in-house sauna, gym, indoor pool, and small convenience store on the first floor?

Heaven.

Thea kicked at the door again and shifted the bags in her arms.

When Bobby finally answered, he gave a small jolt when he saw the mountain of food in her arms. He dove in to take the majority of the bags because Thea was slow to react.

Something about seeing him in reading glasses always threw her.

A hotheaded bruiser on the ice...and a total dork off it.

She just couldn't wrap her head around it.

Bobby kicked the door open a little more, before moving toward the kitchen. Thea slid in and let the door slam shut behind her. She started kicking off her shoes, already talking.

"So, I know you said no harm done, but I was a total bitch today. I never should have said that about you. And I know all good apologies are ruined by the word 'but'..."

"But..." Bobby finished for her, grabbing two glasses from a tall cabinet and ducking into the fridge.

"But, I don't have a good excuse. Being around Ian makes my brain stupid. I was trying so hard to get him to notice me that I ended up being a total asshole to you. As much as I want to get his attention, that's no excuse. I'm sorry."

Bobby placed a tall glass of milk in front of her and tapped it with his own. "Apology accepted. Move on."

Thea rolled her lips to the side. "Yeah, but..."

Bobby gave a long-suffering groan. "You and your dramatics. I'm good, Bea. Move on, babe." Bobby moved to the bags, pulling out all the to-go boxes that Thea had picked up on her way over. "Jesus H Christ. You stop at every restaurant on the way here?"

She smiled and took his instruction to move on. "Just about." She went to a drawer on the other side of the island and started grabbing utensils. "I didn't know what you were in the mood for."

"Clearly."

"And the way to a man's heart is through his stomach." She sensed Bobby pause while he was getting down some plates. "I figured I had a lot of groveling to do to make up for my shittiness."

"Nah, I'd never make you do that, Bea. No groveling necessary. Ian's Ian. He could make a priest curse. At this point, I just figure the negativity just rolls off him and infects everyone around him. We all do shitty things in his presence. It's a compulsion." He gave her a dark look. "One of the devil's many skills."

Thea rolled her eyes and slapped some napkins down on the table next to the take-out.

"Puhh-lease. Ian's hardly the devil." At Bobby's scoff, she tossed a fortune cookie at him. "He's not! He has good in him."

"Ugh, you and your ceaseless faith and infatuation. Save me."

"Hey! He's always nice to me."

"In all *fifteen* conversations you two have had over the last three years?"

Fifteen?! Yeah, right. It was obviously more than that.

And he said *she* was dramatic.

She held up another fortune cookie and gave him a scowl in promise.

He held up a placating hand and plopped down on the high bar stool next to hers at the island, his plate piled high with an assortment of food from each of the take-out containers.

"Fine. He's been nice to you. So have I. So have all the guys on the team. I don't see you panting over Ilya."

"That's because Ilya is emotionally closed off." Thea took a bite of shrimp teriyaki rice and moaned, savoring the rich flavors. She pointed her fork at her plate and whispered to her meal, "You beautiful bitch. You are *just* what I needed tonight."

"I'm serious, Thea. You've never given me a straight answer."

Thea swallowed and took a sip of her milk, staring at the artwork on Bobby's walls. Some Spanish bridge or something, she couldn't remember what he said it was.

"It's hard to explain. My dad seemed to really like him." To put it mildly. "And then, after the accident, I read a sports piece about Ian that showed a side of him that I never knew existed." At Bobby's confused look, she waved him off. "I know, I know. It's hard to explain. But there was something about Ian orchestrating a fundraiser in my dad's honor that just spoke to me, and confirmed my dad's assumptions about him. So, I owe it to my dad and myself to see if something really is there." She shrugged.

Bobby's fork dropped onto his ceramic plate with a clatter and Thea turned to him, eyebrows raised.

"Bobby?"

He coughed hard into his hand and pivoted so he was facing the opposite direction. Then, without a word, he got up from his seat and went into the bathroom.

Panic gripped Thea's chest like a vise. Was he okay?

Thea strained to hear any sound from the bathroom, but there was only silence. Why was that more worrisome?

"Bobby?" she called, her voice tinged with concern.

The faucet was running.

Why was the faucet running?

Heart racing, Thea slid off her stool and took several quiet steps toward the bathroom, her mind racing with worst-case scenarios.

Did he choke?

Was he unconscious on the floor?

Was another person ripped from her life by a horrible accident?

Was she wasting precious moments listening for a hint of sound rather than sprinting to call 911 and trying the Heimlich?

The door was thrown open and she took a couple steps back, unsure whether to look like she was on her way to save him from a piece of errant chicken tempura.

He gave her a funny look, darted his eyes to the kitchen island, and looked back at the now-dark bathroom.

"Do you, uh, need this?"

Embarrassment burned through her body at her blatant and unmistakable overreaction.

"Bobby! What the hell?" She waved her hands frantically to signal that her urgency wasn't about the restroom. "No, I don't need to use it! I was worried sick about you! I thought you were choking or worse in there!" Taking a few steps closer, she searched his face for signs of distress. "Are *you* okay?"

He watched her back, his face conflicted. Bobby settled on a small chuckle and then chucked her chin gently with his knuckles, the fingers slightly damp. "I'm fine, Bea. Something just went down the wrong pipe. All good. Let's get back to it."

Thea watched him plop down onto his stool and couldn't shake the coiled snake that was writhing in the pit of her stomach. She thought back to their conversation. Did she say something shitty again? Thea wrung her hands together to try to get them to stop shaking. No luck.

"Thea?"

She blinked and forced herself forward, taking a deep breath to steady her nerves.

Holy fuck, what if he had been choking for real? She was *so* not prepared for that.

Out of respect for the near-miss disaster, she took much smaller bites for the rest of the meal. And scowled at Bobby's plate whenever he scooped up a too-large bite.

Playing with fire, that one.

"How's the new routine going?" Bobby asked, nudging her playfully with his shoulder. "You've been obsessing over it for weeks. The rest of the Chillers are bitching about you at the bar. They say you're working them too hard for a part-time gig."

"Hey!" Thea protested. "They all knew what they were signing up for. And the routine is going to be amazing once we get some final details figured out." Taking another small bite and swallowing, Thea continued, "But we were a little slow last month in our ice shoveling during the games. We averaged seven seconds longer than usual with that lineup of Crew members. I think it was because Brian wasn't out there." She considered it for a moment, then added, "I'll need to work on switching up lines for ice duty scraping to see if that's better. I don't want any write up from the officials going into the playoffs. If I can show a course-correction, that will work in my favor when management is making their final decisions for the reporter job. It will show that I can take feedback when I'm in my new role."

"*When?*"

Thea raised her chin, hiding her embarrassment. "When," she confirmed. "Kayla said I need to start actualizing and manifesting."

His eyebrows climbed and his eyes crinkled in amusement. "Seems a little hokey pokey, even for a shrink."

"Psychologist is the correct term." Thea narrowed her eyes on him in disapproval.

"Glutton for punishment is better. I can only imagine the shit she gets saddled with on a daily basis."

Thea stuck her tongue out at him.

He laughed and tapped her nose. "You're amazing out there, Thea. You always are. Your crew is one of the best in the league and your efforts do not go unnoticed. So, I'm sure you'll be up in the metaphorical heated seats in no time. Hey, you'll actually be able to wear clothes during the games then."

This again.

Their Chillers outfits left...little to the imagination.

"The outfits are fine, Bobby."

He raised his eyebrows but remained focused on the food on his plate.

"Bobby, I'm serious." She put down her knife before she could stab him, and turned to face him. "We get a choice on what to wear. I chose to go with a more revealing outfit. That was *my* choice."

Bobby paused, his fork mid-air, as he considered her point. "Okay, I get that it's your choice. But doesn't it bother you that the choice itself is expected to lean toward something more revealing? Isn't that playing into a stereotype?"

Thea leaned back, crossing her arms. "It might seem that way, but it's also about reclaiming our power and agency. If we feel empowered and confident in what we wear, isn't that a form of progress? We're not just ice ornaments; we're athletes, performers, and part of the entertainment. It's about owning our image, not being dictated by it."

He sighed, setting his fork down and turned to her. "Okay...but what about the message it sends to younger fans? Shouldn't there be a balance between self-expression and the implications of those choices?"

"And what does my outfit say to younger fans?" Her voice could flay his skin at the implied insult.

He gave her a weary look. "That they have to show lots of skin to get noticed. That they have to sell their bodies to move up in the world."

"Rachel wears more concealing clothing and she's doing just fine." Thea was now shaking for an entirely different reason.

Bobby just pinched his lips together and turned back to his food.

No way, he wasn't getting off the hook that easily!

"And that thinking is why we also focus on community outreach and programs that emphasize skill, dedication, and teamwork beyond just the glitz. We want to inspire, not just entertain. It's about showing all facets of what we do, not just the sparkly costumes."

With an unimpressed look, Bobby settled for, "Call me when the designers let you go out in comfortable, roomy, and *warm* clothing. Then we'll talk."

"Brian doesn't have to show skin to win over the crowd."

Bobby gave a soft chuckle and gave her a small smile. "Brian is a dude. Brian is gay. And Brian is fabulous. He could win over anyone."

"See, we're not just selling sex."

Bobby wisely kept his mouth shut.

"We're empowered to make our own choices about our costumes. We don't get penalized if we go for less-sexy outfits."

"Would your pay get affected if you *butched* up, wore baggy clothes, and stopped the signed photos and lingerie ads?"

Shit.

"People would still want photos with an Ice Crew member," Thea snapped back.

Bobby simply lifted his milk in toast and took a small sip.

"Whatever, dude. At the end of the day, it's my choice. Don't paint this into something it's not. And speaking of narratives, we've also been pushing for more inclusive representations on the crew. Like incorporating routines that highlight diverse cultures during heritage nights. It's about broadening the conversation, showing that we're a part of something bigger than just a game or a performance."

"Fine, fine. You win. It's not a 'sex sells' thing. It's purely an exhibition of skills and hard work."

Thea licked her lips and winced. She couldn't let herself get worked up like this if she wanted to be in charge of on-ice interviews. She had to try to stay neutral. See both sides...

"Well, maybe it's a bit of sex sells."

Bobby burst out laughing, milk spewing from his mouth and nose, and soaking the table in front of him.

Thea couldn't stop her own chuckle.

"Jesus Christ, Bea. Get the mood swings under control, will ya?" Bobby laughed.

Thea tossed a dishcloth that was resting on the table at him.

"I'm just trying to be bipartisan," she protested with a regal sniff.

That sent him into an entirely new roar of laughter, actually causing him to pause in mopping up so he could catch his breath.

"Fucking hell, you keep me on my toes," he muttered as he started wiping up again, using his free hand to swipe at his eyes.

Thea got off her chair and helped Bobby with tidying things up. When they finished, Bobby tossed the combination of napkins and dishcloths on the counter by the sink and sank back down onto his high stool.

"But really, the new routine is going okay?"

Thea leveled him with a sardonic look but settled onto her own stool beside him.

"It's starting out slow. Working through some kinks to get everyone on the same page. It's awesome that management is giving us ice time before and after the game to act as openers for whoever wants to come."

"The longer the people are in the arena, the more they buy."

Thea hummed in agreement. "Exactly. And we've been able to brainstorm some fun games to get the crowd a bit more engaged." Thea paused. "I think it's going to be really fun once we get it all worked out."

"Hey, did you see that triple deke Jason pulled off last week? I keep forgetting to ask you!" Bobby said, his voice fast and eyes bright. "I thought for sure I'd go back to the locker room to find a thousand texts from you roasting him for trying it during such a close game."

Thea rolled her eyes. "I'm trying to be less critical."

He grinned and Thea's heart gave a little bump at the mischief in his eyes. "Of course you're critical. You're Thea. It's who you are." He nudged her shoulder with his own. "And those who know you, know that about you, know where your heart is, and we love you anyways."

Why did he always know just what to say?

With a smile that she tried very hard not to show that she was on the edge of tears, she nudged him back with her own shoulder. "The deke was nice. But mostly I was just astounded by your slapshot from the blue line. Not really your style, Bobbyo. You surprised me."

"You and everyone else," he murmured, scraping the final food remnants from his plate. After a silent exchange, he snagged Thea's empty plate as well and made his way to the sink.

"What do you have planned for the rest of the night? Any hot dates?" Thea asked to his back as he rinsed off their dishes in the sink.

Given that he was in sweatpants, that she was trying hard not to focus on, and in his reading glasses, it was a joke more than anything else. When he hesitated, her stomach gave a dip.

What?!

Thea leaned forward in her seat to try to catch his expression. "Bobby?"

EMBELLISHMENT 21

He turned and his cheeks were slightly pink. A wet hand made its way up to rub the back of his neck, drawing her eyes to his biceps before she forced them back to his face.

Friends, friends, friends.

"Not a hot date, really. Just...maybe a lukewarm date? Hard to tell really. We're still just...trying things out."

Thea's heart started pounding as she stared at her friend.

Her shriek surprised even her own ears. Thank God the rest of his neighbors were teammates, or he'd be getting called in for a noise complaint.

"Since when are you seeing someone?!" Thea's heart was pounding out of her chest.

His cheeks turned a shade pinker, and he adjusted his glasses. "I don't know. Not long. A bit. I don't know."

"Spit it out. Not long or for a bit? Who is she?" Thea was standing now, arms outright in front of her, palms down on the countertop.

He fidgeted again and she fought back the urge to reach out and strangle him.

Spit it out, Davidson!

"Not long. We met at a book signing at the library. We started chatting about what we were reading and exchanged numbers."

"Are they dates or not, Bobby?"

Why was he dancing around the answer?

And why was she so anxious to know?

He turned on her with a dry look. "There have been a couple of dinners..."

"Jesus, Bobby!"

He shook his head. "What does it matter? So, we've been on a few dates. Why do you care?"

Why indeed.

Thea opened her mouth to answer but couldn't find the words.

Why *did* she care so much?

At her silence, Bobby sighed and rubbed at his face with both hands. Then, he looked down at his watch and his shoulders tensed.

What now?

"So, uh, she's getting off work soon and I need to meet her at the movies, but I want to shower first. Are you just going to hang out here tonight to get away from Lila or are you heading home?"

He was kicking her out?

For another woman!?

Why did she want to scream and vomit? Not necessarily in that order.

Rallying herself, she shook her head and moved to the chair where she had tossed her jacket and purse. "Nope, I'm good. I'll leave you to it."

"Thea—"

"No, it's fine. You have a date. A girlfriend even. Maybe. It's okay. It's not like we tell each other everything, right?"

Why couldn't she meet his eyes?

"The—"

With her eyes on her shoes that she had kicked so unceremoniously on the shoe mat earlier, a horrified thought struck her. Would his girlfriend be okay with her and Bobby being friends?

Would he not be allowed to talk to her?

Or hang out with her?

Grab take-out with her?

Her heart started hurting and she felt a squeezing burn in her throat.

She needed to leave.

Slipping her shoes on quickly, she bumped into the wall in her haste. Bobby's warm hand grabbed her at her elbow, preventing her from falling over.

She froze, staring at her feet, breathing hard.

"Thea. It's just a few dates. It's not like we're eloping and moving to Nebraska."

Oh, God. Was she from Nebraska? Would she want to move home once they got married? Would she lose Bobby forever except for the occasional funny Christmas or birthday card?

"Is she from Nebraska?" Her voice was high and tight.

"Jesus, Bea. Take a breath." His hands, now burning hot on her skin, turned her to face him. He moved a hand to her chin and pulled gently, forcing her to meet his eyes.

His concern melted into something kind as he stared at her.

"Thea, you're not losing me. You got me forever. Whether you want me to or not. I'm not leaving. You know how much I love," he paused and swallowed thickly, "this fucking city. I never had a home. This is my home now, and I'm dying here."

Thea winced.

Bobby mimicked her wince. "Fuck. Not what I meant." When she tried to pull away, he tightened the hold he had on her chin. "Listen to me, Sharppe. *Right now.* Your dad was *taken* from you by some dumbass drunk driver. You lost him. Then you found me. I plugged a hole, I get that. But whatever is going on with me and Lucy... you aren't *losing* me. I'm here. Forever." He gave her a little tweak of her chin. "Deal with it." With that, he let her go and took a step back, flexing his fingers slightly.

Where he had grabbed her still burned from the heat of him, making the rest of her body feel cold.

Thea sniffed as quietly as she could and squared up to face him. "She better be okay with you having a girl for a best friend."

Bobby gave her a small smile. "Wouldn't even give her the time of day if she wasn't."

Thea sniffed again and looked away, feeling the heat from his touch transition into her cheeks.

Damn. Talk about overreacting.

Maybe he was onto something about her dramatics. The thought made her lips twitch.

She lifted her chin as she met his eyes and gave him a strict nod. "Damn straight. Remember that, killer. You're not getting rid of me either."

Another small smile graced Bobby's mouth, though this time it didn't reach his dark eyes. "I'll remind you of that once you start dating Ian."

Shit.

They stared at each other for a moment, both lost in solemn thoughts.

Yeah, getting Ian and Bobby together for things would certainly pose a problem if she ever did end up convincing Ian to give her a chance.

That was fine though. Fixable. She had been through worse, and she could make it work. She would have to. There was no way she was losing Bobby; it would be like losing a limb. Ian would just have to play nice. Same with whoever this Lucy character was too.

Still reeling from the rampant emotions of the night, Thea impulsively leaped forward and pulled Bobby into a tight tug, squeezing him tight to her chest but keeping her hips away.

A full-body hug...hip to hip...just seemed...weird.

After a beat, he returned the hug, though not as fiercely.

"I'll see you tomorrow."

"Sure thing, Bea," he said to her neck. His warm breath tickled, and she pulled away, heading toward the door.

Thea pulled the door open and turned back to him, watching him closely.

"Have a nice date?"

Bobby's lips twitched under his tightly trimmed goatee. "Will do."

"Not too much fun."

"Wouldn't dream of it."

"Have you talked to the guys about contacting a prenup lawyer?"

His lips turned into an outright smile, popping bright in contrast to the black facial hair. "Have one being drawn up as we speak."

Thea gave him an efficient nod, her own smile breaking through her bossy words. "I mean it though, have fun."

He nodded.

Okay, moving on.

She gave a small, awkward wave and slipped out the door and into the hall. Music was thumping from one of the apartment suites and Thea hustled down the hall toward the elevator, her heart jittering in her chest.

Why were her emotions all over the place?

Was it the emotional aftermath of her frantic worry from him choking earlier?

The terror of losing yet another person in her life?

Bobby had plugged a gaping wound in her after her father had died years ago, but he was so much more than a stand-in male figure in her life. He was her rock.

Or, maybe it wasn't the thought of losing him to death. Maybe it was the idea that she could lose him to a woman who wouldn't trust their friendship?

As she stepped into the elevator, a burst of delicious smells assaulted her. Here she was, having just eaten so much her stomach hurt, but now that she was smelling some spicy tangs of Mexican food, she was kicking herself for not picking up some of their favorite Mexican dishes and working those onto her dinner plate.

As she pressed the number for the parking garage below the building, she paused.

Was *that* what *this* was?

Was it simply her wanting what she couldn't have? Or maybe the thought of someone else taking what she had?

Thea's mind churned as she made her way home, her thoughts swirling with the complex mixture of emotions Bobby's new relationship stirred within her. Was it jealousy? Or was it something deeper, a fear of losing the irreplaceable bond they shared?

The idea that she might be jealous was absurd...right?

Bobby was her best friend, not a romantic interest.

Yet, the thought of him with someone else, potentially drifting away from her, sent a pang through her chest.

It was ridiculous.

She was just thinking earlier about how he needed to go on a date to remember what it felt like to feel passion so he could understand her preoccupation with Ian.

But it turns out he didn't need help finding a date.

What movie were they going to see?

The new rom com?

The new horror?

Bobby hated horror.

She hoped *Lucy* knew that.

And what about *after*?

Were they going to spend the night together?

Shit.

Okay. So what if they did?

It's not like she had any right to claim Bobby.

What he did in his love life was his business...

Even if it made her stomach clench and riot.

She was happy for him.

...Or at least, she wanted to be.

CHAPTER THREE
March 26, Friday afternoon
Thea

Thea leaned against the glass of the ice rink as the Zamboni hummed and glided across the ice. Lila bounded up to Thea's side, her blonde curls jouncing around with every step.

"Thea! I managed to land the transition we were working on this morning!" she gushed, her bright blue eyes shimmering with excitement.

Thea couldn't help but smile at her roommate's infectious energy. Lila was an incredible dancer...but skater? Not so much. Which made it so she had to work twice as hard as the others to master their choreography.

"No way!" Thea beamed. "We just went over that piece yesterday!"

Lila was practically vibrating. "I know!" Her voice was high with excitement as she bounced on her skates and clapped her hands together. "I'm really feeling more natural on the ice."

Thea chuckled and bumped their shoulders together. "So, you don't need private lessons from one of the Cyclones players anymore, then?"

A blush spread across Lila's cheeks, and she nudged Thea back. "Hey, I'm not going to turn down a private one-on-one." Lila sighed dreamily and looked toward the empty bench, no doubt envisioning Bobby there. "Especially from one in particular."

Thea was surprised by a squeeze, low in her stomach.

Nope.

No way.

No way she was jealous of freaking Lila!

She was *so* not Bobby's type.

Plus, he avoided her like the plague.

Given the level of obsession that Lila harbored and failed at hiding, which was probably for the best.

Maybe that's what Ian was doing...maybe he was avoiding *her*.

Was she being too obvious?

As the members of the Ice Crew laced up their skates and prepared to hit the ice, Thea shook her head. She was flirty; that's who she was, but she wasn't obsessed. She just...needed him to give her a chance.

Similarly, how she needed the Cyclones to give her a chance.

She was more than just a pretty and entertaining Ice Crew member—she *knew* hockey. The ins and outs. She could—no, she *would*—fucking *rock* the open on-ice talent job that they were looking to fill.

She could make valuable insights on the plays, the players, the coaching calls—everything.

They just needed to see past her cup size.

Damn Bobby, for putting that in her head.

Lila squeezed her arm. "Hey. We've got this, okay? We all believe in you, and we'll work hard until we make this routine perfect. Your debut will go well. We're behind you."

"Thanks, Lila" Thea murmured. The Zamboni rumbled past them, and the girls double-checked their laces. With one last deep breath, Thea stepped out onto the ice, her heart pounding with a mixture of nerves and determination.

First, she needed to get this routine perfected.

Second, she needed to get management to offer her the sideline reporter job.

Third, she needed to convince Ian that she was the perfect girl for him.

Then, she could breathe easy: her dad could be at peace.

• • • •●•●• • •

The Zamboni finished its final sweep, and Thea pushed off from the barrier, joining the rest of the Ice Crew on the freshly smoothed surface. As they skated in sync, practicing their routines, she tried to focus on her movements, on the feel of the ice beneath her skates.

Thea's blades sliced through the ice as she launched herself into a series of intricate spins and jumps, her solo routine taking shape under the watchful eyes of her fellow Ice Crew members. With every graceful movement, she felt her dedication to this organization surge through her veins—this was where she belonged: on the ice.

"Looking good, Thea!" Lila called out with a grin.

"Thanks," Thea said breathlessly, flashing her friend a grateful smile. "I just want to make sure I've got it down perfectly."

"Perfectionist much?" Lila teased, twirling around her.

"Maybe a little," she admitted, pushing herself into another spin. "But I need to make sure I'm demonstrating how hard I can work, and how I don't waffle when all eyes are on me. I need management to feel that I *belong* in front of a camera—that I demand that much attention."

"Girl, you've already made your mark," Lila insisted.

Thea felt a surge of warmth at her friend's unwavering support, but her thoughts stubbornly drifted back to Ian and the way his eyes seemed to see right through her.

What did she have to do to make *him* see her?

She twirled into eye contact with Rachel—one of the bitchier Ice Crew members—and was stunned at the venom in her stare.

"Jeeze, she needs to get a grip," Lila muttered, doing her own twirl next to Thea. "She didn't even want the Ice Crew manager job, and now that you have it, she's acting like she's wanted it for years."

Thea stumbled on her skates and went down hard on a knee, catching herself with her fingertips splayed. She couldn't take her eyes off the small white sprinkles that gathered around her fingertips.

Oh, my God!

That was it!

Thea stood and whipped to Lila, who was watching her with concern—it wasn't often that Thea fell during warmups.

"Lila, seriously, I could kiss you right now."

Lila blinked. "Well, I don't really swing that way usually…"

Thea swatted at Lila's shoulder and then pulled her into a tight hug.

"You don't know it, but I think you just gave me the recipe to get everything I wanted this year."

Lila cocked her head and studied Thea with a lost expression. "I guess just call me Santa?"

Thea wrapped her hands around the back of her friend's head and pulled her in, smacking a kiss on her forehead. "I'll call you more than that if this works, you genius."

Without waiting for a response, Thea pushed away toward the far side of the rink, acclimating herself to the ice and thinking of how she was going to get Bobby to agree to her plan.

Operation Get-Ian-To-Notice-Her was on.

CHAPTER FOUR
March 27, Saturday Night
Bobby

The arena was packed, the roars drowning out the sound of the skates slicing through the ice. The anticipation was palpable as the Springfield Cyclones entered the final minutes of the game. Bobby sat on the edge of the bench, watching his teammates execute their lines with precision, a testament to their dedication at practice.

The coach called for a line change and Bobby tightened his grip on his hockey stick and leaped over the wall, his eyes fixed on the puck Ian was charging down the ice with.

Ian took a rogue route to the blue line and paused, throwing off the perfect timing that Bobby was counting on. Bobby cursed, dug in his skates, and tried to bank hard to get back onside.

Whistle blown.

Fuck!

Fucking *fucker*!

Bobby watched a hint of a smirk coast over Ian's face.

He'd bet his entire life here in Springfield that Ian did that on purpose just to screw him over. Ian was still feeling a bit salty about Bobby not losing his spot on the first line with him.

Too fucking bad.

They were on a fucking power play and Ian was pulling this shit.

They just lost their three-on-two-man rush that an unexpected turnover generated!

The players took their positions around the faceoff circle and Ian was quickly thrown out, taking a skate of shame out of the center. Boos from the crowd echoed in the arena.

Bobby and Ty, their other forward, locked eyes. Ty nodded.

All his.

Good.

Bobby slid into Ian's faceoff spot, priming his gloved hand on his stick. He exhaled slowly, narrowing his eyes on the puck...waiting for it to drop.

The tension in the air was thick, a tangible force that seemed to slow time itself.

Bobby's focus was laser-sharp, his body primed for the moment the puck would be released.

The linesperson's arm moved, and the puck dropped.

The clack of their colliding sticks echoed through the charged atmosphere. With a swift motion honed by countless hours of practice, Bobby won the faceoff, passing the puck to Ty, who was already in motion.

Ty handled the puck with ease, skating forward before shooting it back to Bobby, who had found an open lane. The ice beneath his skates felt like home, the weight of the moment fueling his determination. He weaved through the opposing players with a dancer's grace, his eyes locked on the goal.

It wasn't usual to have this much time stickhandling in front of the net, but the other team was in penalty-kill mode and a player short. Now was his chance.

As he approached the goal, Bobby faked left, pulling the goalie out of position, before sending the puck rocketing toward the net, glove side. It sailed past the goalie's outstretched hand and hit the back of the net with a satisfying thud.

The arena erupted, the cheers washing over Bobby in a wave of pure adrenaline.

He pumped his fist at his side, a victorious grin spreading across his face as his teammates skated up for a quick celebration. The camaraderie among them was evident, their joy in the shared success was a testament to their bond as they thumped him on his helmet and back.

Even Ian skated over and 'celebrated' with him.

If nothing else, at least they both had a tacit understanding not to let their...tension...be noticed by the fans or media.

As they dispersed, Bobby glided back to the bench, offering fist bumps to his teammates as he glided along the ice in front of them.

As he went, his gaze inadvertently drifted to the corner of the rink by the Zamboni entrance. As expected, there was Thea, cheering like crazy behind the glass, her enthusiasm unmistakable even from a distance. Her face was glowing with excitement, her support unwavering.

A smile broke across Bobby's face. It was moments like these that reminded him of the bond they shared, deeper than just friendship, but complicated by unspoken feelings and missed opportunities.

Yet, later, as he hopped over the wall for the line change, he caught Ian's eye and Bobby's smile faltered. Confusion and frustration bubbled up again.

What did Thea see in Ian?

Ian: who had tried to trip him up on the ice during a game, who carried an air of arrogance that was overwhelming, who was selfish and spoiled.

What was the fucking deal with her crush?

Why was she drawn to someone who was so...shitty?

Bobby allowed himself to steal a glance at Thea. Shaking his head, Bobby forced the thoughts away. This wasn't the time for distractions. He had a game to finish, a point to prove.

He was just as good as Ian.

In every facet of life.

He should be a *first* pick...not a second.

But he understood all too well that it wasn't his choice; it was hers.

And if Ian was who would make her happy...well, then...

She deserved to be happy.

Chapter Five

March 27, Saturday Night
Bobby

Sure, it was impossible not to admire Ian's skills, but the way he carried himself both on and off the ice left a bitter taste in Bobby's mouth.

It seemed as though Ian always put himself first, leaving the rest of the team scrambling to follow his lead.

The game had been won and the team had just wrapped up their center ice after-game ritual. The players were skating together back to the bench to head down to the locker room. The crowd was dispersing sluggishly but there were a few who waited by the tunnels in the hopes of receiving sticks from the players.

Bobby was stuck behind Ian; forced to stare at the dreaded "Novak" on the back of his jersey as they made their way off the ice.

Would Ian give a stick to an adoring fan?

Probably. He always did.

For better or worse, the fans didn't know just how much of a douche the guy could be.

But Bobby knew.

He just couldn't see how Thea didn't.

Bobby's gaze shifted from glaring at Ian's back to Thea, who was skating onto the ice with the rest of her Ice Crew, trying to engage with the fans who were still hanging around. Cyclones' management was trying to get people to dawdle after the games so they'd buy last-minute merch and food. The Ice Crew hadn't quite received the marketing push that would have told the fans that an after-game show was going to be the new norm, so not many people knew to stay.

It was okay, though. If anyone could turn that around, it was Thea. The woman was tenacious.

Her green eyes were locked on Ian as she coasted up to center ice, a big smile on her face. Her brunette hair was curled and styled in a seductive way that swayed as she leaned forward on her skates, getting more speed. Behind her, Lila waved to Bobby, her blonde curls springing with each animated gesture.

Bobby clenched his jaw. How much clearer could he be? He very obviously avoided Thea's roommate, but the woman just wasn't getting the memo. He *wasn't* interested.

Hmm, missing the signs. Sounded like someone else he knew...

His eyes shot back to Thea, who was now on the other side of the rink, waving at the crowd and doing some fancy dance moves while skating backwards.

"Can't believe she's so into him," he muttered under his breath, adjusting his grip on his stick and shaking his head. "Selfish punk."

"Who, Novak?" Tommy, one of his teammates, asked, overhearing Bobby's comment as they transitioned to the rubber flooring.

Bobby nodded reluctantly, not wanting to give away too much. "Yeah, I just... don't get it," he said, careful to keep his tone casual.

A few players ahead, Ian's stick was hoisted into the air and passed to a kid reaching into the tunnel.

"Hey, can't argue with his skills," Tommy replied with a shrug, continuing down the narrow hallway.

Bobby lifted his stick and handed it to a girl decked out in Cyclones gear. The smile she gave him was blinding.

Well, at least someone was happy to get his stick.

He just wished he was giving it to Thea.

· • • ●• • ●• • ·

The post-game celebration in the locker room was a whirlwind of exhilaration and camaraderie. Bobby stood among his teammates, clapping them on the back and laughing at their raucous jokes. The deathly scent of sweaty hockey gear poisoned the air, made worse by the occasional spritz of nose-burning body spray.

The room buzzed with reporters and staff, all eager for a piece after the Cyclones' triumph.

Catering to the soundbite that the media wanted, Ian played the part they had spent years perfecting.

"Hey, Davidson," Ian called out, clapping him roughly on the shoulder. "Great game, man!"

Lights flashed as the photographers snagged their shots.

"Thanks," Bobby replied, forcing a smile as he pretended not to care that Ian repeatedly made him look bad on the ice.

It was about the Cyclones. It was about their home.

Ian's shitty behavior with Bobby was manageable, as long as Ian remained an asset to the *team*.

As long as Ian was the best man for the job, Bobby would take whatever shit Ian tossed his way.

It was the least he could do for the Cyclones and the management that saved his life.

With Ian's arm around his shoulder, they faced the awaiting reporters as a united front.

More pictures were taken, and recorders were pushed in front of their faces. Reporters fought for their questions to be answered, and the second part of their charade began...

CHAPTER SIX

March 27, Saturday Night
Thea

The dimly lit, semi-private bar was alive with laughter and chatter, as the Springfield Cyclones celebrated their victory. The bouncers at the doors, both the regular and the VIP entrances, knew who to let in and who to keep out. The owner of The Five Hole did an excellent job of creating a small-town atmosphere in the bar that allowed the players to come in and unwind after a game without being mobbed...unless they wanted to be, that is.

The thought caused Thea to turn and watch Ian from across the room, his dark hair still slightly damp from the post-game shower, as he flirted and took photos with a group of puck bunnies.

She picked at her thumbnail, trying to muster up the courage to push through that gaggle of women and demand his attention.

"You look like you just threw back a shot," Lila said, appearing beside Thea with a couple fancy drinks. Lila handed her one of the tall glasses, filled with a vibrant mocktail that seemed to glow radioactively under the bar's neon lights.

"Thanks," Thea mumbled, sipping on the straw without looking away from Ian.

After dealing with the fallout of someone else's excessive drinking, alcohol and getting drunk just didn't hold the same appeal for Thea anymore. She tried to keep her anger and bitterness from affecting her relationships with others who were drinking... but it was a work in progress. Whenever she saw someone getting too drunk, a flare of resentment bubbled up inside her, reminding her of past hurts she couldn't quite let go.

"Go on. Don't be a chicken. Just go ask him out already," Lila urged, though her own attention seemed fixed on something else entirely. She nervously fidgeted with her bracelet, eyes flicking toward Bobby, who had just walked in.

Yeah, she was one to talk.

Thea glanced at her roommate, contemplating Lila's obvious crush on her friend. Bobby was great—funny, kind, and easygoing.

He just wasn't a good fit for Lila. She couldn't put her finger on 'why,' though.

"Earth to Thea!" Lila waved a hand in front of her face, snapping her out of her reverie. "Are you going to talk to Ian or not?"

"Maybe later," Thea replied, her voice laced with uncertainty. She shifted her weight from foot to foot, feeling the floor stick to the underside of her shoe.

"Suit yourself," Lila sighed, though her attention quickly snapped over to Bobby, who had just taken a spot at the bar, signaling for his standard post-game beer. Thea could see the wheels turning in her friend's mind, and she knew Lila was wondering the same thing as Thea, just about a completely different guy.

Thea had spent the last two days completely obsessing over the idea that had hit her at practice the other day. Lila's comment about Rachel and her jealousy about the role she didn't want, yet couldn't have—combined with her own reaction to Bobby dating *Lucy*.

Ick, just thinking the name made her nose crinkle.

But, if *she* got—she wasn't going to say *jealous*—over Bobby dating someone, and Rachel got jealous and wanted what she couldn't have...

What if she became suddenly unavailable to Ian?

What if she became unavailable because she was taken by the one man who sparked Ian's jealous and competitive tendencies more than anyone.

What if she could convince Ian that *Bobby* had won her heart...

Would that spark a flame of interest? A tickle of desire?

If she was able to be wooed by Ian's rival, would Ian let his competitive edge take over?

Would he start to see her differently?

The concept was sound and consumed her every waking second.

The issue was Bobby.

One...he was Bobby. Her best friend. He might think it was stupid, especially given his dislike of Ian.

Two, even if he agreed, they might not be very convincing; their chemistry might fall completely flat.

Three, Bobby actually did have a real-life lady interest right now. Thea didn't know how long that had been going on or how close they were, but asking them to stop seeing each other so he could have a fake relationship with Thea to make another man jealous was ridiculously selfish.

Even if this new girl—*Lucy*— was incredibly cool and claimed to be 'okay' with their fake-dating ruse, the fact that Bobby and his female best friend once pretended to date would likely haunt her. The lingering doubt about Thea's role in Bobby's life would always remain.

At least, that's how Thea would feel if their roles were reversed.

Asking him to put a real relationship in jeopardy for a fake one—could she really live with herself if she pushed for that?

Absolutely not.

She needed to show Ian how amazing she was, but there was no way she could hurt Bobby in the process.

So the fake dating theory was out.

So, for now, Thea would stay the course, her heart racing with a mixture of excitement and trepidation as she watched Ian's every move. One day, she'd find a way to show Ian that she was more than just a random co-worker, but for tonight, she'd stick to admiring him from a distance while brainstorming her next move.

Chapter Seven
March 27, Saturday Night
Bobby

At the team's preferred bar after the game, Bobby's gaze raked across the room to where Thea stood, her bright green eyes gleaming as she chatted with Lila.

She looked so beautiful with her brunette hair framing her face in soft waves.

Fucking Ian—how could he not see how amazing she was?

Truth be told, Bobby was grateful that Ian didn't notice her, because that relationship would be a total shit show.

Not that Thea believed him when Bobby told her that. She had her sights set on Ian and the bull-headed woman was not to be influenced. He usually admired that about her.

Not when it came to her crush on Ian, though.

Her out-of-character reaction the other night when she found out about Lucy had been…interesting.

A more optimistic man would think it was jealousy that had driven her manic response.

A more pessimistic and rational man would assume it was a woman fearing that her stand-in male presence was going to be taken away from her until all she was left with was a random card at Christmas.

And Bobby was never mistaken for an optimistic man.

And yet…he was an idiot. So he would continue to hope.

Taking a deep breath, Bobby made his way over to say hi.

He was a fucking masochist.

Thea's face lit up when she saw him, and his heart skipped a beat at the sight of her genuine joy. "Hey, Bea," he said, trying to keep his voice casual while giving an impersonal, I'm-not-interested-therefore-I-don't-want-to-lead-you-on nod to Lila.

Her crush was just *really* misplaced.

"The new routine went well. I heard some reporters commenting on it to each other in the locker room after the game. I also heard one speculate on whether management was going to consider you for the on-ice job. She said your social media posts were brilliant and that they'd be stupid not to seriously consider you."

The way Thea's face lit up.

Fuck.

It was like he just told her that scientists had found a way to bring back the dead.

Bobby made a mental note to send Peyton Knowles some flowers for planting that little nugget in a fellow sports reporter's head. Peyton had done Thea a total solid.

Thea turned to Lila and they hugged hard, jumping up and down and whooping with joy. Thea then threw herself into his arms.

Jesus.

There was no space between their hips this time.

This hug was all about being as close as possible to each other.

And fuck, was he going to *savor* it.

Bobby pulled her in tight, giving her a small sway back and forth, deeply inhaling her signature citrusy smell.

He closed his eyes and let it consume him.

Fuck, he had it bad.

Thea pulled away and beamed up at him, before looking up to the ceiling and mouthing the words, "Thank you."

To God, the universe, another being, or to a theoretical heaven was unclear.

Regardless, she was appreciating the goodness of The Now.

Thea lowered her eyes to him, and she took him in, frowning somewhat as she stared at him and the bruise forming along his jaw from one of the fights that night.

"I'm, uh, going to grab some more drinks. Be right back." Lila scampered off, her cheeks a vibrant pink as she made eye contact with Bobby.

Bobby glanced at the small high-top table where the women had gotten comfortable and the still very full glass that was near Lila's elbow.

Thea shifted her weight and Bobby turned his attention to her, catching her still studying him.

"The team was great tonight. The drills Coach ran this week really helped. The defense looked much better. You played really well…" She chewed on her lip before looking down the bar where Ian was holding court.

Of course.

The fact that she knew exactly where Ian was…Bobby flexed the hand that desperately wanted to punch the nearest brick wall.

"Considering the stunt that Ian pulled at the end," Thea continued, her eyes flicking momentarily to Ian before returning to Bobby. "And the two times before that."

Three times before that, actually.

"Thanks," Bobby replied, swallowing the bitter taste of jealousy.

She meant it as a compliment, but it felt like he was being compared to Ian—and coming up short.

Per usual.

Then again, she never called Ian to patch a hole in her apartment wall, rather than telling the super.

"I mean…maybe he didn't mean…"

Bobby just stared at her, his eyes narrowed and his lips tight.

Thea wasn't usually biased in her analysis of the game, no matter who was playing. Thea Sharppe called it like she saw it, and she wasn't one to sugar coat it for some dude she had an infatuation with.

She winced and rubbed at the back of her neck. "Yeah, you don't get this far in hockey and make mistakes like that." She coughed and shifted uncomfortably. "I just...don't get it. The jealousy and antagonism. You guys play so well together when the game is on the line. It's only after the game is put away that he usually pulls that shit." She faded off and started chewing at her thumbnail as she glanced down to where Ian was taking a body shot from some bunny.

"Yeah, well..." Bobby shrugged.

What was he supposed to say? That Ian was bitter and jealous? That Ian was offended because years ago, when Bobby did Ian an unasked-for-favor, it changed the course of Ian's career? And that the embarrassment of that unwanted debt caused Ian to act like a dick?

Saying all that didn't make Bobby sound like a pompous jackass *at all*.

It was easier to let Ian's actions do the talking.

Or...it should have been. Thea just wasn't connecting the dots. She had blinders on.

"Sometimes, people just don't mesh well together, Thea. It's not always something that can be fixed."

Just as she was opening her mouth to respond—to no doubt tell him how he needed to extend an olive branch and give Ian a chance—Lila came bursting back, out of breath, snatching Thea up.

"Oh, my God! Brian just said that our post-game routine is blowing up. Said it's playing on at least two sports networks and is trending on social media!" Lila's voice turned shrill, and she shook Thea by the shoulders. "People are recording themselves doing *your* moves!" Lila then lowered her voice. "And they're talking about your chances for the on-ice job..."

Now both women were shrieking and jumping again.

Lila grabbed hold of Thea's hand and dragged her through the throngs of people to the backroom where they could commandeer a TV.

Between one sip of his drink and the next, Thea was gone.

Story of his life.

· • • ◆ • ◆ • • ·

As the last call was made, Bobby found an open wall to rest against and finish his beer in peace. Did he want to spend his night after a game in a bar? No. But, was it a good time to connect with his teammates when they weren't as guarded, so he could get a pulse on any brewing issues? Yes.

He and Ilya split the duties the best they could.

Only Ilya didn't get called 'Mother Hen,' by the guys.

Jackasses.

He grinned to himself as he took a sip of his somewhat-warm beer.

Most of the guys had headed home—or elsewhere—for the night, and he was just waiting for the rest of the troops to leave so he could head out too.

Bobby let his mind wander back to his favorite daydream topic: Thea. They knew each other's likes, dislikes, and reactions. He could walk around a corner in a random house and Thea would know exactly what height to jump so she could launch herself onto his back and tag along as he kept walking. He knew where her legs would sit and where her hands would fall on his shoulders or chest. He knew the sound of her laughter or the way her lip curled when she thought someone was lying.

He knew it all.

And so did she.

She knew when he needed a quiet moment of solitude, and she respected that, giving him the space he needed without question. She knew when he needed a laugh or a distraction, and she was always there with a witty comment or a playful nudge to lift his spirits. She knew that he might want to binge-read a new release all day next to the pool, but he still craved someone to be there, even if they were doing their own thing.

He needed to find a way to stand out in Thea's eyes.

Lucy was fun, but she wasn't Thea. They had discussed that Bobby was emotionally unavailable when they started 'talking.' Which was good, because so was Lucy—she still wasn't over her ex. So, it worked—there would be no broken hearts, as they recognized that they were each other's way to pass the time.

And even though he prided himself on knowing Thea better than anyone...Thea's reaction upon learning about Lucy's existence was one he *never* could have predicted.

Not in a million years.

He sighed, running a hand through his short hair before taking another sip from his bottle.

"Something on your mind, Robert?" asked a grating voice. Ian clapped a hand on Bobby's shoulder briefly before leaning against the wall next to him.

What an insufferable prick.

Bobby tried not to let himself stiffen in irritation.

"Nothing important," Bobby muttered, trying to turn his lips up into the hint of a smile.

You never knew who could catch an errant photo that would go viral.

Ian raised an eyebrow at the taciturn response. "You were off your game a bit tonight. We all have bad days. To be fair, you don't usually let me catch you off guard so often, so I couldn't resist that final time."

Fucking *asshole*.

Bobby stared out at the people making their Texas Goodbyes and tried to think of how long it would take till he could escape as well.

"I wouldn't have fucked with you like that if the game was on the line," Ian said, his tone patronizing. "You know that. A little friendly competition on the ice never hurt anyone. We want the same things."

Unlikely.

Bobby stared down at his still mostly full beer.

"For the Cyclones to be the best," Ian clarified, clearly not reading Bobby's reluctance to have a conversation at all.

"Right," Bobby replied, the epitome of disengaged as he swirled his bottle and continued to stare at it. "All's fair in love and war. As long as the better team wins."

"Right," Ian echoed, looking out over the people making their way out of the bar. "We both want the better man...I mean, team, to win."

Right. Like he was supposed to believe *that* was a Freudian slip?

Fucking hell, this guy was such a douche.

What the fuck did Thea see in him?

Ian continued spewing his barbed pleasantries in Bobby's ear, but Bobby tuned him out. They'd been doing this for years, he knew exactly what bullshit Ian would be saying: 'No hard feelings, it's all in good fun, stop being so serious, it's just a game, they were winning anyways, why did he have such a stick up his ass.'

On and on.

The guy was a real charmer.

Why he insisted on cornering him for these little chats, Bobby could never figure out.

It's not like he meant what he said. It's not like he wanted to be friends with Bobby. It's not like he wanted *anything* from Bobby.

Why did Ian insist on these little chats when they both knew how much they disliked each other?

What did Ian get out of it?

As Bobby watched Thea's figure, arm in arm with Lila, disappear through the exit and into the night,, Bobby knew that he had to do something—anything—to make her see Ian as he truly was. And to see him as more than just a friend.

And though he had no idea how to go about it, one thing was certain: he wasn't going to let a fucker like Ian Novak beat him without a fight.

May the better man win.

CHAPTER EIGHT

March 28, Sunday afternoon
Thea

In the cozy, bustling atmosphere of Springfield's local bookstore, the air was rich with the aroma of paper and worn leather, a scent that always reminded Thea of Bobby. He stood in line next to her, a tall stack of assorted titles cradled in his arms like a precious hoard, his eyes devouring the first few lines of the book on top.

Thea flipped through a glossy sports magazine with half-hearted interest. It was their second time this week picking up new books, yet she still hadn't found the time to delve into the one Bobby insisted she read.

She hadn't had the time...or desire. No matter how 'perfect' it might be for her.

She'd never been a big reader, but for Bobby, she'd try. She'd get around to it.

Eventually.

Despite the vibrant images and compelling headlines that celebrated the prowess of hockey's finest, her attention was intermittently hijacked by an article featuring Bobby, Ty, and Ian. Each sentence praised their on-ice brilliance and teamwork. There was even a small section focused on Ian's charity work and how his latest was hosting a big fundraiser soon. Seeing all of Ian's good work outlined on the page tightened the knot of frustration in her stomach until, in a moment of irritation, she snapped the magazine shut—a sharp clap echoing in the quiet bookstore.

Why was someone so remarkable on paper so woefully blind to the goodness of her best friend?

Even if she was able to go on a date with Ian, disarm him with her excellence, and deep dive into the warm, gooey goodness that was sure to be waiting under that prickly exterior...would it matter?

Could she really, honestly date someone knowing that they were a douchebag to her best friend?

Then again...maybe she'd be the bridge to a real truce.

Thea watched Bobby adjust his grip on his stack of books, his forehead creased in concentration. There was something so inherently Bobby about the way he stood there, lost in literature, which warmed her heart. At some point, he had slipped on his reading glasses and was completely oblivious to the line that had shifted. She grabbed his elbow and gently guided him forward, knowing that there was no way he would notice on his own. As they assumed their new spot in the glacial line, she inquired with a nonchalance she didn't feel, "What's Lucy up to today?"

Bobby's eyes barely flickered from the text as he answered, "Lucy and I are on a break." His voice was as calm and steady as ever, before refocusing on his book.

What!?

"What happened? Are you okay? Did this happen last night? This morning?"

Was it her?

He peeked up at her from under his glasses and her heart gave a little stutter, which she suppressed immediately. *Friends, friends, friends.* Friends can recognize that their friends are 'attractive', but not 'sexy.' *Nope, nope, nope.* She forced her heart to steady.

His forehead wrinkled as he stared at her. Then he shut the book's cover, his thumb saving his page, and gave her his full attention.

"We met up this morning for breakfast. We both decided that it wasn't working all that great, so we wanted to part ways for a bit." His eyebrow climbed as he studied her. "Jesus, Bea, are you okay?"

The words hung in the air, heavy with implications that sent Thea's mind into a tailspin. She fought to maintain her composure as a whirlwind of thoughts and emotions threatened to overwhelm her.

Her grip on the magazine tightened involuntarily as conflicting feelings surged through her. Relief washed over her like a wave crashing against the shore, knowing that Bobby wasn't being whisked away by another woman. But there was also a heartache there: Bobby was awesome—he deserved to find someone who recognized that. The guy was meant to be a husband and dad, and here he was, now not even a boyfriend.

But that meant...

If Lucy was out of the picture...and Bobby agreed...

Was this the universe's way of giving her a boost?

Was the universe trying to tell her that this was the path?

Her father always used to talk about the universe and what it had in store for them. He was a big believer that everything worked out. It was all Thea could do to remind herself of his unwavering faith as they lowered her father into the ground.

But her father had known her better than anyone. And he must have seen something in Ian, otherwise, he never would have told Thea to call him.

Was this her father's so-called 'universe' encouraging her to take the chance of asking Bobby to be her fake boyfriend?

What were the chances that Bobby would become single right now? After all, it would be the perfect way to make Ian jealous and finally get a chance to prove her worth to him.

Around them, the bookstore hummed with the quiet activity of fellow book lovers navigating the aisles, their presence a comforting background to the tumultuous excitement brewing within her.

With a deep breath, she let her dad's faith in the universe calm her racing heart.

She looked at Bobby and took in his worried expression. Thea reached out and patted his arm to assure him that all was well.

"I'm fine. I just..." she started, before clearing her voice to get out the rest of her nerves. "Actually, Bobby, there's a huge favor I need to ask you. It might sound a bit..." she waved her hands wildly by her head. "But please, just hear me out." Her eyes locked onto his, a silent plea for understanding and a desperate hope that he wouldn't outright laugh in her face.

Bobby shifted the books around so he could free his left hand from the stack of books. He reached around his back, the small paperback even smaller in his big hands, and used his ring and middle finger to slide a slim bookmark out of his back pocket in his jeans. Replacing his thumb with his bookmark, he placed it back on the pile to give her his undivided attention.

Ah, Bobby.

Even with the nerves, she wanted to smile at how absolutely adorable it was that he brought an extra bookmark to the bookstore with them.

As his dark eyes settled on her and his face wrinkled with worry, the rest of the bookstore faded away, leaving them in their own secluded world. "What do you need?"

Easy. That was it.

What did she need. That's all he needed to hear.

Thea took a deep breath of the coffee-scented air and—

Was interrupted by the person behind them telling them that more lanes had opened up at checkout.

CHAPTER NINE

March 28, Sunday afternoon
Thea

Gritting her teeth, Thea followed along as Bobby led the way to the checkout counter. After Bobby finished paying, Thea grabbed Bobby's arm and steered him toward the in-store café, where the stronger scent of freshly brewed coffee mingled with the sound of baristas calling out orders.

Finding a secluded corner table, she motioned for Bobby to sit across from her.

Bobby set his bag of books on the floor and lowered himself in the chair. The bruise turning yellow along his cheek made his dark expression even more serious.

Once they were settled, Thea took a deep breath, her hands fidgeting nervously in her lap.

"Bobby," her voice was surprisingly steady given the flutter of butterflies in her stomach. "I want to ask you something really...out there," she semi-repeated her lead-in from earlier.

Bobby leaned forward slightly. "So you said—what's going on?"

Thea glanced around the café, ensuring that no one was within earshot before leaning in closer to Bobby. "It's about Ian," she whispered.

Bobby's eyebrows shot up in surprise and he sat back a bit. "Ian? What about him? What did he do?" The storm brewing in his face was nothing compared to how tightly coiled his body became just then.

"Oh, God, no. It's nothing bad. Don't freak out." Thea reached out and placed her hand on his on the table, ignoring the zing of warmth. "I just had an idea and I wanted to know if you'd help me. I know you don't see the appeal, but I have a plan to make him see me differently," she confessed, her words rushing out in a jumble. "I feel like I need to do this. The universe is *telling* me to do this."

His eyes had flitted down to their hands, but he hadn't pulled his away. "The *universe* is telling you to…"

"I want you to pretend to be my boyfriend."

Bobby shot back, ripping his hand out from under hers, his eyes wide and mouth opening and closing. "You want me to *what*?" he finally managed to choke out, his voice a mixture of disbelief and confusion.

Thea nodded, her heart thundering in her chest as she leaned forward and braced herself for his response. "I want us to pretend to be in a relationship, just long enough to make Ian realize what he's missing out on," she explained, her voice trembling with nervous energy. "He's ridiculously competitive with you. If he thinks *you* have me, his instinctive rivalry with you will demand that *he* win me from you. I know it's stupid but…I need him to give me a chance."

For her father, she *needed* Ian to give her a chance.

Bobby's brow furrowed as he considered her, his expression a mixture of concern and uncertainty. "Thea, I'm not sure if that's such a good idea," he said. "I mean, what if it backfires? What if Ian doesn't react the way you're hoping?"

Thea's shoulders slumped at his words, but she refused to let her resolve waver. "I know it's a risk," she admitted, her voice tinged with determination. "But I can't just sit back and do nothing while Ian continues to see me as just one of the guys or some random coworker. I need to take matters into my own hands. The universe is handing me this opportunity."

"The universe?"

She waved her hands, rolling her wrists dramatically. "It would be too hard to break down all of the signs, but trust me, they're *totally* there."

His eyebrows climbed so high that his forehead creased.

"Bea, I think...are you going to tell Lila?"

Thea blinked and sat back.

Wait. What?

He was worried about Lila?

Did he *like* her?

Is that why he avoided her so much?

A vise clamped down on her throat, giving her an uncomfortable frog to swallow around.

"Um, I haven't thought of that, but I probably wouldn't tell anyone...just in case it got out and made it all...pointless."

"Are you prepared for that fallout?"

Thea swallowed hard and cracked her neck, trying to dispel the tension. "Um...I think it will be fine. It's not like it's going to last for too long, right? A couple of public appearances, I catch Ian's eye, and boom, we can call it off as soon as he makes a move. No big deal."

Bobby didn't look convinced.

"You seem pretty confident that Ian will come sniffing around. What if he doesn't? Ian can be pretty self-absorbed. What if he doesn't even notice our little charade? We could end up making fools of ourselves for nothing."

Thea leveled Bobby with a pitying look. "Have you met Ian? Have you noticed how childish he is around you? Anytime you're getting even a slice of attention, he's like...genetically compelled to insert himself. It will work."

"And this is the winner that you're so desperate to get the attention of," Bobby grumbled.

Thea glared at him. "I don't expect you to understand."

Bobby pivoted, "And what if you find out that he's as much of a dick as I keep telling you?"

Well, shit.

"He won't be."

She hoped.

"He is," Bobby insisted.

"Nope, that's impossible."

There's no way her dad would have liked Ian so much if he really was a douchebag to his very core. He saw something in him that made him worthy of her: his princess.

That was *all* she needed to know.

Bobby studied her for a long moment, searching her as if trying to gauge the sincerity of her words.

"And, what if things get... complicated between us? I value our friendship more than anything, and I don't want to jeopardize that. There's literally a whole wall over in the corner over there," he pointed toward the romance section of the bookstore, "that focuses on fake dating. This is not something new. This has been tried and failed enough times that there is a fucking trope wall devoted to it."

Thea squirmed in her seat and started chewing absently on her nail.

"I think...we'll be fine. Right?" She sounded as unconvinced as she felt. "We know it's just fake. We know the end goal. Some kisses, a little extra touching, some cuddling, fond looks...that's all it is. You've been acting like a bestie to Ian for years and the media never caught on. I'm sure you can sell this."

He stared at her, his internal debate raging.

"Please. I've been looking for a chance to go on a date with him since my dad died. The universe is screaming that this is my chance. I don't want to waste it."

Bobby's eyebrows furrowed. "What does this have to do with the accident?"

Thea winced and tried to figure out a way to confess her dad's intent for her without sounding like she had lost her mind. After a moment of contemplating several ways to articulate it, Thea simply forged ahead. There was no sugarcoating the reality; it was what it was.

"Okay, so I know this sounds nuts, but my dad really wanted me to go on a date with Ian before he died. He was convinced that Ian was my soulmate. Like...really convinced. So, I owe it to my dad—and myself—to give it a shot and see if it's right. My dad was never wrong about stuff like that. He knew me better than anyone." She looked down at where her sleeve was covering her compass tattoo. "There's no way my dad would say all that if he didn't believe it."

Bobby's features softened, a pained expression etching across his face as he watched Thea's voice falter and crack under the weight of her emotions.

With her heart in her throat, Thea leaned forward, begging him, "*Please*? Can we please just *try*?"

Bobby let out a sigh, his shoulders sagging. "All right, Bea," he said softly, his voice tinged with reluctant acceptance. "We can try."

Relief washed over Thea as she reached across the table to grasp Bobby's hand in gratitude. "Thank you, Bobby," she whispered, unable to take a full breath, her eyes burning with unshed tears. "Thank you."

Bobby gave her hand a reassuring squeeze, a small smile tugging at the corners of his lips. "I hope you're right about him and that you find what you're looking for," he whispered.

Staring up into Bobby's familiar, brown eyes, Thea's heart gave an errant skip.

"Me too," she echoed softly.

But as she considered the potential consequences, she couldn't help but wonder: was she risking too much in pursuit of Ian?

CHAPTER TEN

March 28, Sunday afternoon
Thea

Thea's mind buzzed as she began to map out the specifics of their fake dating plan. She knew they needed to be convincing, not just for Ian's sake, but for everyone else who would be watching.

"Okay," she said, leaning in closer to Bobby. "We'll start by showing up together at the next team event. We'll have to explain that we were hanging out one night and something just *shifted*, and now we're an item."

Bobby shook his head, still trying to process everything. "Thea, I really don't think—"

"Shh!" Thea silenced him with an excited grin. "Once Ian sees us together, he's bound to feel something—jealousy, curiosity, whatever. That's when we turn up the heat."

As she spoke, Thea couldn't help but notice how warm and inviting Bobby's brown eyes seemed under the dim lights. She quickly pushed the thought away, focusing instead on the task at hand. "We'll attend functions together, go on dates, and post pictures online to make it look official. But the key is subtlety; we can't make it look like we're trying too hard."

Bobby's fingers drummed on the wooden surface of the café table; his eyes fixed on some distant point beyond Thea. She could see the turmoil in his expression, the way he bit his lip as he weighed the consequences of her proposal. The low lighting cast shadows across his face, emphasizing the lines of worry that creased his forehead.

Bobby sighed, clearly still uncomfortable with the idea. "Thea, I don't know...."

"Don't get cold feet on me now! We haven't even started!"

She felt a strange mix of emotions—excitement at the prospect of finally making Ian see her as more than 'one of the guys,' anxiety over potentially harming her friendship with Bobby, and a nagging worry that perhaps she was being selfish.

"Trust me," she assured Bobby, gently touching his arm. "We'll make it work, and in the end, we'll both get what we want."

"Which is?" Bobby asked, his voice barely a whisper.

"For me to be with Ian," she stated confidently, though her heart fluttered with uncertainty. "And for you...well, maybe this will stop the conflict between you and Ian, and the team will be all the better for it."

"Right," he said after a moment. "The team."

What was *that* about?

Thea studied him. What about that statement bothered him?

"Bobby?" Her stomach was writhing uncomfortably now. "Bobby, *are* you okay with this? Say the word if you aren't. I didn't mean to..." She corrected herself. "Well, I *did* mean to pressure you, but not like 'pressure you, pressure you.' If you are really not okay with this, we'll pretend this whole thing never happened. I want you to be okay..."

She placed her hand on his and he pulled it back...

Holy shit.

Did she just break them?

Her stomach was a full-on writhing wriggle of worms right now. Something was wrong.

As excited as she was before, now she was terrified.

Oh, God.

"Bobby?" Her voice sounded winded and every bit as scared as she felt as he refused to make eye contact.

At her distress, Bobby turned back to face her, pulling his attention from the acoustic guitarist that was strumming on the small, make-shift stage in the corner.

"Right here."

"Are you...okay with this? Honestly?"

The seconds that he spent staring at her were the longest of her life, and that was saying something.

Just as she was about to call the whole thing off, he reached out and grabbed her hand, capturing it within his two large, and surprisingly warm, ones. She found herself momentarily lost in the scent of his skin—a mixture of soap and a hint of aftershave that reminded her of crisp winter mornings on the ice.

"Bea, when have I ever told you no?"

Well, that wasn't really an answer.

She tried to pull her hand out so she could tell him 'Never mind' and run home to brainstorm how to get Bobby to forget this ever happened, but he didn't let her go.

"Bea, I'm fine with it. We'll make it work. Ian will probably react how you think he will. If I know him at all, that would be my guess. I'm just...worried about what you'll find when you actually get him where you want him, and what that means for you...and us." He shrugged and ran a calloused thumb over her knuckles, causing goosebumps to break out on her skin. "But, you're right. I'm single, you're single. As you pointed out, I can be pretty convincing. There's not a reason in the world that I can't help you out with this."

She tugged her lip between her lower teeth, still not sure she was buying it. "But..."

"But, nothing. You want this. You want this so bad that your heart was absolutely breaking in front of me when you thought I would say no." He swallowed hard. "So no, Thea. You don't need to worry. I'm okay. We're going to do this. And you'll get an answer one way or another. And regardless of what happens, you still have me. Like always."

Like always.

The words felt solid. A promise carved in stone.

For the first time in minutes, when she took a deep breath, it actually felt satisfying.

Okay.

She and Bobby were okay.

Thea curled her hand, holding tight to him.

"You have me too, you know?" She wet her lips and tried to make him understand. "He could be the second coming of Christ, but if he can't put whatever shit aside to be kind to you...you have me too, Bobby."

Something undecipherable danced across Bobby's face before he gave her a soft smile and squeezed her hand.

Then he let go and sat back, leaving her clutching at the air where he had been. Cold and...missing him.

Pulling her hand back into her lap, Thea clenched it a couple of times to get the phantom of his palm out of her hand's memory.

Bobby cleared his throat, and she looked up, unprepared for the easy smile on his face. "Okay, Bea. I know you've already got this figured out, so lay it on me. Give me the timeline here: what do you need me to do, and when? I'm your willing soldier."

And he looked it; staring at her with such trust and confidence, waiting patiently for her instructions.

He wasn't judging and teasing. He was just trying to help her find what she was looking for.

For the first time, she noticed the length of his eyelashes, dark and delicate against his skin. It was an oddly intimate moment, and Thea felt her cheeks heat at the realization.

"Okay..." Thea trudged on. "I was thinking we could ride to and from the rink together. It'll be perfect, since everyone will be there."

"Sure," Bobby agreed, sounding totally casual-like they were discussing the weather.

The emotionless way he said it made her take another quick study of him, but his face was a picture-perfect example of engaged listening.

Something about that look made her skin itch, but she couldn't figure out why.

Why was his easy acquiescence causing such a knot to form in her stomach? If she asked him if he was 'okay' one more time, he'd probably ban her from poker night.

"Can you imagine the look on Ian's face when he sees us together?" Thea asked, careful to examine Bobby's reaction to the comment.

"It will probably look a lot like his face did when he got taken out by the open ice hit last night," Bobby offered her a friendly grin.

Again, why did that result in warning bells in her belly?

"You certainly took care of the retribution on that one," Thea grumbled, eyeballing another bruise forming on his jaw under his tightly cropped, black beard.

He rubbed at it and gave her a more mischievous grin that went a long way to settling the nerves in her stomach. "It was a legit hit, but it was still shitty. Third line wasn't delivering the punishments last night. Coach was *pissed*." The way he widened his eyes had the last of Thea's worries fade away as she leaned forward again, resting her forearms on the table.

"What did he say this time?"

Bobby shrugged his plaid-covered shoulders and looked around the café for a beat. Then he turned back to her and grimaced before admitting, "More threats about bumping me down to the later lines if I couldn't keep a lid on it."

"Tommy's been fighting just as much as you and he's not getting the same threats."

Bobby chuckled and leaned back in his seat, sliding his glasses off, folding them up, and putting them in his chest pocket. "True, but Tommy's fights are different. You know that.. And Tommy's play is not the same as mine. There are different expectations. I need to be more selective about my fights but when I hear what they're taunting..." Bobby twisted his neck sharply and she heard the pop from where she was sitting, "it can be challenging to ignore them and just let it happen." He shot her a wry grin. "Don't worry, Coach hasn't threatened to trade me, yet. I think I'll be all right."

Thea's stomach bottomed out, this time for an entirely new reason.

"Trade?" Her voice went high, her chest going tight. "Has he mentioned that before? Jesus, Bobby, stop getting in fights if that's what you're up against!"

"Listen, it was nothing more than an offhand remark made a while back, directed at both me and Ian. He mentioned that if we didn't get our act together, he'd force one of us to go. But really, it's nothing. Just his way of lighting a fire under us. We're okay."

Usually, the coach wasn't one for employing intimidation as motivation. Yet, despite Bobby's unwavering assurance that all was well, Thea couldn't quell the wave of nausea that threatened to overwhelm her. A cold realization washed over her, chilling her to the bone.

All week, her fears had been consumed by the thought of another woman luring Bobby away from Springfield, from her. But it had never once crossed her mind that the real threat could come from within, from a decision enforced by his coach.

She never considered that it would come down to Bobby...or Ian.

And that having one meant losing the other.

Chapter Eleven
March 29, Monday morning
Bobby

Bobby's grip on the steering wheel tightened as he navigated the early morning traffic toward Thea's apartment. His heart, a traitorous drum against his chest, seemed to mock him about the impending performance he was about to give.

As he parked his car, the reality of the situation settled heavily upon him like a weighted blanket, each thread woven with a mix of anticipation and dread.

Thea, radiant as ever, greeted him with a smile that could outshine the brightest of days. Her enthusiasm was palpable, a stark contrast to the anguish churning inside Bobby.

Sure, he had agreed to this façade-to play the loving boyfriend-but now, standing at the threshold of her apartment, the performance felt daunting. Thea's energy, however, seemed to cut through his apprehension, as she ushered him inside with a cheerfulness that left little room for objection.

"Okay, so let's practice before we head out," she proposed. She took his hand, her fingers weaving through his with a familiarity that sent electric shocks up his arm, a physical manifestation of his heart's silent scream that this was no mere act.

They stumbled through a rehearsal in her living room, initially awkward but gradually finding a rhythm. Thea's laughter, light and genuine, filled the room, making their contrived connection seem momentarily real.

"Look at us," Thea laughed, her joy infectious. "This is totally going to work," Thea said, snapping a picture of their intertwined hands. "We look adorable together."

Bobby's heart skipped a beat, but he masked it with a grin. "Convincing, at least," he replied, the words feeling hollow compared to the storm of emotions inside him.

His attempt at a smile felt strained, but luckily she was too busy grabbing her gym bag to notice.

"I know we originally decided that I'd grab a ride home with Lila, but I'm just going to bring my work stuff with me, and work on it while I wait around for your practice to be over. Maybe I'll hit up the gym as well. That way, it's another chance for Ian to see us together."

"Of course," he mumbled as he held the apartment complex door open for her. She breezed by and gave him a bright smile of thanks and strode out into the nippy air.

The drive to the rink was a blur with Thea's excitement a constant hum beside him. She uploaded the picture of their hands to social media, narrating her caption as her fingers flew over the screen: "New relationship, who 'dis? So thankful that our jobs make it so we can ride to work together."

Holy fuck—this was happening.

How was this happening?

Bobby's heart lurched with each notification, a symphony of pings that felt like a countdown to his inevitable unraveling.

On one hand, he hoped like fuck that Ian would notice today and just let them end this charade that was flaying his emotions...on the other, he hoped it never ended.

Masochist.

Thea read the comments from their friends aloud to him as he cruised down the streets. "Ty says, 'What!? No way! When did this happen?!' Jason said, 'About time,' and Tommy said, 'Finally.'" Her forehead wrinkled and she turned to him. "Are they trolling me? Did you tell them?"

Fuck.

Fuck, fuck, fucking, fuck.

He should have given them a heads up.

Bobby shifted in his seat and chewed on what to say.

If he was honest, she would very clearly, and correctly, read into the fact that Bobby had been sporting a crush on her for years...

And if she asked any of the guys later...

Fuck.

This was going to be such a mess.

"They're not fucking with you. They've been trying to get me to date you for years. I keep telling them you're not my type and they insist that we'd be great together. I think the amount of time we spend together just confuses them; they don't have any women in their lives like that. In their minds, girls and boys can't be just friends."

There. That sounded good.

"What do you mean, I'm 'not your type'?"

Jesus H.

He cast an incredulous look at her and felt a jolt shoot through him at how irritated her face was.

Damn, she really was getting persnickety about that.

"Bea...are you really going to tell me that you think you and I would have worked?"

He felt her eyes on him as he drove down the side streets to the rink.

"Why not!? You're attractive. We do everything together. What's wrong with me?"

Absolutely *nothing*.

"How are you insulted about this? The guys thought we should date, I said we shouldn't. I figured you thought the same given that you certainly never said anything. You don't see me demanding you tell me what was wrong with me and why you think Ian is so much better."

Shit. Maybe a little too much truth in that one.

If they made it through the fake dating shit show with their relationship intact, it would be a *fucking* miracle.

"There's nothing wrong with you." She grumbled and sank lower into her seat. "You're fantastic. But I just have this thing with Ian that I owe it to my dad to try."

Their breathing echoed in the confined space of the car, each word a weight added to his already heavy heart.

"And Ian is *not* better than you." She ground out, angrily tucking her phone in her bag.

Well, at least he'd gotten that out of her.

He needed to lighten the mood, stat—given that they were pulling into the underground parking garage, and it was almost show time."

"I know. And I'm glad you agree."

He felt her smile as she pouted at the window.

He threw the car in park and turned to face her. "Are you seriously miffed that I told the guys that we shouldn't date?"

She wrinkled her nose at him. "It's just a little off-putting to know that you don't think I'm a catch."

Jesus.

Slowly, he reached out and grabbed her sharp chin with his fingers. He turned her face toward him and took in her adorable pout. Fucking hell, she was high maintenance and an emotional rollercoaster.

And fuck him twice for loving it so much.

"You, Thea Sharppe, are every man's 'type.' Not a guy on this team, besides married or gay, would turn down a date with you." He paused and revised the statement to be a bit more honest. "They might not come back for a second date, but they'd be there for the first one."

"Hey! Why am I not second-date worthy?" Her voice rang throughout the car as she tried to pull her face out of his hand...and failed.

He rubbed her chin softly to lessen the sting of not letting her go, and for the blow he was about to land.

"Bea, you're perfect. But you're also crazy. And your 'crazy' is not a 'crazy' that just anyone can, or wants, to handle." At her look of outrage, he smiled at her and tensed his fingers on her chin, trying to get her attention. "Your 'crazy' is, unfortunately, a 'crazy' that *I* adore. Maybe Ian will love it as well. But do you think for one minute that Ilya would take you out for a second date?"

She chuckled, leaning into his hand the tiniest amount.

"Exactly. You'd give the poor guy a heart attack with your dramatics. Hell, you give *me* whiplash with your mood swings most days, but I'm still here. So, shake it off, we're here, and we gotta get going." He leveled her with a serious look. "You got your shit together yet?"

She gave him a haughty and indignant look. "As if I ever lost it."

He grinned and slid out of the car, grabbing their bags from the backseat before walking around to her door. Bobby pulled it open and peered down at her. "Of course. You never, ever, overreact. What was I *thinking* to imply such an insult?" He reached out a hand, inviting her to take it. Her small, soft hand molded perfectly to his in a way that made his heart clench. Bobby gave her a tiny tug and pulled her to standing. "Game on, Bea. Ready to win the man of your dreams?"

Thea pulled her opposite thumb to her lips, nervously nibbling at the ragged nail as she eyed Bobby with a conflicted expression.

After a moment, she blinked and squeezed his hand. "I'm ready."

As he shifted and started toward the player's entrance, Bobby caught sight of some empty food containers on the ground by the maintenance shaft and made a mental note to talk to Ty about whose turn it was to leave food out for the stray mystery dog that haunted the parking garage. Was it Ilya's turn? Or Jason's? It was easier to focus on Fido's food schedule than to obsess over how

Thea's hand felt in his—whether he was holding it too tight, too loose, or too...sweatily.

Bobby also determinedly ignored the million texts he felt vibrating from his phone. No doubt his friends were going absolutely nuts and demanding answers.

Well, he'd face the firing squad soon enough.

But for now, Bobby needed to hold his 'girlfriend's' hand and pretend that he hadn't just bared his soul to her.

And he needed to hope that she hadn't noticed his heart had taken residence in the palm of her hand.

CHAPTER TWELVE
March 29, Monday morning
Bobby

"Remember, we've got to sell this," Thea whispered as they entered the building, her eyes scanning for Ian.

Their steps echoed in the vastness of the arena's back hallways, the sound mingling with the distant hum of machinery and electrical equipment. Thea walked beside him, her hand tight in his.

As they neared the locker room, the reality of their impending separation, and how they needed to act, struck Bobby with an unexpected force. The easy banter that had flowed between them in the car now stumbled, faltering under the weight of the unscripted moment they found themselves in.

He stopped in front of the locker room door and looked down the empty hallways.

Were they supposed to stay on script even if no one was around?

"So, this is it, huh?" Bobby broke the silence, his attempt at levity falling flat even to his own ears.

Thea glanced at him; her smile tinged with a nervous energy that mirrored his own. "Yeah, guess so?"

He shoved his hands into his pockets, searching for something to say that could bridge the awkwardness between them. "Guess we'll have to save our award-winning performance for later?"

Thea chuckled, the sound rusty and uncomfortable. "So, it would seem."

Bobby couldn't help but smile at that, the absurdity of their situation momentarily easing the knot in his stomach. "And here I was, thinking we'd be bombarded as soon as we stepped foot inside."

"Apparently, we weren't as hot an item as we thought." Her cheeks flushed. Their eyes met, and for a moment, the world around him seemed to pause.

Bobby saw the flicker of something in Thea's gaze, a quicksilver flash of emotion that he couldn't decipher. It was gone as quickly as it appeared, leaving him to wonder if he'd imagined it.

Then, without warning, Thea stepped closer, her movement bridging the gap between them with a boldness that took his breath away. Going on tiptoes, she leaned up, hesitating for just a heartbeat before her lips brushed his cheek in a feather-light kiss.

The contact was brief, barely more than a whisper against his beard, but it sent a jolt through him, electrifying and unexpected. Thea's cheeks burned even brighter, her eyes wide as if she was surprised by her own confidence.

"Have a good practice," she murmured, her voice a soft song that lingered in the air between them.

Bobby stood frozen. "Yeah, you too," he managed to say, though his voice sounded distant, like it belonged to someone else.

With a shy smile, Thea turned and walked away, leaving Bobby to watch her retreating figure. He touched his cheek, the warmth of her quick kiss seared onto his skin as a tangible reminder of the blurred lines between their act and his all-too-real feelings.

The locker room's familiar smells and sounds enveloped him as he pushed through the doors, but his mind was elsewhere, replaying that moment with Thea over and over. He changed into his workout clothes, knowing that there wouldn't be much time between film and weights.

As he was pulling his shirt over his head, the door to the locker room swung open and some of the guys pushed in, all chuckling with each other.

Until they saw him...

They froze in the entrance, staring at Bobby.

He fought a blush, cursing himself for feeling like a nervous middle schooler.

"So, uh...congratulations?" Ilya broke the silence, pushing past Ty, who was motionless and blocking his path. The tall blonde giant made his way to his locker stall, dropping his own bag and placing down his blender bottle on the bench in front of it.

"Dude, what the fuck?" Ty's expression was one of betrayal.

Yeah...Ty knew exactly what Thea meant to him. The fact that Bobby didn't text Ty to tell him, first, about them getting together...
Shit.

He needed to have a chat with his best friend to explain the situation. Ty wouldn't share the details with anyone. He should know the whole story. But the other guys...

Tommy jostled his way around Ty and wrapped Bobby in a giant bear hug. Bobby wasn't a small man, even so, Tommy made him feel petite. Tommy's aftershave caused Bobby's eyes to water, but he gave him a weak hug back when he remembered that he needed to act the part.

A solid thwack on his back had him catching himself before toppling over.

"Fucking hell, man. Nice work!" Tommy gave him another smack, this time on the shoulder, and then made his way to his own cubby.

Jason ambled over and rested a hot hand on his shoulder, giving him a gentle shake. "Congrats, man. Happy for you two."

Ty was still studying him, a frown now marring his face. His square jaw was set in a way that did not bode well.

Judging by the way Ty jerked his head toward the door, he wanted answers. Now.

With a sigh, Bobby grabbed the stuff he needed for the film review, and the gym after, and followed his irate friend.

A chorus of 'ohs' and 'someone's in trouble' echoed from behind them as they made their way into the hall and up to the film room.

"So, uh..."

"Just stop." Ty ground out, as they passed one of the maintenance crew pushing a trolley down the hall. Taking a back hall rather than their usual route, Ty led them halfway down before stopping and turning to Bobby. "Is she in trouble? Does she have debt? A stalker? Some other threat? Fuck," Ty scrubbed at his face. "Is she pregnant? Is she using you as a stand-in Daddy?"

Damn. Apparently Ty wasn't buying this for a minute.

"I—"

"Fuck, Bobby. There's whipped, and then there's *fucking* whipped."

Bobby jerked back at the sting of Ty's rebuke. "That's not what—"

"Fucking hell, Bobby! Open your eyes! She's not once shown an interest in you! So, why the hell now? What changed? And don't tell me she isn't using you. Your face says it all. If this was real...your face would show it."

Fuck.

Well, so much for the idea that he could sell ice to an Eskimo.

He might be able to fool the media, but not the people closest to him. Thank God his mom lived in Tampa and wasn't hip on video calls.

He'd have to work on his voice inflection for his weekly phone home.

Ty's indignant look at the delay in Bobby's explanation forced Bobby to refocus.

"Okay, you're not...wrong. We have a deal. She needed help with something, and I volunteered."

"Volunteered?"

Bobby failed at hiding his wince. "Was asked..." he corrected weakly, knowing just how much Ty was going to *love* that.

Ty scowled.

"Better. Now the rest of it. The actual truth, not the watered-down version that you want to give to make me not want to ban her from every future poker night for fucking with your emotions for years."

Fuck, Ty was a great friend. Even so, Bobby wanted to punch him in the throat for blaming Thea for something she had no idea she was doing.

"She's not leading me on."

"In the pool, when we play chicken, who does she choose?"

Shit.

"Whose arm does she link hers through when we're out walking around town?"

Bobby squeezed his lips together.

"Who did she text a picture of a lingerie set to when she wanted to know which had a better 'Valentine's vibe?'"

Fuck, he had forgotten about that one.

"Love is supposed to feel good, Bobby. Not like..." Ty gestured at Bobby, disapprovingly. "This."

Bobby glanced away, unable to look Ty in the eye, because he was right.

But his love for Thea went deeper and was just *different*. It felt good to help her now, even if he knew it would hurt worse, later.

"Ty, she just has this thing. She needed a fake boyfriend, she asked me. I could have said no."

"You don't say 'no' to her! Ever!"

Bobby sighed and ran a hand through his hair as he glanced down the empty hall.

"You know she's got this hang-up for Ian..."

"Yeah, I think everyone but Ian knows that."

"Well, she thought that if it looked like we were together, it would...instigate Ian."

Ty reared back and stared at him, opening his mouth only to shut it, repeatedly.

Jesus.

Bobby let out another whoosh of air and gave his friend a sad smile. "Yeah, that's me. The Trojan horse she's using to catch the attention of a guy who I think is a total douche. And the one who agreed to do it. And it sucks, but dude, what could I do? She wants this so bad. I don't think he's a good fit for her, but she needs to learn that herself. The sooner she learns it, the sooner she drops this insane infatuation." Bobby's chest heaved up with the size of his inhale. "I don't know man. She's using this to catch Ian's attention, but what if this is my chance to catch hers?"

There.

He said it.

He gave his stupid hope a voice.

The words hung there between them, and the anger slid from Ty's face as he stared at Bobby.

"All right then. Time to make you *Super Boyfriend*. I know you're out of practice, but we'll make it work. But you're going to need to work on your demeanor, Darcy. Thea isn't an Elizabeth; she wants drama and romance. Setting up Lila with a Bingley isn't going to cut it."

Bobby's eyebrows shot up as his friend turned him and started pushing him down the hall. "You read it?"

Ty winced. "My date wanted to watch it."

"The book is better," Bobby remarked casually, his chest feeling lighter than it had been since Thea had proposed this ridiculous scheme.

"Sure it is. Anyway, we need to iron out some details. You need to be prepared. You need to be charming. And you need to be convincing."

"I can do that."

Ty laughed, "Did you hear me say 'charming'?" He wrapped a big arm around Bobby's shoulder and pulled him in for a one-arm semi-hug. "I've got your back, bud. There's some...*potential*...here.

You'll woo the pants off Thea in no time. She'll be asking 'Ian who?' in less than a week."

"That's the hope," Bobby muttered as they turned the final corner before the film room.

As they entered and took their seats among the chatting men, Ian turned to him, a grin on his face. "There's just one condition. I want your firstborn to be named after me. No excuses. I'm Uncle Ty and there's going to be a Little Ty. Naming rights are only fair."

Ian plopped down in the seat behind them, a smoothie in one hand and a protein bar in the other. "What are we talking about fellas? Who's having a Little Ty?"

A few of the other guys started taking random seats throughout the room as the coaches mingled up front, waiting for the stragglers to come in. Tommy, Jason, and Ilya grabbed seats near them as well.

The twinkle in Ian's bright blue eyes didn't encourage the nerves in Bobby's belly.

Sure enough, the shit starter began laying the groundwork.

"Oh? You didn't hear? Bobby finally sealed the deal with Thea. Took him forever, especially because of her conviction that hockey players aren't good boyfriends, but he finally wore her down. There's no way he's losing her now." Ty's voice echoed around the room and Bobby could have sworn he literally saw the soundwaves with how loud they felt.

Ian's expression was...

Well, if so much wasn't on the line, Bobby would have laughed.

The confusion had caused his face to twist into an amusing contortion, a mix of disbelief and intrigue. "Bobby, you sly dog," Ian drawled, his acidic voice dripping with faux astonishment. "Here I was, thinking you were all about hockey and nothing else, and you've been working on this secret romance this whole time."

Bobby forced a chuckle, his heart pummeling his ribcage like a battering ram.

He had to sell it.

Show time.

"Yeah, you know me, Ian. Always full of surprises," he replied, hoping his voice sounded steadier than he felt. "But after the game the other night, well, you know how it is." He swallowed and tried to project as much confidence as possible. "I had a fucking great game. Combine that with a fight and a bruised face that needed tending. It was easy. You know how she is. She wants the best in everything. After that game, I managed to convince her I was it."

The false bravado was almost comical in how many curious looks it was generating from his friends on the team.

Like the wingman he was, Ty played along.

"After she turned down that proposal from a Spartans' player a couple of years ago, I thought no one would ever meet her standards. I'm glad you showed her you're the one, brother." Ty patted Bobby on the shoulder, the picture-perfect bro happy for his buddy.

Ian's eyes darkened. "You didn't have that good of a game…"

Tommy laughed from two seats down. "Fucking hat trick, man, as well as a Top Ten SportsCenter goal, and still managed to get in a fight and lay someone out. Seems like the trifecta to me."

Bobby couldn't stop his grin. That Tommy didn't even mention his mistakes—some of which Ian had orchestrated to make Bobby look bad—was just icing on the cake. Bobby couldn't have planned this to go any better.

Ian's jaw was twisted to the side as he dragged his unimpressed look from Tommy back to Bobby. "I wasn't under the impression that Thea was a…hard lay." He raised his hand in a quick appeal, anticipating the reaction that such a slur against a person's girlfriend would generate. "No offense."

Ty stiffened but Bobby had spent the last twenty-four hours preparing for the shit that Ian was going to say to get under his skin. He had years of practice, the fact that it was now aimed at Thea, made him want to break Ian's fucking nose, but that would be giving

Ian a reaction—something that he learned years ago was a bad move. If he appeared unphased, Ian moved on faster.

Bobby gave a friendly shrug and met Ian's eyes. "If you can name one guy on the team, or anyone in the NHL that Thea has dated besides me, I'll let you cold clock me at practice later." After a beat, he added. "With or without a glove—dealer's choice."

The guys around them stilled and swiveled toward them. Their attention was making Bobby's skin prickle, but he kept a level, easy expression on his face as he looked at Ian. Ian's eyes were darting around the room, he was searching for a name...and coming up blank.

Thank fuck.

With a smile that Bobby tried to make as joyful as possible, he gave a nod to Ian and turned around in his seat, giving the man his back.

Down by their knees, Ty presented Bobby his knuckles.

Grinning in earnest now, Bobby gave Ty a discreet fist bump and directed his eyes to the screen where the coaches were now pulling up the game film. An assistant coach pulled the door shut before flicking down the lights as chatter died and their head coach started strategizing their upcoming game against the Maple Leafs.

As Coach Montgomery started playing the video, Bobby sent a giant thank you to Thea's 'universe' that Thea had never shared about any of her relationships on social media. She had remarked that morning in the car that posting about a relationship was a new thing for her followers—of which she had thousands—and she wondered what it would do to her engagement and public perception. There was a moment of worry that being seen dating a player would affect her on-ice reporter application, but she was a determined woman, and the feminine rage she would unleash if she was judged for that during any further interviews would burn the sports world to the ground.

Thea would be okay.

He was just thankful that he was her first.

Even if he wasn't her last.

Chapter Thirteen
March 29, Monday afternoon
Bobby

The men had only a sliver of time before ice practice, the perfect window for a quick workout. The atmosphere was charged with an undercurrent of tension that hummed beneath the surface—thanks, in no small part, to Ian's simmering antagonism–as the team made their way down the hall.

Bobby's mind was a whirlwind of thoughts about the coach's words, about Ian's taunts, and, most prominently, about Thea. She had mentioned earlier that she was going to work out for a bit, and he was just hoping she'd be gone by the time they got there.

Then again, given that her day job was literally a mix between fitness influencer, model, and sports analyst, he shouldn't have been surprised to find her still grinding away.

Her latest sponsors did not disappoint.

That outfit was...

He had to suck in a deep breath so he wouldn't pass out.

Her outfit was eye-catching, to say the least—a vibrant splash of red in the otherwise monochrome gym. Thea's getup was a seamless blend of style and functionality that hugged her form in all the right places, accentuating her toned physique. Well, the parts that *had* fabric at least. The various cutouts and cropped parts left inches of tantalizing, delicious skin to admire.

But the outfit wasn't just sexy; it was empowering, radiating the confidence and strength that was so inherently Thea.

The guys turned to him when he paused at the entrance.

Shit.

Was he supposed to go to her?

Ignore her?

They were still co-workers...was it crossing a line to greet her?

Or was that what she wanted from him?

Holy fuck, why was it suddenly so hot in here?

Bobby tugged at his shirt collar but felt no relief.

It was Ty who broke him from his reverie, giving him a slight push toward Thea. Bobby stumbled forward, thankful for Ty making the decision for him.

As he approached, Thea's gaze found him, and the world seemed to freeze.

Her smile was like a beacon, radiant and genuine, drawing him in despite the storm of doubts raging inside him.

It was the same smile she always gave him.

Her joy to see him wasn't for show.

And wasn't that the rub?

As he approached, he couldn't stop from worrying what his next move should be.

Should he embrace her?

Kiss her?

What did their audience expect from Springfield's newest power couple?

Thea's eyes flickered behind him to the group of players staring at them, no doubt finding Ian, before she returned her eyes to Bobby.

With a grace that seemed to belie the awkwardness of their situation, Thea closed the distance between them, rising on her tiptoes to plant a brief, but firm, kiss on his lips.

His skin caught on fire. Not only his lips, which now tasted of her citrus bubblegum, but the spot on his chest where she had placed her hand as she leaned up.

A place where her hand was still resting.

As she pulled away, Bobby was left momentarily dazed.

Thea's smile was triumphant, reveling in the ability to debut their relationship in front of her *dearly beloved*.

Bobby fought a lip curl.

Ian, for his part, watched with a mask of indifference that didn't fool Bobby. The flicker of annoyance, the tightening of his jaw, betrayed his true feelings.

Ty, however, looked pleased as punch and gave him a dorky thumbs up with a huge cat-got-his-cream smile. Well, at least someone was happy.

The weight room echoed with the clinking of metal and the muted thuds of weights being set down, a symphony of determination and discipline.

"Good skate earlier?" Bobby couldn't quite find the brainpower to form a complete sentence, not while standing in front of her in that sexy outfit, with the taste of her on his lips, the feel of her on his skin, and the smell of her in his nose.

Thea's chuckle filled the space between them, easing the tension that had knotted Bobby's insides. "It was decent," she replied, her hand finally retreating from his chest, leaving a trail of warmth in its wake. "But I think some of the upper management was hanging out on the main level, looking down at us while we worked. I made sure to be extra amazing."

Her eyes sparkled, but Bobby noted worry among the confidence. "I'm sure everyone they've talked to has had nothing but good things to say. If the sports channel this morning was anything to go by, you're a hot commodity." He paused and studied her for a minute, before squinting with a frown. "Did Boston really call you?"

Her loud laugh burst through the barren room, echoing off the hard walls and rubber flooring. She leaned forward and rested her head on his chest, shaking him with her giggles. "Oh, my God! No, they haven't! Is that what the news is saying? I wish! I'd look fantastic in black and gold."

Bobby, finding his footing in their banter, teased her back. "Oh, is that so? Here I was thinking you were a Springfield girl for life. Do your fans know this about you, Benedict Arnold?"

Thea's smile widened, her gaze locking with his in a challenge as she put a quick hand over his mouth. "Shh, don't say it too loud. I have too many endorsements to risk a traitorous scandal like that."

Bobby nodded sagely, crossing his fingers over his heart, and trying not to reach out and nip the hand on his lips.

Thea beamed up at him, then blinked like she'd been blindsided. She ripped her hand back and crossed her arms across her chest, looking around the room quickly, not settling on any one thing.

Was she looking for Ian?

Hence the signature blush that was now gracing her cheeks.

Fucking hell.

Bobby cleared his throat, also looking around, not noticing Ian anywhere. He then turned back to Thea. She was watching him, but when their eyes met, she glanced down at her shoes.

"So, yeah, no call from Boston, or any other place. Cyclones are my ride or die. Dad genetically engineered my DNA to make it so. Couldn't shake them if I wanted to." She gave a wooden laugh and nudged the ball of her foot into the floor in a subtle twisting motion.

"Keep getting those fitness clothing companies to send you outfits like that and management won't want you wearing anything else when you're reporting on the ice."

She straightened and dropped her arms, swinging her head up to face him.

"What's wrong with my outfit?"

It was physically impossible not to lean back and assess her outfit, or lack thereof. "Not a single, fucking, goddamned thing." It wasn't supposed to come out as a hungry growl.

But it sure did anyway.

She blinked.

He froze.

Shit.

He straightened and raised his eyebrows at her, hoping to play it off. "It's perfect. Not a thing wrong with it. It's great."

Her cheeks were as red as her outfit, and her bright eyes were blown wide as she took him in, trying to process the change in his voice.

He laughed; the sound more relaxed than he felt. "Only on paper. In reality, I have no idea how well it holds up under one of your workouts, so you'd have to be the judge of whether it's practical as it is ...sexy."

He could have used a less seductive word—but hadn't he just told himself that he needed to walk the walk? He needed to be boyfriend material. Which means, he needed to start putting those teasers and nuggets in her head. He needed to stop filtering his attraction so much, especially if he wanted her to notice him in a new light.

"Um," she blinked rapidly a couple of times and reached up to tuck a nonexistent hair back behind her ear. "Yeah, it's...practical. And very...supportive...in the," she waved her hands near her push-up bra that was designed by the gods. "You know, chest...area."

He stared down at her cleavage for a beat longer than he normally would have allowed himself and then tore his eyes back to hers. He tried to ignore his own blush and the uncomfortable need to adjust himself in his shorts.

"Uh, yeah. I can, um, see that."

He needed to get his shit together. Bobby had to stop treating Thea so carefully and doggedly platonic. If he wanted a real chance with her, he needed to show her the side of him she had never seen before. He had to treat her like any other woman he was genuinely interested in dating, not just as his best friend.

Bobby gestured to her whole outfit. "It's sexy as hell, so it's a winner in my book. Wear it over to my place any day of the week and I'll buy you whatever you want to watch for a movie that night. As long as I can watch you lounging around in that, I don't even care if it's one of your reality shows."

Thea's mouth dropped open the barest amount, just enough to show a sexy tease of white teeth. She started breathing a little heavier, so naturally, her fucking breasts had to start moving up and down enough to call his attention back to them. Rather than fight the urge as he had trained his body to do for the last few years, he let his gaze drop, taking a second, then another, before forcing himself back up to her face.

Fucking hell, he'd need an ice shower after this, or he'd be benching with the Eiffel Tower in his shorts.

Thea gave a small cough and in a tight voice said, "Ah, so it's the spandex that does it for you?"

"It's not the spandex that's making an impression," Bobby admitted, allowing his gaze to openly appreciate her once more, making her blush—a victory in its own right. "It's the woman wearing it."

Thea gave a nervous giggle, her eyes gleaming with a mix of pride and something else—something warmer, softer.

The air around them shifted, charged with an unspoken tension that Bobby had never allowed to form before. They met just after her father died and she hadn't needed a *boyfriend*, she needed a *friend*. He was more than happy to fill that role, because, as he told her earlier, her particular brand of crazy was exactly his preferred flavor. He hadn't even known her well, but even riddled with grief, he still knew *that* about her. Instantly.

And as the years passed and they grew closer, Bobby didn't know how to level up from the friend zone.

Didn't even know if he wanted to risk it.

Being friends with Thea was better than losing her completely if she felt awkward about his feelings.

So he never let her get those...vibes...from him.

But she was sure as fuck feeling them now, if her dilated pupils were anything to go by.

Okay, Bobby, strike while the iron's hot.

He closed the distance between them just a little. "So, about this workout," he started, lowering his voice like he would if he was picking up a woman at the bar or a club. "You planning on teasing us all with this little number, or...?"

Thea tilted her head, a shocked small smile forming as she stared up at him with wide eyes. "I think a little teasing is never a bad thing." The way her eyes darted back and forth from his own and the little exhale she gave that coasted across his lips...*fuck*. He needed that ice shower. Stat.

Bobby allowed his lips to form in a wolfish grin, leaning forward even more, placing their faces within inches of each other's, the thrill of the challenge igniting something in him. He whispered low and seductive, "That's fine, Bea. Tease away. But just remember, what goes around comes back around. And I'm not known to be hasty in my retribution. Just ask the guys on the ice."

With that statement, Bobby gave her a quick kiss on the nose, chuckled her gently on the chin, and turned away to the team huddled in the corner starting on incline presses.

"I'll be waiting!" Thea called with a laugh.

Without turning around, Bobby held up a hand as a wave of acknowledgment. He could almost feel her resulting smile.

The warmth on his skin shifted and a sharp tingle on his neck caused him to turn his head the slightest amount, only to see Ian spinning on an air bike not far from where they had been standing. Bobby hadn't clocked him earlier.

As he saddled up to the workout equipment, he tried to think back on whether he or Thea had said anything incriminating, but he didn't think they had.

Bobby couldn't decide whether he was relieved about that or not.

Given the contemplation growing in Ian's narrowed eyes, Bobby was leaning toward regret that he hadn't let something slip.

Because he didn't trust that look *at all*.

CHAPTER FOURTEEN

March 29, Monday afternoon
Bobby

Bobby's breath fogged in the icy air as he watched his teammates glide around the rink.

Ty skated over to him, a broad grin on his face.

"Hey, lover boy! How's Thea?" he teased, elbowing Bobby gently. "Didn't look that fake to me."

"You don't have to sound so giddy about it," Bobby grumbled, trying to brush off the comment and focus on scooping and balancing, puck after puck.

"And you're telling me that you *aren't* feeling giddy? Dude, you had her fucking panting after you with only *one* flirt session in a *public* gym. How are you *not* on cloud nine?" Ty's incredulity tempered his excitement for Bobby.

"I'm...It felt weird to turn it on her. To use that...shit...with her. It felt...manipulative."

"You mean, that for once, you actually said what you were thinking and let your guard down just enough to actually do something that you wanted to do? You're not her fucking father, man. You don't have to parent her."

Bobby stiffened and whirled to face Ty, dropping the puck with a clack.

"What the fuck did you just say?"

Ty shrugged, his practice shirt tugging with the movement. "I know you liked the guy and got close with him on our road trips and shit, but you didn't owe him some unbreakable vow to treat his daughter like a nun."

"I was being respectful!"

"You were being a chicken."

Silence fell.

"Well, damn, what are we having here?" Tommy iced the boards behind Bobby and inserted himself into their little standoff. In a lower voice, Tommy continued on, "Coach is eyeballing you two and your voices are starting to carry. Get your shit together, fast, or Coach will pull a *Miracle* and make us sprint till we're all vomiting. Got it?" At the menacing look in the bruiser's eye, both Bobby and Ty went back to focusing on the drills that they had been doing.

Jason skated over, joining the group. "You know how much I love good gossip, so fill me in. How's it going with Thea? She seemed ready to jump you in the gym, earlier."

"You noticed that too?" Tommy reached out and yanked a bit on Bobby's head, rocking him back and forth. "I thought we were extras in a porno that no one told us about."

Bobby's cheeks flushed as he remembered Thea's hands on his chest, the warmth of her breath on his lips, and the taste of her citrus gum. He forced a laugh, attempting to maintain a casual façade. "We're fine. Things are still new so we're...navigating it."

"I bet," Tommy said jovially. "Navigating and exploring and *plundering*. Fuck, those are the best parts, especially when you know it's wrong." His voice took on a distant, distracted tone and the men turned to him in confusion, not that the giant was paying attention.

Ian skated over and chose that brilliant moment to try to start another round of shit.

The other guys just rolled their eyes and skated away, abandoning Bobby to deal with his pissant teammate.

"So, you and Thea really are a thing."

We have a Sherlock here, folks.

"I guess I just thought Ty was exaggerating. Especially with all that talk about you having such a good game. You and I know it was fine, nothing to go down in fame though. I thought Thea came from a hockey family. Shouldn't she know that?"

Was Bobby really supposed to answer that?

Coach blew his whistle and Bobby made his way behind the net to get in line for the next drill.

Ian followed.

Fucking lichen, that one.

"So, let me know when you're done playing house with Thea. I don't usually buy used goods, but given the outfit she had on today, I might make an exception. She looks like she knows how to handle a stick, if you catch my drift. And after she's done with you, she might be craving a guy with a little more...balls, ya know?"

Bobby's hands convulsed around his stick, as he forced himself to stare at the skates of the player in front of him in line. His muscles tensed with the urge to whirl around and silence Ian with a single blow.

The rink seemed to shrink, the brisk air thickening with the weight of his fury. Every nerve in his body screamed for retribution, for the satisfying crunch of his fist meeting Ian's smug face.

But he forced himself to stay rooted, to swallow the rage burning in his throat like acid. The skates in front of him pushed forward and Bobby woodenly took over the vacant spot, using every ounce of willpower to focus on hockey instead of giving Ian the satisfaction of seeing him lose control. Not here, not now. But the fire simmered beneath his skin, a fierce heat that threatened to consume him whole.

What did Thea see in this fucking guy!?

And why the fuck was he helping her direct his attention to her?

Channeling his anger, Bobby sprinted away as soon as it was his turn.

Like a man possessed, he flew over the ice, sailing by the defenders, and landing puck after puck in the net.

But the exercise and intensity were doing nothing to dissipate his wrath.

Thirty minutes later, the coaches mixed some of the lines up and unwisely, set Ian and Bobby on opposite teams.

Unwilling to take second place to Bobby, Ian increased his intensity—but not enough.

Bobby deked him out of his skates, again and again.

The grim satisfaction he got for making Ian look like a fucking college kid also did nothing to temper the feelings burning him up.

The tension between Ian and Bobby spiked as they collided, sending icy shavings spraying across the rink. The hit and resulting pain finally dissolved the haze that had been consuming him.

"Jesus! What the fuck, Bobby," Ian snapped, his dark eyes narrowed and intense, as he sat up and readjusted his helmet

"Stop being such a little bitch and take the hit, you little snowflake," Bobby goaded back, the bitterness in his voice impossible to hide.

"What the fuck was that?" Ilya growled from next to him.

"What did it fucking sound like?"

He didn't have the patience for Ian's shit anymore. Enough was enough.

Ilya gave a jolt before frowning and assessing Bobby, brow creased with concern. "Bobby, you okay, man?"

"Fucking great." Bobby rolled his eyes, still glaring at Ian as he dusted himself off and skated away. "No, I'm not fucking okay. I listen to his shit every fucking day. None of you say shit to stop him, which is fine, because I don't need you to protect me from whatever garbage he wants to spew at me. But I've swallowed it down for the good of the team for fucking *years* at this point. So, if you have a problem that I just don't feel like putting up with his particular brand of asshole *today*, one day out of hundreds, then you can kiss my ass."

Bobby skirted Ilya and skated hard into the drill, channeling his frustration into the play.

As he skated off his rotation after another goal, he made his way over to the next station. He felt eyes on him and turned, catching Ilya's lingering gaze.

Now that the heat of the moment had worn off, Bobby felt like a total jackass for snapping at Ilya when his issue was with Ian.

He'd grab Ilya after practice and apologize.

As for Ian...well.

Why Ian was perfectly amicable with them and not Bobby was complete bullshit.

They came up the ranks together. They played on the same fucking line. Hell, they used to be friends even. Now, Ian was just...bitter and unforgiving.

Not that Bobby had shit to apologize for.

But, crashing into Ian like that? He needed to recenter himself and get a grip on his emotions.

He could have hurt Ian, or himself, which would have totally fucked the team over for playoffs.

Bobby needed to do better.

He would do better.

Bobby took a deep breath and forced his attention back to the ice. He couldn't afford to let his feelings for Thea, and his jealousy of Ian, interfere with his performance.

But as he skated through the drills, dodging checks and firing shots, he couldn't escape the truth: he was in too deep.

And as much as he tried to fight it, his love for Thea and his desire to make her happy was tearing him apart.

Chapter Fifteen

March 29, Monday evening
Bobby

Practice had been grueling, though not because of the drills from their Coach.

At least it was over.

Bobby was dripping sweat as he grabbed his drink from the bench, and when he glanced toward the Zamboni gate where his teammates were exiting the rink, he sucked in a breath when he noticed Thea. She was sitting in one of the side seats there, her feet up on the back of the seats below her, her concerned gaze fixed on him.

How much had she seen?

Bobby watched as his teammates disappeared down the tunnel, their laughter echoing through the emptying arena.

Well, time to pay the piper.

Slowly, he started to skate toward the exit, not breaking eye contact with Thea. Without missing a beat, he transitioned from the ice to the rubber walkway that ran along the side of the Zamboni tunnel. He leaned against the wall and waited for Thea to scramble down to talk to him, finally feeling the chill of the arena as his sweat cooled on him.

She appeared a moment later. "Hey," she said cautiously, giving him a worried smile that caused his heart to clench.

"Hey," he replied, struggling to keep his voice casual. "Get a lot of work done?"

"For sure," she agreed carefully, still watching him. "Caught a lot of your practice too."

Fuck.

"Of course, you did. Ian was here," Bobby agreed, forcing himself to be as neutral about it as possible.

Thea winced and looked toward the now-empty rink.

"Are you okay?"

"Fine."

She gave him a wounded look.

Which he ignored.

Hell, day one, and they were already spatting with and lying to each other. Maybe this was a real relationship, after all.

"He said something to you." It wasn't a question.

"Nope."

"Bobby—"

"Thea, stop." Thea reared back as if he'd struck her and he sighed, rubbing his face with his hands and wincing at the ripe smell born of his movement. "You see something in him that I don't. He's a talented player. He's an asset to this team. I owe this administration everything and I will always do anything in my power to make the best moves for this team. But I still think he's a shit human being. I've told you that. You," he pointed at her, and she winced again, "do not agree. We both know that we do not agree on the subject of Ian. Fine. We agree to disagree. We don't need to hash it out again and again." Thea's eyes were wide and full of hurt but he plowed on, unable to stop the wave of frustration from boiling over everything in its path. "I can deal with the shit he says to me. If he says shit to you, I will also deal with that too, in an entirely different way, whether you want me to or not. But I'm here. I agreed to this, and I'll stick to my end of the deal. So, don't worry, I'll be your good little lapdog and pant just how you want. But just know that if he steps out of line with you, he'll have me to answer to." With a definitive nod, Bobby turned for the locker room, trying to erase the memory of Thea's wide eyes reflecting the hurt he'd wrought upon her.

Chapter Sixteen

March 29, Monday evening
Thea

Thea leaned against Bobby's locked car, staring absently at an unusual stack of open take-out containers lining the floor along the wall of the mostly empty parking garage. Her arms were semi-folded across her chest, her nub of a right thumbnail resting at her lips as she waited for Bobby to leave the arena. She had replayed their earlier conversation in her mind countless times, grappling with the hurt she had seen in his eyes.

What had Ian said to him this time?

There was no doubt that he had said something—she'd watched it all go down.

What surprised her was Bobby's reaction. He was usually so good about ignoring Ian's teasing.

Had Ian crossed a line?

And if he had…

Was it just good-natured competition? Or was it something else?

What if Bobby was right about Ian being redeemable?

If so, why would her dad ever think they were a good match?

Footsteps echoed through the hollow garage and Thea looked up, dropping her arms to her side as Bobby rounded the corner.

Thea's heart skipped a beat, anxiety churning inside her chest. She wanted to help him, but how could she do that when she didn't know what was wrong?

Bobby slowed his pace as he neared his car, his expression guarded and apologetic as he took in her waiting form.

She gave him a solitary eyebrow raise while she crossed her arms menacingly.

As if he could scare off Thea Sharppe with a little temper tantrum.

He'd certainly dealt with his share of her emotional outbursts over the years, so she could handle his little fit from earlier.

Honestly, his outburst wasn't even that bad. Just out of character.

Like his behavior at practice.

Thea straightened up as he stopped in front of her, her eyes searching his face for any sign of what he might be feeling. She opened her mouth to speak, but Bobby held up a hand to stop her, his expression serious, yet determined.

"Let me go first," he said, his voice steady but tinged with emotion. "I need to apologize for what I said earlier. My attitude was shit. I didn't mean to lash out. I was...frustrated, and I let it get the best of me."

Thea's shoulders relaxed slightly, a small sense of relief washing over her. "It's okay," she replied softly. "Honesty, it's actually nice to see you overcome with emotion for once." Thea leaned toward him and whispered like she was imparting a state secret. "I was starting to think I was overly emotional. Now I know you're just as much of a dramatic mess as me, you just hide it better."

His eyes were serious, but his lips twitched under his neatly dropped beard. "I don't know if I'd go that far."

"Psh, please. You're a fucking mess. Thank God you found me. My drama puts life into perspective for you. I should be saying 'you're welcome.'"

"You're a true public servant," he added, nodding along gravely, his eyes sparkling as he gazed down at her.

She felt her belly warm at the tenderness in his expression and she tried to force the butterflies down and back into the closet where they belonged.

"Do you think I should go back to school and become a psychologist? Apparently I'm really good at it. I'll give Kayla a call and see if she wants to team up. We'll be psychologists to the stars."

Bobby hefted his bag up a little higher on his shoulder and gave her a soft grin, his eyes still shining on her in a way that made her want to squeeze her legs together. "I think she's already working that route and I don't think there's a spot for you in her business plan. As talented and natural as you may be." He tacked on the end with a flash of white as he smiled big.

More heat curled in her belly.

What the fuck was happening to her?

"Well, anyway," she coughed and glanced around the parking garage, now feeling uncomfortable meeting his eyes. "Ian goaded you by saying something shitty. Something you probably won't tell me?" He gave her a small smile but then ultimately shook his head. "Yeah, I didn't think so. So, he ticked you off and for the first time in years, you let it get under your skin. You should probably vent it out a bit more often there, champ. That way you don't go Vesuvius on his ass. At least not where your coach can see you."

That wiped the smile off his face.

Yeah. Shit.

"He have some words for you after practice?"

"A few."

"Anything we're worried about?"

Bobby looked away and Thea felt fear bloom in her stomach. Bobby was *never* cagey.

What had the coach said?

"Bobby?"

"Nothing that warrants repeating. No worries, Bea. It's all good and handled."

What did that mean?

She glared at him, showing him exactly how unimpressed she was by his silence.

Bobby reached out and grabbed her chin in his fist, giving it a gentle sway. "It's all good, Thea. Put it out of your mind."

Thea swatted his hand away and narrowed her eyes further.

He sighed and looked up at the roof of the garage. "Do you want to hear my plan or not?"

"I do, as long as you aren't a bitch about it."

His face was still upturned but she could see the outright smile bloom.

Why did her toes want to curl at that?

Bobby sobered and leveled her with a serious look. "I know I was shitty earlier. I'm working through some things. I'm relieved that you're being...you...about it. But regardless, I'll do my best not to direct that frustration at you again. It wasn't cool."

"Neither is your obsession with historical romances, but I love you anyway. So, let it go. I have."

They looked at each other for a beat too long before glancing away. Both of them shifted on their feet.

Bobby coughed into his fist and broke the awkward silence. "Okay, consider it 'let go.' But if I made you feel bad about asking for my help, I wanted to apologize. I'm here for you, no matter what," he said earnestly. "Even if I don't always agree with your decisions or desires, I'll always support you."

Something about the 'desire' part of his sentence didn't fit quite right. Yeah, she felt like she needed to go on a date with Ian, to see if they were a good match or not...and yes, he was attractive, talented, and smart...

But if Bobby really hated Ian that much...was it even something he could truly let go? Even for her?

Thea looked up into Bobby's sincere face, doing her best to smother the tingles that were now traveling south. Had he always looked at her so...intently? It was distracting.

"Thank you for apologizing, but it's not necessary. We all need a release valve. You're mine. Now I'm yours. I'm actually feeling like this evens out our friendship. I can finally offer something of value."

His face turned dark and little wrinkles erupted on his forehead as he took a step closer. "Thea—"

She reached out and quickly placed a finger against his lips.

Woah, they were soft.

She hadn't noticed before. Never had a reason to.

She sure as fuck did now.

She pulled her hand back like she had when she was seven and had touched the hot stove on a dare from her brothers.

"It's all good. Let's move on. You know heart to hearts make me squeamish."

"So, we're okay?" he asked, holding out his hand to her.

Thea nodded, taking his hand in hers and giving it a reassuring squeeze. "Yeah, we're okay. Always, Bobby."

Bobby pulled Thea into a hug, holding her close for a moment before stepping back. He then reached around her for the passenger door, pulling it open for her to climb inside.

As she slid in, tucking her bag at her feet, Thea breathed a sigh of relief. She felt like she was going to melt into a puddle of relief right then and there.

It was okay.

They were okay.

Jesus, as her heart started to thump hard in her chest, she realized just how worried she had been about all of this. Her bravado and adrenaline were wearing off and now she felt boneless as she clumsily buckled her seatbelt and took another heaving breath.

Bobby made his way around the car and slid in beside her, tossing his bag in the back seat before starting the car.

"Dinner?" Bobby asked while resting his hand on her seat and pivoting to back out of the spot.

Thea's lips curved into a relieved smile. His fridge was no doubt still overflowing from the other day, but getting take-out was their *'thing'*—their *normal*–so takeout would be *perfect*.

"I'd love that," she replied, her voice breathy and Bobby gave her a quick look before turning his attention back to the road.

A thought struck her, and she leaped on it to dispel the tension. "Though, I already took off the spandex, so dinner and a show will have to be for another day."

Out of the side of her eye, she saw Bobby turn to her. She practically felt his eyes raking down her body. "Shame," he added in a husky voice.

Oh.

Woah.

Her breath caught in her throat, and she used all of her willpower to keep her face neutrally pleasant and facing forward.

Well, that didn't quite relieve the tension as she hoped.

Was he serious earlier, when he was admiring the outfit?

Her heart started racing harder in her chest and she felt a little lightheaded as she took in quicker, yet still practically useless, breaths.

Oh, *God.* She pinched her knees together in her seat and tried her hardest not to focus on the feelings that were burning through her body.

Was he being honest earlier?

Why did the idea of him visually devouring her in the spandex make her body feel so hot and gooey?

Ian wasn't around. Why did he say 'shame?' and in that tone of voice, no less.

Was he Method acting? Did he just want to stay in character so he wouldn't slip up later?

She cracked her window and let the frigid air blast into her face.

"Thea? Want me to turn the heat down?"

Fuck, yes.

Instead, she settled on, "Uh, no. I'm all right. Just a hot flash, you know? Women things."

If he was any other guy in the world, he would have steered the conversation elsewhere, immediately.

But because he was Bobby, he reached forward, grazing her knee as he reached to pop open the glove compartment.

Now she couldn't get the idea of him resting his big hands on her knees and how that would feel out of her head.

She swallowed hard.

"Check in there. It should be stocked for you."

Stiffly, she reached forward, ignoring what the movement did to the center of her, and grabbed the small pack that Bobby had in his glove compartment. Feeling antsy, she crossed her legs and almost groaned at how good it felt.

Holy shit, what was wrong with her?

She tried to focus on unzipping the packet, but she couldn't stop picturing Bobby's hungry look in the gym earlier as he looked, again and again, at her body proudly displayed. The way his face darkened when he inspected her bra...

She fought back a groan and blindly slapped her hand on the window control to bring the window down.

"Jesus, Bea. You want me to pull over?" He cracked his own window to allow for better airflow, but the air pressure shift did nothing to ease the roaring in her ears.

He pulled the bag out of her hand, and quickly dug an item out. "Midol? Tampon? Advil? I think I have a heating pad in the back that can plug into the outlet there." His voice was barely audible over the roaring wind coming through the window and pelting her face.

Holy shit.

Taking a heaving breath, she closed her eyes, trying to ignore the pressure building in her.

"I'm fine, Bobby. Just give me a minute." She waved her left hand vaguely, trying to get him to put the emergency period pack away. That was so typical of Bobby to have it stocked for her. Her heart squeezed in her chest, and she welcomed the distraction from something else in her that wanted to pulse and squeeze.

After a few minutes, Thea had herself under control enough that she rolled the window up and flipped the sun visor down so she could use the mirror to assess the damage. Her hair was blown everywhere, so she efficiently tried to fix it while staring at her too dilated eyes and flushed skin.

She looked like a total mess.

Thea felt Bobby's eyes on her, and she cautiously turned to face him. His eyes were narrowed as he inspected her, looking for anything that he could help with. Luckily, the man had to drive, so he had to turn his eyes back to the road again, breaking the spell that had caused her to hold her breath under his scrutiny.

Okay.

Okay.

So, what?

She knew that Bobby wasn't some blushing innocent virgin or something.

She knew he'd had girlfriends over the years.

Even a few puck bunnies when he first started if some of the comments made by the guys at poker night were anything to go by.

Okay.

She took another steadying breath before turning to him.

"You're welcome."

He whipped to give her a curious look before looking back to the road. "For?"

"Providing you with constant dramas to distract you from the turmoil in your own head."

His teeth flashed as the stoplight ahead of them changed to red. The car slowed and once he stopped her leveled her with an incredulous look.

"You are absolutely one in a million, Thea Sharppe."

She gave him her most winning smile. "And don't you forget it."

The affectionate look he gave her caused the fire she had just smothered to reignite.

Damnit.

Friends, friends, friends.

"So...Burgers?"

A tsunami wave of relief had Thea sagging back into her seat.

"God, yes."

"You got it."

As the light turned green and Bobby eased forward, Thea felt a sense of nervous contentment settle over her.

Whatever was going on with her was a fluke. Some insanity from him flirting with her today and the emotional turmoil they had worked through after. She was just feeling raw and out of sorts.

They were okay.

That was all that mattered.

Those crazy feelings would go away as soon as she had a delicious meal in her stomach and didn't feel as raw.

She was sure of it.

CHAPTER SEVENTEEN

March 30, Tuesday evening
Thea

The next day found Thea navigating the familiar halls of the arena, her steps quickened by the mile-long to-do list that game nights demanded. Dressed in a never-before-seen version of her Chill Chaser uniform, she exuded confidence outwardly, but inside, anguish churned in her gut.

Her body's reaction to Bobby last night still lingered in her mind, replaying over and over again.

What was wrong with her?

It had to have been the emotional whiplash that she was going through that week, combined with hunger and exhaustion from working out.

It had to be...

As she distractedly marched into a three-way junction, she nearly fell on her ass to avoid a collision with Bobby, who was coming from the other hallway. With fast reflexes, he caught her arm, steadied her, and then steered her in the direction she had been heading.

He looked every bit the professional athlete he was, his strides purposeful as he fell in step beside her, no doubt headed toward the trainers' room. "Hey, Bea." A warm smile graced his full lips.

Well, the fake dating thing wasn't rattling *him*.

Why did the lack of nerves on his part make her feel so...shitty?

"Hey," she replied, her voice catching. She cleared her throat to settle the flutter of nerves in her stomach. No dice.

"Check out the fancy new outfit." Bobby let out a low whistle. "That's quite the get-up. Not that I'm complaining."

Thea felt heat rise to her cheeks at his comment. "Yeah, I wanted to switch things up a bit," she tried to sound nonchalant, but worried it came off as more defensive than anything.

Bobby didn't seem to think so.

"It suits you. Not as good as your workout gear yesterday but I think if you wore that out on the ice, the team would be booed when we had to kick you off to play." Bobby replied, a hint of flirtation in his tone. "If any of the guys even wanted to play after they saw you in it, that is. This fresh look is great though. With all those sparkles, I bet you look stunning out there on the ice."

Thea's heart skipped a beat at his words, her stomach doing somersaults. She mentally berated herself for reading too much into his comment.

She self-consciously plucked at some of the sparkling sequins and crystal-studded frills that looked awesome when flying around her.

"I especially like these bits; they make you look like an ice queen." He gently poked some of the crystals in her hair, and the CZ-studded crown. "I've always had a thing for Elsa."

The butterflies were now flapping so hard it felt like the yearly migration in her belly.

Why was Bobby so completely oblivious to the tension between them?

Was it really just one-sided?

Almost as if he sensed her unease, Bobby started asking about the new intermission ice games with the fans they had planned for that night.

His easy smile and relaxed demeanor were a stark contrast to her new self-consciousness.

As they chatted, Bobby kept turning to look at her, which was nothing new.

But the way his eyes lingered on her...

"How have the fans been tonight?" Bobby asked. "Lots of talk about the pre-and post-game entertainment you guys are doing?"

Thea chuckled, grateful for the distraction. "Yeah, lots of talk. Also, lots of requests. One charmer in particular thought it would be a good idea to slip me a porn studio card." She dug into her barely-there spandex shorts and pulled out the offending card. Unbelievingly, she held it up between two fingers, shaking her head.

Bobby's eyes narrowed on the card, and he snatched it out of her hands.

"Bobby!"

"I'll take care of it." His stony expression was set.

She tried to snatch it out of his hands.

"Bobby!" She gritted her teeth, trying to pry his hand open. "Give. It. Back."

"No."

"Bobby!"

He stopped and pulled her to a standstill, causing the people in the hall to part around them like water to rocks in a stream.

"I'm your boyfriend. I'm your pro hockey-playing boyfriend." He paused and then continued. "No way I'm letting this go without a phone call." He placed his hand on her exposed lower back and started ushering her down the corridor.

Prickles danced up her spine.

"Or a visit," he added under his breath, eyes laser-focused on the floor in front of them.

When she tried to stop walking to protest his interference, Bobby ignored her and kept steering her along.

"Robert Orion!"

He scowled but continued marching her forward.

She probably should have guessed his reaction—at his heart, he was a protector—of course he'd do something about a guy he thought was bothering his girlfriend.

Actually...they would be having this same conversation whether Thea was his pretend girlfriend or not.

Classic Bobby.

Unable to help herself, she grinned and gave him a small flirty shove, enjoying how thick his arms were under her hands.

He looked down at her, registered her beaming smile, and the glower faded from his face. With his own grin, he shook his head, and wrapped a tight arm around her shoulders, tugging her close as they continued their walk down the winding staff hallways, steps in perfect sync.

Had they always walked in sync? Or was this a strategic move on Bobby's part to sell their act?

Why was she noticing?

Or caring?

"You shake off whatever was bothering you last night?"

"Uh, yeah. Just needed...a good night's rest."

Bobby looked at her curiously, but she focused on the ground in front of her.

For the first time ever, Thea found the silence between them awkward. "I don't know. Maybe it's just how close it is to...you know...." Thea's chest started to ache at the reminder of her grief...and with the guilt she felt for using her dad's death as a cop-out.

When had she become such a coward? Uck. If her dad could see her now...

Bobby nodded, his expression sympathetic. "Yeah, that's understandable."

Tucked deep into his shoulder, she caught a comforting whiff of his crisp, wintery smell and took a deep inhale—then stopped herself.

What was she doing!?

Ian wasn't even around! They were pretending *for Ian*, to get his attention, not...not...to date just for the fun of it.

She wasn't Bobby's real girlfriend—no matter how genuine this felt.

Before she could dwell on it any further, they got to the end of the hallway where it forked off again. Left was the way to the ATs', and right was the way to the Chill Chasers' locker rooms.

Bobby glanced down at Thea. "Duty calls. I'll catch you after the game?"

Thea nodded, pretending like her mind wasn't a mental train wreck. "Yeah, after the game."

Catching her off guard, Bobby leaned in for a moment, his lips pressing against her jawline by her ear. Or was it her neck...

Whatever body part it was technically called...it didn't matter...the feel of his warm breath, soft lips, and scratchy beard had her toes curling in her cute, efficient sneakers.

A spark of electricity shot through her body, igniting the fire she had previously attributed to frayed nerves and exhaustion.

Thea's breath hitched in her throat and her heart raced as his warm breath tickled her skin, sending shivers down her spine.

What was wrong with her?

Before she could process her thoughts any further, Bobby dragged his lips away. Slowly. Thea was left breathless, her cheeks flushed with embarrassment as she struggled to regain her composure.

The smug but pleased look on Bobby's face only served to turn that flame into a blaze.

As Bobby sauntered off down the hallway, Thea was left standing there at the junction, her mind spinning, and her legs unable to move.

Lost in her thoughts, Thea jumped out of her skin when she felt a hand at her elbow.

"Hey, you okay?" a deep voice broke through her reverie. With a deep breath, Thea turned to the man behind her and gave him a weak smile. Ty gave her a curious look as he cocked his head, taking in her flushed skin and bewildered expression. "Thea?"

Thea swallowed hard and tried to force a little more oomph into her smile and frantically thought of an acceptable excuse besides the fact that she might be developing feelings for her fake boyfriend who was her real best friend. "Fine. Just worried about the post-game skate tonight after all the publicity last weekend. I'm hoping it goes well. Combine that with the silence from management about the reporter job and I'm just letting myself spiral. I'll be fine, just lost myself for a minute."

Ty's forehead wrinkled as he studied her, then he looked down the hall where Bobby had retreated moments before. In the blink of an eye, his face cleared, and a carefully blank, pleasant expression took over, but there was a satisfaction there that made her stomach tighten.

"I'm heading to the trainers to get my knee taped, so I'm sure I'll see Bobby there and can ask him, but just wanted to check, you guys are still coming to poker night on Friday?"

Ah, some semblance of normalcy.

"Yes, of course! Wouldn't miss it." A thought struck her, and she shot him a return question. "And you're still coming to our Chill Chaser fundraiser *tomorrow* night at The Five Hole, right?"

"Like Bobby would let us forget." Ty ruffled her hair with a brotherly grin. "Just kidding. We'll all be there. It's a unique way to connect with fans while still raising money for cancer research—that's a win win." He glanced down the hall briefly before turning back to her. "I gotta get going, but good luck tonight. I'm sure you'll do great, and I'll see you tomorrow."

Thea watched Ty as he strolled down the hall, a sense of contentment settling in her chest—thank God Bobby had someone like Ty to have his back. Sure, Ty was *relatively* new to the team, but he and Bobby had known each other for years. It was a brotherhood that some people went their whole lives without experiencing. She was glad that Bobby had someone like that to watch out for him when she wasn't around. Unless he was on the ice, Bobby tended to let people walk all over him.

How could Bobby's intense compliments send butterflies fluttering in her stomach, and Ty's loyal friendship with Bobby provide her with such a comforting warmth...yet the prospect of finally dating Ian left her feeling utterly...empty? No thrill, no emotional stir—nothing at all but the satisfaction of checking a box....

· · · ● · ● ● · ·

During the game, Thea found herself stealing glances at Bobby whenever she could. That night, he was moving with an agility on the ice that made him untouchable. It was breathtaking. Whether it was his speed, his anticipation, or his stick skills, the other team just couldn't stop him.

After a sharp whistle to bring the teams in for a faceoff, Bobby let himself coast the corner, looping around behind the net. As he rounded where Thea was standing, their eyes met, and for a moment, the world ground to a halt.

Thea's breath caught.

"Hey, Ice Girl," Bobby called through the glass with a grin. Shivers erupted down her body as she balanced the tray of beers in her hands.

She couldn't tell if she actually heard him over the roar of the crowd or whether she just knew his voice so well that she could read the words on his lips while her brain predicted what his voice would sound like when saying them.

Thea smiled back, her heart racing in her chest.

Okay, so she was definitely reacting to *him*...but it was simply because she was getting the flirtatious attention from a handsome, intelligent, well-read, athletic man. If Ty turned on his charm with her, she'd be feeling the same way...probably...maybe....

It was just basic biology—she needed to stop stressing about it.

Before she could give him a thumbs up, Bobby was gone, lining up at the edge of the faceoff circle.

Out of habit, she glanced toward Ian on the other side of the circle...and caught him staring at her, a determined expression on his face.

CHAPTER EIGHTEEN

March 30, Tuesday evening
Bobby

Bobby drove directly home after the game, leaving Ilya to manage the boys at the bar. Despite having one of the top five games of his life just an hour before, Bobby couldn't get his mind off Thea.

If he closed his eyes, he could flawlessly envision her smile.

If he listened hard enough, he could hear her boisterous, no-holds-barred laugh ringing perfectly in his ears.

Bobby forced himself not to punch his steering wheel with frustration at how fucking stupid he'd been.

He wanted Thea—*needed* her—more than anything in the world.

Yet, to her, he remained invisible, hidden in the shadow of Ian's '*dazzling*' presence.

Fuck.

He needed to set up a visit with Kayla—get his brain sorted. He hadn't felt the need to see her for a few months now, but with the way his head and heart were tearing him apart...a visit with a psychologist couldn't hurt.

His heart heavy, Bobby leaned his forehead against his steering wheel while waiting at the red light, mentally reliving Thea's intermission performance on the ice tonight. He was never able to catch them live, obviously, but he always made sure to watch the replays before heading home, or—if he was on 'mother-hen duty'—the bars. Every seductive and talented move she made only served to remind him of what he couldn't have outside of their charade, and the pain was almost unbearable.

Why in the world had he agreed to this?

He could flirt until his heart gave out, but it felt like none of it helped her to *see* him.

Probably because she was so blinded by Ian and this obsession to live out her father's vision for her.

Not that Ian gave her the time of day.

Hell, she literally had to start dating his worst enemy to get Ian to look twice.

But fuck, it was actually *working*.

Bobby hadn't missed the way that Ian's eyes were drawn to Thea. She had just been a part of the furniture before. A houseplant in the corner that he'd seen a thousand times. Now, she was the statement piece.

It's not like Bobby could take a page out of Thea's playbook and date someone in front of her to make *her* jealous. He was supposed to be shacking up with her and that would totally ruin the whole façade.

But...

He didn't love the idea...but Thea had gotten jealous as hell over the unknown-to-her-Lucy...

So, maybe Bobby did have a way to catch Thea's attention, though, he needed to be careful that he did it in a way that no one got hurt.

Bobby's head spun with all the ways this could go wrong, but it was do-or-die time: he had one chance to make Thea see him, truly *see* him, and as more than just a friend. He had to find a way to break through Ian's blinding light, even if it meant risking everything he held dear.

Especially with how Ian was taking the bait; Bobby needed to move fast.

He needed to capture Thea's attention.

He needed to turn it up and be Thea's boyfriend public—and private.

He needed to blur the lines. Start to get her frazzled and confused. Make her *feel* something.

Something about *him*.

Taking a deep breath, Bobby pulled into the parking garage under his complex.

He didn't know what the future held, or if his plan would even work. But one thing was for certain—he couldn't keep going on like this, trapped in a never-ending cycle of heartache and longing.

It was time to take a leap of faith and pray that somehow their friendship could withstand the storm that was brewing just beneath the surface, or better yet, that their 'ship' would break through the tsunami and bring them to honeymoon island.

CHAPTER NINETEEN
March 31, Wednesday
Thea

As Thea drove home after the game, conflicting emotions churned within her. On one hand, she felt a sense of relief that her awkward encounter with Bobby the night before had prompted her to drive herself to the arena earlier, sparing her from another awkward ride home. On the other hand, she couldn't shake the small, nagging feeling of guilt for not embracing the opportunity to further immerse themselves in their fake-dating charade by riding together.

Once inside her apartment, Thea returned Bobby's texts with false bravado, assuring him she was all right and congratulating him on such a stellar game.

She tossed and turned all night long, desperate to figure out what her reaction to Bobby meant, and what it meant for her end goal of scoring a date with Ian.

Restless and anxious, Thea went to her closet and pulled out her dad's final work notebook.

It hurt to see all the blank pages he left.

Sniffling softly, she flipped through his countless notes, interviews, and one-on-ones that he had conducted in what ended up being his final months. He had worked with the Cyclones for years and had adored his job. While traveling with the team, he used to call her from their away games and give her the play-by-play, despite knowing full well that she had watched it air live.

She had always loved the sound of his voice, the logistics he used to analyze the play progressions.

God, she missed him.

It was why she *needed* the on-ice job. Only weeks before he had died, he had told her that she would be great for a job like that. Then for an opening like that to become available for the Cyclones? It was the universe trying to help her out. It had to be.

She lost her dad in every other way.

She couldn't lose that piece as well.

After a short cry, Thea turned to the last pages, dated on the day he died, and ran her fingers softly along the edges of the words.

If she wanted these pages to last the rest of her life, she needed to treat them gently.

Thea stared at his chicken scratch and random doodles, feeling her heart tear. Some of his thought bubbles had quotes and stats. Others had questions he wanted to ask players later.

Circles, stars, underlines, and traced words covered the messy page. Thea had a bittersweet smile as she lightly traced her dad's nonsensical notes. He never was very elaborate, but he always knew exactly what it meant when he looked at them later.

God, she used to love dissecting them with him. They would sit for hours and look through his old notebooks.

On the very last page, he had a list of books that she guessed he wanted to read, the name "Tim McGraw," and a variety of questions and resulting notes from his interview-filled day. Thea let out a soft chuckle as she looked at his book list. How he was inspired to add books to his TBR pile while making notes during his interviews that day would always be a mystery. But it was so typical of him.

Thea pinched her lips together as she forced herself to breathe through a renewed urge to cry.

After a moment of deep breathing, she refocused on his notes, taking in the stats that he had jotted down: a few for Ilya, Bobby, Ian, and a couple other players. Poor Bobby—looked like that was a rough year for him stat-wise. The thought made her lips twitch. They hadn't known each other but she'd have to ask him about his season at some point to see if she could get a rise out of him.

Her eyes drifted to Ian's box of stats—they were fantastic. Actually, scattered randomly throughout the page were various mentions of Ian's accomplishments that season. Her dad had even written "Selke?" with a box around it.

Thea shook her head and slid her fingers down the page. At the bottom of the page was a small box with a brief summary of verbs that he thought about Ian Novak. Directly to the right, was more of his messy scrawl, but this part he had underlined so many times that his harsh lines had dented the thick paper.

"413-555-0110. *Thea's soulmate. Have Sharon invite to cookout. Grandbabies.*"

From there was an arrow, leading to a heart bubble that had the bulleted words, "*Call Thea. Lunch. Job. Cookout.*"

Thea looked back to the emphasized phone number that she had memorized years ago.

She mouthed the number, head nodding slightly with the rhythm she had defaulted to over the years.

"Oh, one, one, oh," her voice was barely audible in the room, but it still felt too loud—too harsh. She pinched her lips together, mentally continuing the number, her head still bobbing at the imaginary beat. As the page before her started to blur, Thea ducked her head and finished on a broken, "Oh, one, one, oh."

She had stared at that damn number every night for months after her dad's death, debating whether she should do it—call Ian.

Before she could work up the nerve, Peyton Knowles—a kickass Springfield sports reporter—released a piece about Ian organizing a giant fundraiser with a local foundation that worked to prevent drunk driving. Thea's wound was ripped open again at the bittersweet happiness that someone who was notorious for not doing charity work would do something like that to honor her father's memory.

That Ian would cease his well-publicized distaste for marketed nonprofit work to honor a man that he had only known for a year or so? Thea's heart had felt shattered yet soothed at the same time.

Even so, after that big gesture, she felt like she couldn't call him up out of the blue.

It would be too forward. Too creepy. Too stalkerish.

Ian would totally be freaked out by the daughter of a dead man he had admired just randomly calling him up and asking him out on a date.

Then, once she started working for the Cyclones, things got even trickier, and she tried to figure out how to honor her father's secret hope for their relationship while balancing her professionalism at work.

Then she met Bobby.

And the gaping wound that her father's death had caused started to hurt a little less. With that lessened pain came the somewhat-release of her obsession with that fated phone number. Thea wasn't ready to finish typing the 'oh, one, one, oh' and call Ian quite yet. She was still a mess.

Thea needed to heal first.

At the time, she rationalized that she wasn't giving up on that goal, just...postponing until she was ready to do it right.

A year after her father's death, Thea felt she was ready—with all the credit going to Bobby for being her rock—and she was finally brave enough to take charge and fulfill her father's final wish for her.

And when she finally called the number, she was met with a message saying that the number had been disconnected.

Go figure.

It wasn't a problem of getting Ian's number at that point—she could have stolen it from Bobby's phone at any point—but the idea of going up to Ian and saying, "My dead dad thought that we are soulmates, so do you want to go grab pizza?" just didn't feel right.

So, ever since, it was one lame attempt after another to catch Ian's attention.

But she was sick of waiting—playtime was over.

This fake dating plan *had* to work.

Thea *had* to create this opportunity to really get to know Ian.

It was the last thing her father had wanted for her!

So, even though Bobby thought Ian was scum...her dad had seen some potential in Ian...so Thea would too.

After all, her dad had never been wrong.

A tear dropped onto the page and Thea stopped her torture. She closed the book, placed it in the fireproof safe, and slid it back into her closet, trying not to scream at herself for letting moisture touch her father's precious pages.

Thea curled up in bed, replaying every favorite memory with her dad, and sobbed silently up at the ceiling above her. She hadn't seen Lila outside of practice or games for the last couple of days, so she wasn't worried she'd wake her, but just in case, Thea did her best to be silent.

Why did life have to be so confusing?

She had lost her dad; but she had also found Bobby. She had also found the men on the Cyclones, who treated her like a sister. She was a shoo-in for the promotion, but when it came to getting Ian's attention, she needed to force her best friend into an awkward position of pretending to date her. Why couldn't Ian just get his head out of his ass and notice her all on his own?

Why did she have to come up with this stupid ploy just to get him to look at her!?

However, given the way she frequently caught Ian's eyes on her only after two days, Thea knew she finally had his attention.

All thanks to Bobby.

She turned over in bed again and punched the pillow to flatten it out. Thea then slammed her head down and tried to calm her racing heart.

Bobby.

The reason she couldn't sleep.

Yeah, there was no way she was going to the arena or practice center tomorrow. If she ran into him, she'd have no idea what to say!

'Hi, I know we're best friends, and just fake dating, but when you smile at me, or even frown at me, I want to strip naked and rub against you. And I'm confused, because I'm supposed to be soulmates with Ian, but I can't seem to get the thought of you in nothing but your skates out of my head.'

God! She was such a fucking mess!

Fortunately, and also unfortunately, Thea had organized a small fundraiser for the Chill Chasers, and with the same nonprofit that Ian had worked with years ago, for tomorrow night...and the players were the big draw.

That included Bobby.

So, though she could blame her lack of texting on being busy prior to the event...she wouldn't be able to avoid her fake boyfriend forever.

CHAPTER TWENTY

March 31, Wednesday
Thea

The Chill Chasers had arranged a small fundraiser for cancer research at the Cyclones' favorite bar, The Five Hole, and even though the entry tickets were expensive, the atmosphere was down-to-earth—which was perfect to draw in an everyday fan who wanted to meet the players after work while still in their jeans and work boots.

The buzz of laughter and conversation filled the air as Thea made her rounds, taking pictures with the fans. Decked out in their most alluring outfits, the Chill Chasers were a sight to behold as they mingled among the excited crowd. The Cyclones players in attendance were sporting their sweaters and handing out unfettered access to conversation, pictures, and autographs.

She owed the guys *huge* for doing this for her and the Chasers.

The atmosphere was electric, with patrons generously filling up the donation jars, managed by stand-in volunteers. The fun incentive of performing a dance or song for donors had everyone eagerly anticipating their favorite Chill Chaser or Cyclones player taking center stage.

Lila, her blonde hair cascading around her shoulders like spun gold, stood chatting animatedly with Bobby by the bar. Her bright blue eyes sparkled as she shared a funny anecdote, eliciting a barely-there, I'm-only-doing-this-to-be-polite, reserved smile from him.

Jealousy stirred inside Thea as she watched Bobby talk with Lila. It shouldn't, Bobby wasn't *hers*. But there was no denying the clench in her chest when she saw Bobby's small grin aimed down at Lila and Lila's mooning gaze beaming up at him.

Unable to stop herself, she headed over.

"Hey, hun," Thea greeted, trying to sound casual as she leaned in to give him a chaste kiss on the lips. She felt the warmth of his skin against her mouth, a sensation that, despite its innocence, still sent goosebumps down her spine. The quick peck that she planned turned into something a little more lingering as she found herself hesitant to pull away.

"Hey, Bea," he replied, his voice steady and warm. "You look great tonight."

"Thanks," she said, tucking a stray strand of hair behind her ear, suddenly feeling self-conscious about her appearance.

Was she trying too hard?

She glanced briefly at Lila, who was now excusing herself from their conversation, her cheeks flushed and her lips tight.

Shit. That was going to be a problem. But then again, who flirts with their roommate's boyfriend?

After all, Lila didn't know it was fake.

Thea refused to feel guilty. So, what if Lila had harbored feelings for Bobby long before Thea. What mattered was that he had chosen her.

Sort of.

"Everything okay with Lila?" Thea asked as she watched her friend walk away, the curiosity gnawing at her.

"Uh, yeah. She's just a little nervous, I guess. She really doesn't want to have to sing," he answered, picking up his beer bottle and taking a swig.

Thea tried to focus on the words coming out of his mouth, but all she could think about was the subtle scent of his cologne, the way his eyes crinkled when he laughed, and how his presence made her feel like she'd stepped onto the ice for the first time again—excited, nervous, and alive.

"Hey, are you okay?" Bobby asked.

"Absolutely. Just a little tired. Been working like crazy on getting this to come together. Thank you, again," Thea said quickly, placing a hand on his arm and silently berating herself for getting lost in her own mind.

"Of course. It's a good cause." He looked around, then gave her an impressed nod.

She had to agree—not that bad for a low-budget, dive-bar fundraiser.

When she saw bright red staining the corner of his top lip, a short laugh burst from her.

Before she thought too long about it, Thea gently wiped the bright red lipstick from Bobby's mouth with her thumb, her knuckles brushing against the soft bristles of his beard.

His warm breath on her fingers caused a completely different warmth to warp speed its way through her body.

"Your beard is looking quite impressive," Thea commented with a teasing smile, unable to stop her fingers from running along it one more time.

"Thanks, I've been working hard on it," Bobby quipped, a playful grin spreading.

She pushed his shoulder, so he swayed backward in his seat. "Brat."

"Only because you taught me."

All around them, people were paying the Chill Chasers and a few brave players to do outrageous things—singing karaoke renditions of classic love songs, doing tequila shots off a bouncer's belly, even waxing their legs at the side tables.

"Can you believe some of the things people are paying for tonight?" Thea asked, shaking her head in disbelief. "Chill Chasers and Cyclones, turning into circus acts."

"It was a fun idea. I didn't think it would work, but you marketed it well. Having the boards plastered everywhere with ridiculous and embarrassing suggestions also helped," Bobby replied, his eyes twinkling with amusement. "That reminds me, I heard you did a killer dance routine earlier. I missed it!" His disappointment didn't outshine his teasing tone.

"Ugh, don't remind me," Thea groaned, rolling her eyes. "I'm never lip-syncing *Coyote Ugly* again. If I still had the soundtrack in CD form, I'd burn it. The whole movie set an impossible standard."

Their laughter was interrupted when Bobby's eyes landed on one of the Ice Crew, Rachel, who was provocatively dancing with a group of donors. Thea's body instantly stiffened, her eyes narrowing as she watched her sometimes-nemesis prance around the room.

"Rachel," she muttered under her breath, unable to hide her disdain. "She's been pissing me off. She barely put any effort into fundraising."

Bobby glanced over at Rachel again, his expression unreadable. "She seems to be doing all right," he said noncommittally, taking another sip of his beer.

"All right? She's coasting on her looks and charm, while the rest of us were cold calling donors and stopping by shops to drop off donor forms," Thea grumbled. "Do you realize how awkward it is to compete with adorable Girl Scout troops for sponsorships and fundraising dollars? Or homeless agencies? Or foster kids? Or...all of those causes?"

Bobby hummed in acknowledgment. "The world could use a lot of help."

"Ain't that the truth," Thea sighed, taking a sip from her water bottle, and glaring back at Rachel. "I just wish people would see past her pretty face and recognize the lazy, schemer beneath it all."

"Nah, she's *fine*. You're just jealous. You guys are frequently butting heads, so what? I butt heads with Tommy all the time. We *all* do. Doesn't make him a dirtbag. Just makes him confrontational and loud about it. Rachel's fine."

"Fine?" Thea whipped around to glare at Bobby, her chest swirling with a mix of anger and hurt.

Bobby's gaze flicked back to Rachel for a moment before settling on Thea, his expression shifting from disinterest to discomfort. He shrugged, taking a slow sip of his beer before admitting, "Yeah, she's fine. Friendly. You and she are just too alike to actually get along. It's fine. It happens."

Thea's jaw dropped, her disbelief palpable. "How do you know her?" she demanded, her hand on a hip.

Bobby blinked in surprise, clearly not expecting her reaction. "What?"

"How *well* do you know her? What makes you think you can make that statement with such confidence? *How well do you know her, Bobby?*" Thea repeated, her voice rising in pitch as her irritation grew. "Robert Orion Davis, the third. Answer me," she added, emphasizing each syllable of his full name.

Bobby winced, clearly realizing that there was no escaping this conversation.

"We...uh...dated," he confessed, causing Thea's eyes to widen with shock, adrenaline rushing through her.

"Dated?" She couldn't believe it. "Dated how? Like Dated? Or like *Dated* Dated?"

"What does *Dated* Dated mean?" Bobby asked, his brows furrowing.

"*You know what it means!*" she exclaimed, slapping his arm in frustration.

Bobby let out a small chuckle, but the amusement didn't quite reach his eyes. It was clear that he understood what Thea was getting at, but he wasn't about to divulge any more information than absolutely necessary.

As they squared off, locked in an unspoken battle of wills, the atmosphere around them seemed to crackle.

Thea took a deep breath, trying to regain her composure. She had no right to be angry or jealous over Bobby's relationships, but the thought of him being romantically involved with someone like *Rachel* was just...too much. She couldn't help the unbidden images that clouded her mind, making her stomach tighten with an unfamiliar ache.

How could he date someone whom he knew Thea disliked so much?

Thea froze.

Shit.

Okay, she was a hypocrite *and* an asshole. And possibly developing feelings for her very-not-into-her best friend and she didn't know what that meant for the guy who she was trying to win the attention of.

Wonderful.

Bobby took another sip of his beer, his eyes flicking between Thea and Rachel across the room. Something was working in his eyes, but in another first, Thea couldn't decipher what it was. Shock rippled through her when he actually answered her question, "Dated *dated*, I guess."

Thea's jaw dropped in horror.

"Are you kidding me? You had *sex* with Rachel?!" she hissed, her body stiff in anger and disbelief. "You can't sleep with co-workers! That's just asking for trouble."

Bobby gave her a dry look, glancing over at Ian with a pointed look on his face. Shit. Well, it's not like she didn't know she was a hypocrite...

Before he could say anything else, Thea's palm connected with his arm again, making him wince at the impact.

She slammed her bottle down on the bar in front of him and whirled back to him. "*You can't just go sleeping with Rachel!* She's the devil," Thea hissed, her hands now on her hips as she glared at him.

Bobby laughed, clearly not taking her outrage seriously. "She is not. She's nice. You're biased...and jealous." He reached out and cupped her chin, giving it a nudge, which caused her cheeks to flush an even deeper shade of red. "So, she has more followers than you and got the coveted calendar spot. Let it go."

Thea stiffened, her chest tightening at the reminder of her hard work being overlooked. "I worked my ass off to get July and then they gave it to her a month after she took an 'unexplained absence'! It was...nepotism!"

It wasn't her fault for the bitterness that seeped into her voice.

He raised his eyebrows, and she wrinkled her nose.

"Fine. It wasn't *nepotism*, per se. But it *was* bullshit," she grumbled petulantly.

Thea crossed her arms defensively, trying to keep her emotions in check while Bobby studied her face with a concerned frown.

"Hey, come on. You can't seriously be mad about this, can you?" he asked gently, reaching out to chuck her chin. "It was *ages* ago and it's not like we were ever a real thing. We're still friendly though and catch up when we see each other at work or events, but she hasn't called me—or me, her—in years." The way his voice inflected on that last part had Thea wondering if he meant it as a question or a statement. She couldn't tell.

Maybe he couldn't either.

Thea looked down, her heart aching with a strange mix of jealousy and hurt. She knew she had no right to be upset about Bobby's past relationships, but the thought of him sleeping with Rachel—or anyone, for that matter—left a bitter taste in her mouth.

Bobby signaled for another beer, ordering something different. Apparently he could support his best donors only so much. If she wasn't so ticked at him, she would have chuckled.

"Please tell me it was only once," Thea whispered, stepping closer to him, pleading for reassurance. Her heart pounded in her chest, begging for a different answer than what she expected.

Bobby lifted his new beer to his lips, his eyes dancing with mischief. "I never kiss and tell," he replied cryptically, leaving Thea's question unanswered.

She clenched her fists, struggling to control the explosion of emotions threatening to overwhelm her. But then Bobby's gaze shifted to another passing Ice Crew member, and the bomb detonated.

"Hence why you don't know I also slept with her," he said nonchalantly, nodding at the girl who had just walked by. Thea's hands flew to her hips, fingers digging into her sides as she tried to process what he had just said.

"I can't believe you," Thea spat, her voice trembling. "You're living this secret horndog life and I never even knew! Am I the only Ice Crew member that you haven't slept with?"

She watched as Bobby paused, pretending to think about it. Thea's breath hitched, and she snatched the bottle from his hand, taking a deep gulp of the cold liquid. It did nothing to soothe the fury raging within her.

"Nah, not just you," Bobby finally answered, a smile playing on his lips. "I haven't slept with Brian. Or Peter. Though, not for lack of trying on Brian's part."

Thea stared at him, dumbfounded.

Every word out of Bobby's mouth felt like a slap to her face, and she couldn't understand why it hurt so much. They were just friends, right? That's all they had ever been.

"Hey, I'm teasing," Bobby called, tilting his head to look into her eyes, his voice softening as he noticed the tears pricking at the corners. "Baby, Thea, I was just joking. I took it too far. Bea, it's okay, hun."

Thea opened her mouth to respond, but no words came out.

For the first time in their long history together, Thea found herself speechless in front of Bobby Davidson.

He cupped her chin and pulled her face up, to meet his gaze again. "I took that too far, honey. I'm sorry, Bea. I was just teasing." He rubbed his thumb across her chin and up to her quivering lower lip, where he pressed firmly on it, his expression turned ravaged. "Baby," he whispered in a broken plea.

The raw burn she felt last night returned again and she felt her nostrils flare. Shit.

Bobby didn't allow her time to dwell on it, pulling her against him in a tight embrace. The smell of his crisp cologne and the faint scent of winter from his jersey filled her senses, drowning out everything else. She was startled by the intensity of it all but allowed herself to melt into his familiar warmth.

Then he leaned back to see into her eyes, their bodies still so close that she could feel the heat radiating from him. His dark eyes were intense, making her heart pound in her chest. She was suddenly aware of how close his lips were—so tantalizingly close. How easy it would be to just...lean in...

He said something then, but the words felt muffled by the beating of her heart. His gaze flickered down to her lips and his own pouted slightly as if considering something.

She barely had time to catch her breath before his lips met hers.

It was everything she'd never known she wanted - sweet and passionate at once that sent shockwaves through her body. She clung onto him as if he was the only thing keeping her grounded, returning his kiss with equal fervor.

It was only when they broke apart, both panting heavily for air, did she realize what had just happened. The raw emotion in Bobby's eyes matched the wild pounding of her own heart. Suddenly, whatever it was she was upset about seemed far less important than the fact that Bobby—her Bobby—had kissed her with such passion.

She opened her mouth to speak but found that words refused to come. *Again.*

Bobby's lips curled into a small smile as he studied her, reaching up to gently tuck another stray strand of hair behind her ear. The small gesture sent a wave of tenderness washing over her, mingling with the fiery desire that still simmered beneath her skin.

Suddenly, everything felt overwhelmingly real and impossibly surreal at the same time.

She was standing here, in Bobby Davidson's arms, moments after sharing a kiss that had rocked her world. And all the while, she knew Ian was out there somewhere, thinking she was pining for him when really her heart seemed to be veering in a completely different direction.

"Thea?" Bobby's gentle inquiry pulled her out of her thoughts.

She blinked up at him, suddenly aware of how intensely he was watching her. "Yeah?" she managed to croak out.

His smile widened just a fraction more as he brushed his thumb across her cheekbone. "You're beautiful when you're lost in thought," he said softly. Then he sighed, leaning his forehead against hers for a moment as if gathering his own.

Caught off guard by the open affection in his gaze and his unexpected compliment, Thea felt heat creep up into her cheeks. She wished she could say something clever or at least coherent in response, but she was having enough trouble breathing, trying to use words coherently right now would probably kill her.

Did he just kiss her to distract her?

Or was he just trying to fulfill his fake dating duties and he knew Ian was watching?

It sure as fuck *felt* real.

Bobby reached for her chin, his touch gentle but firm, and titled her face back to him. "Good. Now that you look a little more like yourself, I have to ask: *Coyote Ugly* bar dancing is out, but what about top ten hit serenades?"

Thea could only blink up at him.

What?

Bobby gave her a grin-wink combo that sent shivers down her spine, sliding off his stool with an ease that only he could possess. He leaned in, cupped her chin again, and planted a gentle peck on

Thea's lips, the warmth of him making her heart race. A sudden jolt of electricity coursed through her body, leaving her vibrating.

"Excuse me for a moment. I need to place my order for a dance and song. I think I need to see my *girlfriend* sing 'Jealous'. Somehow, I feel like you and Nick Jonas were friends in another life."

His words hung heavy in the air, the word "girlfriend" echoing in Thea's ears.

Thea blinked, trying to process what had just transpired between them. Her cheeks flushed a deep shade of red, and she found herself unable to tear her gaze away from Bobby's retreating form. As if on autopilot, her hand reached up to touch the spot where his lips had brushed against her skin, the ghost of his kiss lingering like a sweet promise.

As the night wore on, Thea found herself torn between wanting to be near Bobby and needing to keep her distance. Each time their eyes met, or their fingers brushed against one another, it felt like walking a tightrope—thrilling and terrifying all at once.

She was just feeling protective.

Protective and *slightly* jealous. Like...the slightest amount.

All this fake dating stuff was messing with her head. Especially with her being so keyed up to land a date with Ian, her 'perfect match.' So, she was clearly already looking for those favorable traits in a man, because she knew Ian was coming along.

She was just having a tough time directing those headlights away from Bobby.

Everything would be fine.

He was still her best friend; her body was just a little confused at the moment.

As soon as Ian gave her an opening, she'd prove it to herself.

The feelings with Bobby were false, just like their relationship.

CHAPTER TWENTY-ONE

April 2, Friday night
Thea

Days later, Thea reluctantly found herself back in Bobby's presence.

Up until then, she had successfully avoided him, explaining it away by saying she was too busy with endorsement photoshoots. But Ty's regular poker night was a staple in their schedule, and this was the first time that they were supposed to attend together as a 'couple.' The original plan was to rub their 'togetherness' in Ian's face.

But now...

Now, the idea made her squeamish.

She cursed herself out for her stupid, flighty emotions.

Especially as her palms started to sweat and her breath caught whenever she and Bobby made eye contact.

After Ty texted everyone and said that they were having it at Ilya's that night, Thea shot a quick message to Bobby that she could drive herself to the party.

When she finally arrived, Thea let herself in and made her way to the dining room where everyone was sitting, waiting for the stragglers to roll in. As all eyes turned to her, her face went hot and she gave an awkward wave, avoiding Bobby's stare.

The conversations were still going on around them, but at Kira's probing look, Thea realized she needed to rally...for appearances. Thea forced herself to walk over to Bobby, like it wasn't causing her mouth to get as dry as the Sahara and leaned down to give him a quick peck on his upturned face. If her fingers lingered a little bit on his cheek as she gave him her *Spiderman*-reenactment-kiss impersonation, then she did her best to convince herself that it was only for show.

She did her best to ignore the tightening in her navel and turned to drop her bag and coat in the corner, only to startle when she saw that Ian was watching her from the doorway. Giving him a weak smile, she pivoted and deposited her items before moving to take the empty seat next to Bobby: her usual spot.

As she was adjusting herself in her seat, her eyes flicked up to sneak a peek at Bobby, only to find him studying her, a curious yet pleased look on his face.

Ducking her head and fighting the heat on her face, she quickly pulled out her phone, opening and closing the apps compulsively just to look like she was doing something important.

The brightly lit room hummed with laughter and the clinking of glasses. People randomly made their way in and out of the kitchen as they dug into plates piled high with savory Russian dishes before heading back to the dining room-turned-poker table.

How many times had Thea sat in this very seat next to Bobby, either here or at any of the other guys' houses? She knew exactly how he'd organize his poker chips, and which snacks he'd grab for the plate that he'd place between him and Thea.

The arm slung around the back of her chair was new though.

As was the distracting way he was softly twirling random strands of her hair as the game commenced.

She didn't have a family history of heart issues, but she was mentally scheduling a visit with her doctor to get checked out.

"Your bet," Ilya said, eyeing Thea curiously when his voice seemed to make her jump out of her skin.

"Right, sorry." Thea tossed a few more chips into the pot, her cheeks flushed from the wine and the constant barrage of flirty teasing coming from Bobby. As he brushed her leg with his own under the table, she felt a zing rip through her, and she ripped her knee away.

Which was ridiculous. It's not like they had *never* touched before! She was a touchy-feely person—it's who she was. Hell, how many times had she lost all her money early and then proceeded to rest her head on his shoulder for a light doze for the rest of the night? Countless times.

So, why was a leg brush under the table causing little shocks that made her want to squeeze her knees together and moan?

"Excuse me for a moment," Thea murmured, sliding out of her chair.

"Everything okay?" Bobby asked, concern etched across his face.

"Absolutely, I just need some fresh air." She tossed her cards face down on the table, ignoring the fact that the river showed that she had two pairs, and hurried to escape the suffocating room.

She stepped onto the back deck, the cool night air filling her lungs as she leaned against the railing and gazed up at the star-studded sky.

What was wrong with her? Would these feelings go away as soon as they dropped this charade?

No—she didn't have real feelings. It was simply the fact that everyone kept mentioning how perfect they were for each other that was getting to her head.

They would go away as soon as they 'broke up.'

Thea closed her eyes, letting the chilly breeze soothe her tangled thoughts.

"Hey," Bobby's voice called from behind her, startling her out of her reverie. "Mind if I join you?"

"Of course not," Thea replied, offering him a weak smile as he stepped onto the deck and leaned against the railing next to her, mimicking her pose.

For a moment, it felt as though time had stopped, allowing them to just be themselves without the need for pretense.

"What're you thinking about?" Bobby asked, his gaze never leaving the night sky.

"The fancy-schmancy Speakeasy Gala tomorrow," she admitted, a shiver running down her spine as the words left her mouth. "Have to look like the perfect couple, again."

Bobby chuckled. "We're getting good at that, aren't we?"

"Like *expert* level," she retorted, the corners of her mouth tugging into a small smile.

The silence that followed was comfortable and familiar, a stark contrast to the chaos bubbling inside of her.

"You're going to be gone all next week too," Thea said after a while, her voice barely above a whisper. She always hated the two weeks leading up to her dad's death anniversary.

Calling it a 'death anniversary' always felt strange. But 'death date' didn't sound any better. In her mind, she always thought of it as the apocalypse that cost her her North Star. Her compass. Her lighthouse. All snatched away in an instant.

"Yeah," Bobby replied, his voice thick with...something. "It'll be over before you know it." He turned to look at her, a sad look on his face. "Will you be okay during the week? Do you think that you'll head down to Hartford at all, to see your mom?"

Thea closed her eyes tight and fought off the bite in the air, rubbing her biceps with her hands. "I'll be fine. Always am, aren't I?"

"Are you?"

He said it so gently that her heart ached.

"I'll be fine, Bobby. Don't worry about me. I'll run down to visit Mom one of the days and check in but..."

Bobby sighed and hung his head, looking at the frost-tipped lawn in front of them. "Yeah, I know."

To say that Thea wasn't on board with her mom having a boyfriend so soon after her father's death was an understatement.

"How long would it take you to be okay with her dating?"

Never.

Thea bit her lip and refused to answer. Despite the whole fake-dating charade, she really did try her best not to lie.

Bobby hummed and shifted so he was behind her, covering her body with his own.

Oh.

Oh, wow.

Thea adamantly refused to acknowledge how snug her ass was pressed up tight against his hips.

Mom is dating, mom is dating, mom is dating.

Jesus, he was *warm.*

She forced herself to settle and just enjoy his presence. They'd done something like this before...surely...right?

Was this for show? Or an act of tender comfort?

No one was watching, but that didn't mean that no one would come out...is that what Bobby was expecting?

"Thanks for worrying about me, though," she whispered, her chest tight. "It means a lot to me that you care."

His hand found hers, giving it a gentle squeeze. "Always, Thea."

As they cuddled, bathed in the dim glow from the light coming through the thin white curtains of Ilya's dining room, Thea couldn't ignore the growing attraction she felt for Bobby. The line between their charade and reality had never been blurrier—and she was struggling to resist the magnetic pull between them.

Before either of them could say anything else, the back door creaked open and Ilya's sister, Kira, popped her head out, with Tommy leaning over the top of her, only his head showing, too. Kira raised an eyebrow at them, a playful smile on her lips. "Are you two planning on joining us for the next game?"

"Or are we interrupting something?" Tommy chimed in, grinning mischievously. "If so, can I join?"

Kira rolled her eyes and slapped somewhere behind the door, laughing as she pushed him back into the house. "Ignore him," Kira told them. "But seriously, we're starting another game if you want in on the last round."

"Of course, we'll be right in," Thea replied, trying to shake off the heaviness of the moment she had shared with Bobby. She slowly unburied herself from under his large frame and immediately felt the sting of the fresh April air. As they made their way back into the house, Thea noticed the lingering warmth of Bobby's hand on the small of her back.

In the dining room, the atmosphere was electric. The room buzzed with banter as Thea and Bobby took their seats at the table again. When Bobby settled in beside her, his hand brushed against hers. A shiver ran down her spine, and she felt her heart race.

It wasn't real. It wasn't real. It wasn't real.

She just needed to keep reminding herself of that.

An unbidden thought caused her to chew on her lip: if she was feeling these emotions due to all their friends' comments, did Bobby feel them too? Or was he able to block them out?

Trying to distract herself, Thea glanced around the room and met Ian's intense gaze from a table over where he was playing with another set of players—Ty and Ilya had learned years ago to split Ian and Bobby up.

Thea ducked her head and tried not to dwell on the penetrating look that Ian was giving her.

Guilt pummeled her again.

She should feel victorious that she was catching Ian's eye finally. Yet, somehow, it was falling flat.

All because of these stupid, confusing feelings toward Bobby.

Thea would have to confront her feelings at some point. But for now, she'd focus on the cards in her hand and the laughter of her friends—and try not to think about what might happen when their charade was over.

CHAPTER TWENTY-TWO

April 3, Saturday evening
Thea

Thea stood before her mirror, the soft glow of her vanity lights reflecting off the sequins of her flapper-inspired dress. With every movement, the shimmering fabric seemed to come alive in a cascade of light and color when she ran her fingers through the matching-colored fringes.

Butterflies danced in her stomach, taunting her with the knowledge that she'd be spending the evening with Bobby.

And Ian.

When had *that* become such a source of tension?

With all the pointed looks from Ian lately, she would bet her treasured Peloton bike that he'd be asking her out soon. Then, Thea and Bobby could go back to normal, and she could forget all about these stupid feelings that everyone was pushing onto her.

Like, really.

What was she supposed to feel when Bobby nailed her with his pretty brown eyes, stellar wit, and thick biceps?

Of course, she was going to feel butterflies!

The guy was a freaking professional athlete! He'd probably banged more puck bunnies than half the team!

Just because he had never lasered those skills on Thea didn't mean they weren't there.

She was actually pretty lucky that he had never tried out his skills on her for real—she would have been a puddle on the floor.

But the fake dating...*that he was doing for her*...necessitated that he turned that part of him on.

Thea took a heaving breath and leaned forward into the mirror so she could finish her makeup.

"I mean, really, I'm only human, and Bobby is...Bobby. Of course, I'm feeling girly and excited around him when he's playing the part. It's just a natural response to his charm and charisma," Thea mumbled while painstakingly outlining her lips in a bold red.

Just as she finished smacking her lips together and giving a test pinch of her lips around a thin piece of fabric, the doorbell to her apartment chimed, and Thea cursed Lila for being so absent lately.

If only her roommate were here to ease the tension that was threatening to strangle her when she was alone with Bobby.

Lila's presence would certainly knock some sense back into Thea's raging and starving hormones.

Maybe it was just her dry spell that was fucking with her head.

She paused her last-second fidgeting with her crimped waves and headband.

Oh, that was a thought.

She lowered her hands from the single feathered headband and twirled the long fake string of pearls at her chest.

Okay, that was totally it!

She was freaking sex starved.

No wonder she was all discombobulated around Bobby right now.

Combined with everything going on—it all made sense.

She needed to take the edge off.

But Thea could hardly go out to a bar and hook up with some stranger while she was 'dating' Bobby.

She would need to figure out something to reset her to normal if this charade went on much longer, though.

But that was a problem for another night, she had kept Bobby waiting long enough.

Thea took one last look in the mirror before heading down the hall and to answer the door. Her heart skipped a beat as she opened it, anticipation and anxiety blooming within her chest.

Bobby leaned against the doorjamb, his dark hair immaculately styled and his perfectly trimmed facial hair framing a reserved smile. His suit was period-appropriate and sharp, making him look like he'd stepped right out of a classic movie scene. Her breath caught in her throat.

"Hey," Thea said, trying to sound casual despite the rock sitting in her windpipe. "You're looking quite dapper."

"Thanks," he replied, his voice lower than usual. "You too. As always." His eyes wandered down her body, taking in her whole outfit, right down to her long, elegant gloves, and era-appropriate shoes. A small grin tugged at his mouth as he looked up at her, keeping his chin down, so he raised only his eyes. "Perfect."

Thea mentally congratulated herself for not combusting right there.

"Shall we?"

Bobby gallantly raised his arm, and Thea wrapped her elbow in his and allowed him to escort them to his car. As they climbed into Bobby's car and drove to the event hall, stilted conversation filled the space between them, punctuated by lingering glances that she didn't dare to interpret further.

She was sex-starved, of course she'd start imagining things.

However, Bobby's hands did grip the steering wheel a little too tightly...and his jaw was set with a rather determined yet pained expression on his face.

Maybe he was feeling the burden of their fake-dating celibacy as well.

Join the club, Bobbyo.

Securing a parking spot proved to be a superhuman task, yet Bobby deftly maneuvered his sedan into a space that, to Thea's eyes, seemed impossibly tight. His triumphant smirk, as they strolled away from the masterfully parked car, was punctuated by the confident chirp of the locks engaging at the press of his key fob. The cocky assurance in his stride peeled away Thea's lingering tension as she laughed and leaned into his warm body.

"Dork."

"Backseat driver."

She chose not to dignify his jibe with words. Instead, Thea stuck out her tongue causing him to grin widely down at her before linking his arm through hers and escorting her into the building.

And once again, those damn butterflies started erupting out of their stupid, little chrysalises in her belly.

This was *Bobby*. *Her* Bobby. She needed to straighten her head out.

Hell, maybe *she'd* call up Kayla and make an appointment.

The grand entrance of the 1920s-decorated venue loomed before them, adorned with strings of pearls and shimmering chandeliers. The lights danced like stars, casting an ethereal glow on the classically dressed attendees milling about.

"Wow," she breathed, taking in the opulent scene. "This is incredible."

Bobby's lips tipped up in a soft smile. "It really is. A bit different than the fundraiser at The Five Hole on Wednesday."

"Hey! We did all right!" Thea protested with a scowl. "It's not like we were working with a big budget. Plus, our *little* fundraiser raked in several *thousand,* so take *that* and s*hove it where the sun don't shine*."

"Easy, Bea. I was just teasing." Bobby let out a soft chuckle and patted her hand reassuringly. He then guided Thea through the swarm of people standing around chatting and drinking.

Thea shot a quick look at Bobby's slicked and neatly combed hair. "Don't tell me you're wearing actual clothing from the era...."

He grinned but didn't look down at her, nodding at a person they just passed. Out of the corner of his mouth, he mumbled, "You don't see any vents in this puppy, do you?"

Thea laughed and leaned harder into his arm, only to pull back when she realized how squished up against his arm her boob was.

Oops.

"I see them! Over there by the dance floor!"

Bobby turned his head and shifted their direction, heading toward the table that housed their small group of friends.

"Ah, the party can finally start!" Tommy boomed, jumping up and slinging an arm over Bobby's shoulders from his opposite side. "Bobby's here. Finally! Time to get wild."

The men chuckled and tossed cloth napkins from the table at Tommy, causing him to unravel himself from Bobby and collect the weapons of war.

A chorus of greetings rang out from their friends.

"Look at you two," Ty remarked, a satisfied look on his face. "You both look like you stepped right out of the Roaring Twenties."

"It's like the Great Gatsby come to life," Kira chimed in, inspecting Thea's elaborate dress and giving her an impressed nod of approval.

"Thanks, girl. You were right, the dress is perfect for me."

Kira held up her hands in defense. "Don't look at me! I asked Bobby for a list of approved dresses that wouldn't make the historian in him mad, and he sent me a few to choose from. I chose mine and then sent you the second best."

"Of course you did," Timmy chuckled from a few feet away.

"You could have taken a leaf from Bobby's book. Look how handsome he is!" Kira inspected Bobby with a big, open smile. "Really. You look so...*debonair*."

"Debonair? Really?" Jason patted his own slicked-down hair. "I'm dressed *exactly* the same! I even gave up the sick bowler hat that I wanted because of Bobby's message to the group chat telling us that it wasn't era-appropriate to wear inside, and he'd make us pay if we violated the sanctity of a true Roaring Twenties-inspired Gala."

Thea couldn't have stopped her grin if she wanted to.

She patted his arm softly when she felt him stiffen. "Bobby is just a fan of the times. Would you like it if some group of kids got to the mountain lodge in full boarding gear and then never even went out, but instead, filmed social media videos down at the lodge all day?"

Jason's handsome face went red. "What's even the point if they aren't going to go up and board down?"

Time for the final nail in the coffin.

"And then, when they did decide to go up, they took forever, giggling and screwing around in front of the lift and making everyone wait while they fucked around?"

Their group fell silent as all heads pivoted to Jason, who looked like he was doing his best imitation of a goldfish having an aneurysm.

Bobby's soft chuckle blew across her ear, and he leaned in and pressed a soft kiss to her jawline.

"Thanks for the defense, Bea. But I'm more than capable of defending the no-hat indoors rule."

She turned and looked up at him, unable to stop herself from touching his bristly cheek for a fleeting moment. "I know. But so can I."

Bobby's pretty brown eyes crinkled, and she once again marveled at just how thick and long they were.

The amount of mascara she had to put on to achieve that length and fullness was ridiculous.

"Okay, then," Tommy jumped in, clapping his hands together eagerly. "Bobby is debonair. And Kira's date's a no-show. Who has the next drama?" The big man had to duck as Kira hurled napkin after napkin at him, forcing him into a yelp when a small spoon was added to the mix.

"You really do look debonair," Thea assured Bobby with a smile.

"A real-life Jay." Tommy squinted at Bobby. "Well, let's hope that's where Bobby's comparison ends."

Thea looked back up at Bobby.

Huh?

"Well, Bobby's finally got the girl, so he's already got one up on Jay," Jason chimed in.

"Took him long enough though." Ilya added as he made his way to their small circle.

"Right here," Bobby gave a mock grumble.

"Just stay away from any pools. We need you for playoffs, and you know Coach's ultimatum," Tommy instructed sternly.

Ultimatum?

"Or enraged husbands," Kira stood and elbowed Tommy to the side to take his spot next to Ilya, completing their little circle.

Okay, what?

Enraged husbands?

Thea was starting to lose track of the conversations as everyone fired off random comments, warnings, and jokes, all in an attempt to pull a smile from Bobby.

Was Jay a player they knew from the league?

A friend?

What was the pool comment?

And the thing about husbands?

Her head was spinning. She'd never seen so many people focus on Bobby all at once.

And the miraculous part was that he seemed right at home with it.

Was this their dynamic usually?

She tried thinking back—was he usually their...she didn't know what to call it...centerpiece? Their glue?

Bobby was always so reserved and content to sit back whenever they all got together.

But she had never really seen Bobby like this before—or maybe she had, and she just hadn't noticed? His quiet confidence as he chatted and mingled, his genuine interest in each conversation, and the way his dark hair fell effortlessly over his forehead all caught her off-guard. He didn't need showboating or loud antics to make his presence known; his magnetic personality drew people to him naturally.

But...it was freaking *adorable*. Thea watched countless teammates approach Bobby and check in: to elicit a grin, earn a chuckle, get a smile.

Even his friends, who clearly wanted to wear their fancy period hats, had resisted because they knew it would rub on Bobby's nerves, not that he really would have said anything about it.

Holy hell.

He was *totally* their dad.

Thea couldn't stop her chuckle. She was dating the team's dad.

The team's hot, intelligent, and super fantastic anchor. Their mentor. Their friend.

Their protector.

Hers too.

Bobby peered down at her, a questioning look on his face, but she just shook her head and leaned her head against his arm, letting his kids get his attention with their various antics.

Minutes passed, drinks and hors d'oeuvres were brought around by the various waitstaff, and their group continued their lively banter in their own little bubble.

It felt like the first time in ages that she was content to just sit back and watch the night play out in front of her.

Ilya made random walks around the room, checking in on the various players and their dates, but always circled back to their home base by the dance floor.

During one rotation, Thea caught Ilya frowning as he watched Kira laugh at something Tommy said and then slap his arm. When Ilya turned away with a small scowl, he caught Thea watching him and froze. Thea forced herself to take on a vacant but polite expression, pretending that she saw nothing of interest.

After he stalked away, Thea let out a small sigh of relief.

Oof.

Little sis was going to get a stern talking to tomorrow.

Judging by the storm in Ilya's eyes, so was Tommy.

Got it: Captain's little sis was off limits.

Tommy needed to check his mailbox for the memo.

Jason kept checking his phone but otherwise was his normal unflappable self as he chatted with Bobby.

Thea snuggled deeper into Bobby's warm side.

When was the last time she wasn't trying to be the center of attention?

Jeeze. Had she always been such an attention whore?

Probably.

Bobby felt her nestle in and peeked down at her. "You okay?"

"Totally."

"You sure? You're quiet tonight."

"The table dancing comes later."

His lips twitched but he stayed after her. "You sure? If you need me to take you home at any point, I can. We just needed to come by for a bit to show our support and write a big check. We've been here long enough that I'm sure marketing won't kick up a fuss if we need to leave—"

"Bobby Davidson, I said I'm fine. I promise."

His eyes squinted as he inspected her, and she tapped his nose. "You need glasses, old man."

"Just for reading."

She'd heard that before.

"Dude. Just embrace it. They're hot. Wear them. No one's going to give you shit."

"They're hot?"

Why did he look so shocked at that?

"Uh, yeah? Have you *seen you* in glasses? It's a social media wet dream. There's a whole corner of the digital world that would eat you up if you exposed your closeted near-sightedness and love of books. Those readers are thirsty bitches."

"Ha. And you're not?"

"I prefer my men in workout clothes, thank you very much."

"The meat heads?"

"Exactly." She tried to keep a haughty look on her face and failed at the twinkle in his eyes. Man, he really did light right up when he was happy.

"What if the meat head in gym shorts was reading a book?"

She gasped and placed a hand on her chest. "Meat heads don't read! I want my meat head dumb, subservient, and worshiping the ground I walk on. I don't want one of those new age men who think they deserve equal pay!"

Bobby threw his head back and laughed hard enough that the people standing near them all turned to look at them. Thea shot them a quick smile but then looked back at Bobby.

"Well, my love, I'm sorry you got saddled with me. I burn the books as soon as I get home. It will be a regular Fahrenheit 451 when I get home."

"What?"

If anything, his eyes grew brighter and deep creases formed in his cheeks as he beamed down at her. Slowly, he reached out and tucked a wayward strand of hair back from her face and around her ear, trailing his fingers leisurely across her skin. The caress caused goosebumps to erupt and her heart to flutter.

"Oh, my Daisy. We need to add a few more books to your reading list."

She cocked her head at him but couldn't seem to say any words, her heart was lodged in her throat from his soft contact and adoring smile.

As the band struck up a lively jazz number, the infectious beat filled the air, pulling people toward the dance floor.

"Shall we?" Bobby asked, extending his hand toward her. Thea hesitated for a moment before placing her hand in his, feeling a thrilling shiver as their fingers intertwined.

"Finally! I thought you were going to make me ask Tommy to dance," she said, her voice barely audible over the music.

"Nah, Tommy may act like an oaf, but the dude's got moves. You should see him at dance improv."

Wait. What?

Before Thea could ask, Bobby spun her out away from him.

As they moved onto the dance floor, Thea found herself lost in the rhythm and the warmth of Bobby's touch as he spun and twisted her around the floor.

Bobby was the epitome of fluid grace on the ice.

He was on the dance floor too.

The lively jazz music filled the air, its infectious rhythm weaving through the throng of partygoers.

They laughed and teased each other, their movements fluid and playful as they swung to the roaring music.

Would she have come as his date if they were just friends? How many of these types of events had she missed out on over the years?

Even now, was she here just for the sake of her charade or would he have asked her to come anyways?

Unfortunately, she really didn't know.

God, was she really that self-centered that she never saw the influence and impact that Bobby had on everyone, not just her?

"You're really good at this," Thea gasped, breathless while trying to keep up with Bobby's expert footwork.

"Years of practice with my sisters," he admitted, grinning. "And maybe a few old movies."

Their laughter and panting mingled as they continued to wildly flail, kick, and step.

Thea fought off the joy that threatened to overwhelm her, his wintry smell and the feel of his skin against hers was making her head spin.

Across the dance floor, Ilya twirled his sister Kira, their movements harmonious until Jason swooped in, stealing Kira away with a mischievous grin.

Not to be outdone, Tommy cut in moments later, whisking Kira out of their reach.

Ilya and Jason turned to each other, contemplating dancing together in a hilarious deliberation before opting to find different dance partners instead.

Laughing, Bobby gave another tug on her arm causing her to spin around, only to be halted by his waiting hand.

The dude had *moves*.

And judging by the smile on his face as they danced the night away, he loved using them.

Had her cheeks ever hurt this bad from smiling so much?

What a glorious pain to have.

Then again, she was always feeling some sort of happiness, or peace, or challenge, or...self-reflection even, when she was with Bobby.

No matter what she was feeling with him, it was always *natural*.

Except for the attraction. The attraction was manufactured and a total placebo effect from their charade.

Too many meddling cooks in the kitchen making comments, too many confusing signals that her brain was having a tough time remembering were fake, and too many sex-less nights.

Which is what she reminded herself of *repeatedly* as the heated intensity in Bobby's eyes seemed to reach out and touch her, igniting that newly familiar burn.

The music crescendoed around them, and Bobby pulled her in for the final notes, holding her close.

Everyone else started clapping but Thea was frozen, staring up into Bobby's face and trying not to let herself look at his lickable lips.

She tried to think of something witty and clever to say, but all she could focus on was the warmth of his hand on her waist and his unwavering gaze.

"Are you having fun?" Bobby asked softly, his voice barely audible above the applause.

"More than I ever thought I would."

"Good," he whispered, his breath tickling her cheek, sending shivers down her spine.

Their eyes locked again, and the world seemed to fade away, leaving only the two of them in a bubble of their own making.

Before she could spiral into further self-doubt and concern, a deep voice cut through the haze of their connection. "Can I cut in?"

CHAPTER TWENTY-THREE

April 3, Saturday evening
Thea

The spell broke as Thea turned to face Ian, who stood there with an expectant smile on his face.

"Thea?" he asked, extending a hand that was both inviting and slightly calculating. Caught in a moment of surprise and conflict, Thea glanced at Bobby, feeling his reluctance to let her go as his grip on her waist tightened just a fraction, firm but gentle.

Confusion twisted her insides, unsure how to react to the man she had been chasing for so long, especially now with the unexpected emotions coursing through her veins for Bobby.

Forcing a smile, she accepted Ian's outstretched hand, causing Bobby to release her reluctantly. The transition from one dance partner to another was smooth but charged with something that left her feeling squished and uncomfortable in her own skin.

It was fine. This was fine. This was the end goal.

She should be happier, damnit!

"Uh, sure," she stammered, glancing back at Bobby, who wore an unreadable expression.

Was he hurt? Relieved? Happy for her?

As Ian pulled her away, Bobby offered her a small, forced smile before he wandered back to their table to join the card game some of their friends had started.

Thea tried to focus on her dance with Ian, but her thoughts kept straying back to Bobby.

The moments that she and Bobby had been sharing since this charade began... did they feel as real to him as they were to her? Was he also confused and floundering?

Doubting every look, glance, touch, laugh, smile?

She could still feel the ghost of his touch on her skin, and she ached for something she hadn't even realized existed until now.

Damn everyone to hell for messing with her mind.

And damn herself for causing this stupid, fucking shit show!

Why couldn't things just go back to normal, damnit!

"Are you okay?" Ian asked.

"Sorry," she replied, forcing herself to smile. "I'm fine, just lost in thought."

"Must be some thought," he chuckled.

"It's something."

She couldn't bring herself to find a new topic.

As the music continued and Ian guided her through the steps, Thea tried not to compare this dance to the one she had shared with Bobby.

Why wasn't she smiling so much that her cheeks hurt?

Why was she squirming away from his heavy hand on her ribs?

Why was his grip so chilly?

And had he just wolfed down a tray full of shrimp cocktail?! Uck! Fucking damnit!

Why was she not on Cloud-Fucking-Nine?!

The universe was giving her a chance and instead, she couldn't wait to get back to Bobby!

Ian started making small talk as the dance swung directly into a livelier number, though the speed prevented them from engaging in any substantial conversation.

Ian's attention was solely on her, but Thea couldn't stop from continually glancing to where Bobby was sitting, chatting with some women who had approached him for pictures and autographs.

Fucking puck bunnies.

Thea set her jaw and turned back to Ian.

At his small frown, she consciously fought to remove the scowl from her face.

Way to make a good impression, Thea.

Then again, that's what a real girlfriend would do, right?

She was just acting the part...

A part of her wasn't buying it as easily this time, but she stuffed it down and turned up the wattage of her smile at Ian.

He took the bait.

Ian leaned in, his voice low and smooth as silk. "You know, I took college dance classes. Top of the class. They actually asked me to join the theater program, but I had to decline because of hockey commitments."

"You don't say? That must have been an interesting experience."

If he was top of his class, then why was he clunkier on his feet than Bobby?

"Definitely. I'm glad it's paying off. Remind me sometime and I'll tell you about the time I saved one of the dancers from getting hit by a bus. Who would have thought practicing all those jetés would pay off?"

Forcing her eyes back from where they had wandered over to Bobby, again, Thea nodded quickly at Ian. "That's incredible. I can't wait to hear all about it. You know, when it's not loud and crazy. And we aren't winded." She gave him a sheepish smile and a confident grin spread across his face.

"Nah, this is nothing. You should see the sprints that coach makes us do at practice." He paused and shot his eyes over to where Bobby was now leaning against a wall chatting with Ilya. "Wait, was Bobby tired just from dancing?"

Ugh, really?

"No! Of course not. I was just saying that it's hard to have a conversa—"

"Wow, can't believe a little dancing wore the guy out." A smarmy smile slid across Ian's face—doing little to detract from his handsome looks, but still had Thea's back straightening. "Must be from all the sleepless nights worrying about his spot on the team." He nodded sagely, unaware of Thea's stiffening form. "I'd be sleepless too. The guy loves the city and here he is....faced with the choice of leaving or getting his shit together. That's a tough pill to swallow. I don't blame him for feeling a little out of sorts." His words took on a slight slur and Thea took a second look at his eyes.

Well, they certainly were a little more glossy than usual.

Though, his balance didn't seem to be impaired...maybe it was just the lighting?

"So, go easy on the guy. I'm sure he's dealing with a lot," Ian continued.

Thea blinked and stopped her head from falling from her shoulders.

"What?"

"Just go easy on him. So he's a little off. It's to be expected."

"Uh. No. I mean...you're *defending* him? From *me?*"

He reared back and this time he swayed a little too much.

Fuck. Ian was *totally* sloshed.

Ian raised his eyebrows at her. "What? I'm not a monster. I feel for the guy. Just because I think he's an arrogant, know-it-all-prick, doesn't mean that I don't think he plays good hockey...when he gets his head out of his ass."

"Oh..."

What more could she say to that?

Thea darted another quick glance at said quiet hockey player with a heart of gold who offered her his unwavering support....who was now getting chatted up by even more puck bunnies!

Son of a bitch! Didn't they know he was taken for chrissakes?

Thea gritted her teeth and refocused on Ian's now running diatribe.

The alcohol was absolutely hitting him, and his sentences were becoming increasingly slurred and choppy, often changing topics jarringly.

She cringed inwardly as he slurred a compliment, a bit clumsy and unsteady. A wave of disappointment washed over her, tainting the success of the moment. She finally got him one-on-one, and he wasn't sober—or even just a little buzzed—but full on drunk as a skunk.

Why did alcohol have to ruin *everything*?

"Anyway," Ian continued, swaying to the slower song that was now playing, "I think my travels have really given me an edge when it comes to culture and sophistication. Something I'm sure you can appreciate."

Thea nodded politely, but was plotting an excuse to use the restroom ASAP.

She had guessed that Ian would make a move soon, but being confronted with it head on was an entirely different matter. And with him being so...incoherent right now.

Unsubscribe.

What had her father seen in Ian that made him such a desirable match for her?

If anything, she would have thought that her dad would have preferred Bobby. Bobby's genuine nature was more appealing by comparison, his quiet confidence speaking louder than Ian's boastful words.

"Your father always said great things about you," Ian added, as if sensing her thoughts. "I think about him a lot. What a sad honor it was to be part of his last interview. Man, you should have seen him scribbling in that notebook of his as we all chatted. I'm sure not even half of the interview even made it into the final cut in the exclusive but damn, he was the best. The way he read the players, understood the game, and could carry a conversation, all while taking random notes to himself in that damn notebook. A legend."

Thea swallowed a lump in her throat and blinked hard to get rid of the tears collecting in her eyes.

Just what she needed—to be seen crying at the gala. That'd look great in pictures.

"Are you okay?" Ian watched her closely, squinting through his alcohol-induced fog.

"Um, yeah," Thea replied, forcing a smile. "It's just... it's been a long night."

Ian nodded. "I know how you feel. But as they say, a great dance partner can make all the difference." He leaned in closer, his breath warm on her cheek, heavy with the scent of whiskey and shrimp.

How much had he been drinking?

How in the world had she not noticed it sooner?

How was he getting home?

She'd mention Ian's intoxication to Ilya—he'd make sure Ian got a DD.

As the music shifted into a new song, Ian moved as if he was going to keep dancing with Thea. She placed a polite hand on Ian's arm, subtly keeping him at a distance.

All she wanted was to get back to Bobby.

"Thank you for the dances, but it's time I get back to my date," she said, her voice carefully controlled.

"Of course," Ian replied, grinning cheerily. "I'm always up for a challenge."

What?

"Ok, then," Thea offered noncommittally, her smile weak and confused.

What the hell just happened? Was she living in some alternate reality?

Was she really looking forward to escaping Ian, the dad-approved-guy-for-her...for Bobby? As she cast one last look at Ian's drunken, unfocused expression before turning to walk back to

Bobby, Thea answered her own question: apparently, yes, yes, she was.

And wasn't that quite the pickle.

She wasn't quite sure what to do with that information quite yet.

She was just feeling confused and lonely.

Not a big deal.

And it would be over soon enough.

As her stomach pitched, she tried to figure out if the thought of the charade being over brought on relief...or disappointment. Thea shook her head and put the concern away—she'd deal with *that* later.

With a half-hearted smile that felt more like a grimace, Thea weaved her way back to Bobby, who was smiling softly at her, his eyes bright and clear.

It felt like a soft, warm blanket settled on her shoulders.

Home.

Thea gave a grateful smile to the best man she knew, and was rewarded with a happy grin in return. She tucked herself under Bobby's outstretched and welcoming arm. The sigh of relief she let out when she sank into his side was audible enough that Ty barked out a laugh.

She didn't know what to do with all her confusing ass feelings, but she knew where she should be spending the rest of the evening—and it wasn't on the dance floor with Ian Novak.

CHAPTER TWENTY-FOUR

April 3, Saturday evening
Thea

After a lively auction, a delicious dinner, a sentimental speech, and more laughs, Bobby led Thea back out onto the dance floor.

"This is the closest I get to seeing the Ice Crew skills I only ever get to watch on a screen. I need to take advantage of the moment," Bobby justified.

Who knew when the next time they'd be dancing like this was...if ever.

Especially, if their fake-dating scheme got Ian to ask her out.

Thea had a suspicion that Ian would grow jealous of the way that she and Bobby were dancing.

She was choosing not to think too long about that...and what it would mean.

"Consider this my audition for the Chill Chasers after hockey runs its course," Bobby joked as he twirled Thea around. Now that they were in the final hour of the event, the band had switched from the roaring twenties tunes to more modern dance hits. The music, now bumping with the latest chart-toppers, seemed to pulsate with a life of its own, urging everyone to forget the world beyond the ballroom.

If she was surprised that Bobby could dance to the oldies, she was speechless at his moves for the current songs.

"Where have you been hiding these skills?" She laughed again as he effortlessly maneuvered the latest viral group dance steps, but in reverse, as he stood in front of her, facing her.

He shrugged with a sheepish smile. "I know The Five Hole doesn't have much of a dancing scene, but do you think I just hermit at home when my Ice Princess is busy?"

Oof.

Damn, she had been a total douche.

She hid the sting of his accurate claim with an eye roll and a fancy spin. But she couldn't stop herself from asking. "Why are you friends with me? Seriously? I'm the queen of drama. I'm spoiled. Self-centered. And stubborn. Why the hell do you put up with me?"

She tried to turn her question into a joke, but he saw through it and immediately stopped dancing.

Thea mimicked his frozen state.

Bobby stepped forward, crowding her, and then gently grabbed her chin between his calloused fingers.

In a low, serious voice, Bobby put all her worries to bed. "Thea, you're not that. You're passionate, fiercely loyal, and one of the most genuinely caring people I've ever met. And stubborn? Sure, but that's because you believe in things with your whole heart. You don't see it, but you light up a room just by being in it—not because of the drama, but because of the energy and life you bring. I '*put up*' with you," he paused, his gaze softening, "because you're my best friend. Because the good so vastly outweighs the occasional bad. I even adore all your wild and impulsive dramatics. And even though your lack of interest in any of the books I loan to you is a knife to the heart, in this crazy world, you make things interesting and real." He smiled to show he was teasing. "You're you, Thea. Perfectly imperfect. Do you think I'd let just anyone drag me onto a dance floor all night long? Only you, Bea."

He released her chin and offered a half-smile, his eyes twinkling with a mix of humor and sincerity. "Now, don't let me hear you talk about yourself like that again." He then chucked her chin playfully before tapping her on her nose and contradicting himself. "But if you get a case of the self-doubts again, as always, I will listen, I will tell you you're wrong. And I'll help you bring yourself back to the awesomeness that is *you*. Always, Thea. I promise."

Thea felt a warmth spread through her, a mixture of relief, and an affection for the man in front of her.

"I love you, Bobby," she said, her voice soft as she looked up at her absolute best friend. "Like a lot. Thank you for being in my life."

He looked like he wanted to say something...but then snapped his mouth shut and chose something else.

"Like you'd let me escape even if I wanted to. Your dad once told me a story about how you used handcuffs on your brothers to keep them in your room while you interviewed your stuffed animals."

Thea tipped her head back and roared out a laugh that was so unexpected that her stomach hurt. She collapsed forward into Bobby's strong chest and felt his arms around her, but she couldn't focus on anything but trying to breathe and wipe the deluge of tears pouring from her eyes.

Giving up, she swiped messily at her eyes, saying fuck it to the smudged makeup that was sure to happen, and beamed up at Bobby.

His smile was soft and beautiful as he stared down at her—and there went her breath again.

"I forgot about that," she whispered roughly, unable to look away.

"I remember other stories he told me." Bobby paused and gave a comical look, as if he just realized something. "Or maybe he was *warning* me...Now I'm not sure."

Thea slapped at his chest with a weak thwack. "*As if.* I was his princess."

Bobby continued to stare down at her, his look turning even more tender, and Thea's toes curled, and she felt the need to squeeze her legs together.

"You certainly were."

Oh.

Oh boy.

"Stop aiming those puppy dog eyes at me. I know what you're doing. Playing on the 'dead family' card to get out of an honest dance-off with me. I get it," Bobby goaded. "You're frightened—intimidated by my liquid grace. I can't blame you really. I just expected more from—"

Thea gave a playful push to his chest, causing him to back up a few steps. She stalked after him, unable to stop the spread of a mischievous grin.

Leave it to Bobby to save her when she was spiraling.

"All right, all right," Bobby held up his hands in surrender, trying to suppress the grin on his face. "But don't think I'm going to go easy on you, Sharppe."

With a laugh, Thea stepped forward and brazenly met his gaze. "I would expect nothing less, Davidson."

For a moment they stood there, staring at each other. Around them, the dance floor was alive with movement and energy, but for Thea, the world had shrunk to just two.

As they resumed dancing, a sense of gratitude washed over her.

Gratitude for Bobby, for his unwavering support and friendship.

Gratitude for this moment, this fleeting reprieve from the chaos of their lives.

And gratitude for the simple joy of being alive and surrounded by love.

With each step, each spin, Thea forgot the promise she made to herself to live up to her father's dreams for her: her career limbo, her need for Ian to date her, her desire to become everything he wanted for her.

For the moment, in their place was a sense of peace, of contentment, of pure, unadulterated happiness.

And as the final notes of the song faded away, Thea found herself smiling up at Bobby, her heart overflowing with love and appreciation. "Thank you," she whispered, her voice barely audible over the music.

Bobby drew her closer, their bodies mere inches apart. "Anytime, Thea," he murmured, his voice low and full of emotion. "Anytime." The intensity of his gaze sent a shiver down her spine, and she found herself holding her breath in anticipation as he leaned in, their lips almost touching...until a commotion pulled them apart.

They both turned to the darker edge of the dance floor where Derrick, a younger teammate, was slurring and staggering—his steps unsteady, and his eyes were half shut.

Thea's stomach knotted with frustration and dread. She clenched her jaw, the sight stirring up a torrent of bitter memories. Each wobbly step he took felt like a slap, reminding her of the havoc that alcohol could wreak.

Bobby's own body was tense as he watched Ilya grab Derrick's arm and say something in his ear. The smaller man pulled away, offended at something Ilya had said and Bobby swore under his breath and pulled away from Thea, leaving a cold shadow in his place.

"Give me a sec," Bobby murmured, heading closer to where Ilya and Derrick now stood with Tommy and Ian.

Despite Thea's distaste for excessive drinking and the soul-wrenching pain it sometimes caused, Thea followed.

"Guys, I can drive myself home!" Derrick insisted, his words slurring together.

Concern flashed across Bobby's face as he took in his younger teammate. Without hesitation, he stepped forward, and clasped the man's shoulder in a brotherly way. "No way, man. Let me drive you home. You can't even walk a straight line."

The...kid....looked up at Bobby with such hero worship that Thea was reminded once again about how ingrained Bobby's quiet leadership was to the team. She always knew he was a pillar for them; it just took her until tonight to realize that he wasn't just their rock-he was their freaking *sun*.

And they were his little planets that all just wanted his quiet approval.

She couldn't stop her small, proud lip tilt as she watched Bobby reason with Derrick. Derrick, for his part, was clearly not processing a whole bunch, but Bobby had such a calm, non-confrontational manner, that the younger player didn't get violent about it.

Thea had seen her fair share of drunks get belligerent when it was implied to them that they weren't fit to drive.

Something about that challenge just...

Thea rubbed at her chest, trying unsuccessfully to ease the ache there.

Why were people so pigheaded?

Was their pride really worth the risk of crashing into a mom in a minivan with kids? A sixteen-year-old who just got their license? A dad who was his daughter's entire world...

Thea swallowed back her tears.

"Derrick. What if I drive you? That way, Bobby can stay here and enjoy the final bit of the night with Thea before they head home," Ilya interjected.

But Derrick seemed to have a hero-worship of Bobby, drunkenly-and emotionally babbling about how much he appreciated Bobby's leadership and kindness on the team.

Derrick started crying as he asked Bobby if he could call Derrick's mom sometime and tell her that she made the best whoopie pies he had ever tasted.

"I know I've never actually shared any with you, but she'd absolutely love that, man. You'd make her whole week. Month. Year. You're her absolute favorite. She's always asking about you and..."

"Of course, I'll chat with her," Bobby assured the rookie, who was now leaning his forehead into Bobby's chest and shoulder. Bobby gave him a rub on the back and asked softly. "What would she say if I told her that you wanted to drive in this state?"

There was a loud, wet, sniff that had Thea wincing at how juicy it was.

"She'd tan my hide, that's for sure."

Bobby gave his back another set of soft pats. "That's what I thought. Now, don't make me make that call, all right? The only call I'd hate more than that, is calling that lovely woman and telling her that her son died because he was too foolish to take the hand that was offered to him."

Derrick looked up at Bobby, his eyes glistening in his youthful face. "You're here with your girl. I can't do that. I'll...drive slowly. Then text you when I get home."

"No fucking way, kid. Not happening." Ilya jumped back in.

The rough words coming from a surprise participant in the conversation startled the kid and he stiffened and straightened away from Bobby.

Oh hell.

There it was.

"You know what? I'm fine. I'll find a girl, get her to drive or something. I'll be fine."

Derrick began to pull away and Bobby stopped him with a firm hand.

"Actually, I wanted to ask...you still driving that Shelby?"

The man swayed on his feet and blinked at the change of tacts.

Damn, Bobby was *good*.

A freaking master.

Made sense why he babysat the boys on alternate nights with Ilya. They had a good cop, bad cop, thing going on.

"Yes?"

"Fucking *fantastic*. I've been eyeballing it ever since you brought it to the arena last year and I haven't had a chance to ask to drive it. You cool with me giving it a spin?"

Derrick swayed and Tommy sidled up next to him, his bulky frame holding the smaller man straight so the media hounds wouldn't smell blood in the water.

"When? Tonight?"

Bobby nodded, his face excited and totally convincing.

The man needed an Oscar.

"Absolutely. It's a classic. I've been wanting to get my hands on one for ages but just haven't gotten around to it." Bobby paused for a moment, his eyes heading to the ceiling as he did some mental calculation. Then he leaned forward in glee. "You still living up past Holyoke? Up ninety-one?"

Derrick nodded, a confused frown dancing on his face.

Bobby wrapped a sudden arm around Derrick's shoulders and pulled him tight into a side hug. "Perfect. A little highway ride for me. You know any of the cops out that way in case we get caught speeding?"

A confused nod was his only response.

"Perfect. Let's get going. I want to get out of here before all the crowds all get on the road."

Bobby turned them so they were facing the exit, but Derrick stopped and stared blearily at Thea, "No, dude. I can't—"

Okay, time to help.

"Don't say no on my part! Bobby's totally been eyeballing your car for ages. You should see the photo he has up in his office. Why he went with a Stingray when he had the option to get a Shelby, I have never been able to figure out. Don't tell him no, it will break his heart. I'll catch a ride home with Kira."

Sure, she laid it on a little thick, but she wasn't lying about the Stingray.

She had given him so much shit when they left the auction yard that day.

Bobby had such buyer's remorse and she teased him relentlessly. Just the thought of it now made her smile at him...where she caught him looking at her with such a grateful, soft smile, that her toes curled in her shoes.

Damn.

Derrick seemed encouraged by her comments and finally relented, handing over his keys to Bobby. "Only because it's you, man."

"Thanks, Derrick." Bobby took a few steps to Thea, and dipped his head, rubbing his bumped-from-being-broken-too-many-times nose against her own. As her breath caught at the intimacy of the movement, Bobby tilted his head just enough to lay a sweet, wet, open-mouthed kiss on her. As his tongue reached out and touched her lip and tongue, Thea gripped his sleeves at his elbows so she wouldn't fall over. Or pass out.

With a final caress and a sealing kiss, Bobby pulled away, staring at her with such adoration that Thea couldn't stop the warmth from gushing through her.

Oh, holy fuck.

Shivers shot down her spine.

Thea's heart pounded hard against her ribcage as she contemplated the possibility of falling for Bobby, for real. The sparks between them were undeniable, and a future where they were more than just friends was freakishly easy to imagine.

But as quickly as the thought appeared, she pushed it away, unwilling to risk their friendship—or their plan—for a fleeting fantasy. They had a goal: get Ian to ask her out. Simple. She made a promise to herself, and she wasn't in the habit of letting people down, especially herself.

This was just a combination of self-actualization, dancing, laughing, and nostalgia.

These feelings weren't *real*.

Well, maybe the arousal was.

But that was to be expected.

Anyone with a pulse would be turned on by Bobby when he leveled them with that dark, adoring look.

"Thank you. Text me when you're home safe," he whispered before turning and guiding Derrick toward the exit.

Ilya bent down and looked at Thea with a highly entertained smile on his lips. "I'll, uh, follow them, and give Bobby a ride back to his car. I'll make sure he gets home."

Still unable to form words because her lips were still experiencing electroshock therapy, Thea just nodded her understanding.

Kira sidled up next to Thea, swinging an arm around her shoulders. "I got her, bro."

"Thanks, kid," Ilya said before making his own way to the exit.

Thea continued to stare at where she had last seen Bobby's back disappear, unable to forget the feel of his lips on hers.

While she knew Bobby's actions were necessary, she couldn't help but feel a pang of loss at the early ending of their night together.

With a deep breath, she turned to Kira, who was waiting patiently by her side.

"Ready to go?" Kira asked, her voice filled with understanding.

Thea nodded, her mind still reeling from the events of the evening. "Yeah, I think so."

As the women grabbed their things, Tommy and Jason swung by and demanded that they walk them to Kira's car.

The alpha protectiveness set off Kira's independent streak and Thea let herself get distracted...somewhat...by Kira and Tommy's bickering as they all made their way out into the chilly night and to the parked car.

"Thanks for sharing Bobby with Derrick tonight. Probably not what you had planned. Especially with us being gone for a week starting tomorrow," Jason said.

A mixture of pride and sadness swirled within her, leaving her feeling strangely hollow.

"Uh, yeah. Of course. Well worth it if it stops Derrick from making an unwise decision." Thea rolled her lips together and tried to think about her reaction to Bobby's kiss.

"We all make stupid decisions. Some of us are just luckier than others." Tommy chimed in from Kira's other side.

"The sheer amount of shit that Bobby and Ilya clean up for us is unreal," Jason shook his head in amazement.

"Saint worthy," Tommy agreed.

"I have a call in to the Pope," Jason joked with a mock somber expression.

"Hey," Kira said gently, placing a reassuring hand on Thea's shoulder. "You okay?"

Thea tried for a convincing smile but by the concern in Kira's expression, she totally failed.

"Just didn't realize how tired I was, I guess."

"Bobby keeping you up at night?"

Tommy let out an *oomph* when Kira placed a solid elbow in his gut.

Jason watched them with a small smile on his face. "Children, both of them."

Thea's smile was more genuine this time.

"Ilya will make sure that Bobby gets home okay. Don't worry. This isn't the first time that Bobby's saved one of us from a drunk driving catastrophe and it won't be the last." Jason gave her hand a pat from where it was resting locked into the crook of his arm as he escorted her down the hard dark, and damp sidewalk.

"Well, not the last for Ilya. Will be for Bobby if he doesn't stop taking on the enforcer role. I keep telling him to leave it to me. Coach is fed up with it." Tommy gave a shrug with a single shoulder, still refusing to remove his arm from around Kira. Her face was petulant but didn't seem overly bothered by its presence.

"If Ian would stop starting shit that Bobby felt he needed to defend, it'd make things a lot easier," Jason noted.

Tommy shrugged again and kept looking forward, his eyes scanning every dark alley or road. "Sure, but it's not just that. Ian can play dirty for sure, but he also antagonizes the shit out of Bobby. And the amount of times that he fucks over Bobby on the ice...well, it defies coincidence. Especially when it only happens when we have the game in the bag. I've had a few run-ins with Ian about it. He always swears it's friendly and that Bobby and he have an understanding. I'm not so sure."

Thea bit her tongue.

She always just figured that the guys on the team knew about the animosity between the two men. She hadn't considered for a minute that even their own teammates might not know the depth of their dislike of each other.

"Yeah, I've noticed that! They always stay as far away as possible at events and parties. What's up with that?" Kira looked up first at Tommy but when she didn't get an answer, she swiveled to look at Thea and Jason. "Nothing? You got nothing?"

It wasn't her place to say anything, so Thea just settled for, "I'm not sure. They just give each other a lot of shit. I've never been able to get a reason why out of either of them."

"It wasn't always that way. It just kind of went to shit a few years ago. Not sure why." Jason looked like he was thinking back...and coming up blank.

"Might have been all the drinking. That was a bit of a problem," Tommy said absently, eyes still scanning for any possible threat.

Thea's body stiffened as she stared at Tommy, her mouth hanging open.

"What?" Her loud bark echoed across the parking lot.

Tommy winced and shot her an apologetic look. "Sorry, not Bobby. Ian. Ian was partying pretty hard a few years ago. He and Bobby were killing it, and the team was having a killer run. Everything they touched on the ice turned into a fucking goal. And off the ice, everything that Ian touched turned into alcohol. Fuck, Bobby once accused him of drinking before a game."

"Fuck, yeah, I remember that," Jason said in a surprised voice. "I forgot all about that."

Tommy shrugged. "Something about that, then, maybe? Don't know."

A car up ahead beeped twice and then started, lights shining in their faces as they walked toward it.

"Remote start," Kira said to Thea. "Give it an extra minute to warm up."

Now that Kira mentioned it, it was pretty chilly.

And wet.

And Bobby was driving a Shelby at midnight on I91.

Jason grabbed hold of the nape of her neck and gave her a gentle shake. "He'll be fine. He's smart. He's not going to do anything stupid that could take him from you. Not now that he has you."

"Finally," Tommy chimed in, approaching the car and pulling the door open for Kira.

Finally?

Why did all the guys keep saying that?

It wasn't the first time the guys had mentioned the fact that Bobby might have held a torch for her for years. Then again, they clearly weren't the most observant, either, if they didn't notice the animosity between Bobby and Ian.

As they said their goodbyes, and Kira pulled out of her spot and away, Thea stared out the window, lost in her thoughts.

She replayed the evening in her mind—the dance with Bobby, then Ian, the tension between him and Bobby, and the connection that seemed to grow stronger with each passing moment. Had she made a mistake in prioritizing Ian's attention over her growing connection with Bobby?

A heavy sigh escaped Thea's lips as she watched the city lights blur together in a kaleidoscope of colors.

There was no denying the chemistry between her and Bobby; it had been like a physical force, drawing them together despite her best attempts to resist.

What would have happened after the fundraiser? Would Bobby have kissed her again? How far would they have taken their charade?

Would they have let their teasing flirting consume them and spend the night together: sharing a night of passion after emotions were strung too tight and needed release?

And why did the thought of that leave her with a strange mixture of excitement and dread?

This was all just part of the plan, she reminded herself—a means to an end. It didn't mean anything, and she couldn't afford to let herself get caught up in it.

But even as she tried to convince herself of the truth of her own words, she couldn't shake the feeling that something had shifted between them. And she wasn't quite sure how to handle it.

Long after Kira dropped her off at her empty apartment, Thea tossed and turned in her bed, wondering if her world would ever be the same again.

CHAPTER TWENTY-FIVE
April 12, Monday
Thea

Thea stepped onto the ice, her skates gliding smoothly over the surface as she inhaled the cold, sharp air of the rink. The guys had arrived back home to Springfield that morning, but she hadn't heard a peep from Bobby. In fact, she hadn't heard much from him since the dance.

She thrust out hard, feeling the skate slice into the smooth ice as she powered her way around the rink.

Every time they had texted or chatted this past week, it had been her reaching out to him.

Years, they had been friends *for years*, and she had never felt like their relationship was forced.

For years, they'd send each other funny memes, impressive sports clips, news articles—*anything*—while he was gone for away games.

This week?

Silence.

Or, pretty damn close to it.

She tried to land a simple axel, one she had done thousands of times, and totally botched it, catching her toe pick on the ice.

Fucking hell.

The crash to the ice was solid and unforgiving, stealing the air from her lungs.

Son of a bitch.

Thea sucked in a shaky breath and stood back up, giving a half-assed wipe of the snow that had collected on her black leggings.

She gritted her teeth and thrust off again, viciously dragging her toe pick on purpose, just to feel the ice tear under her.

Fucking bitch.

She pushed hard for the corner and then went for another axel, landing this one perfectly, despite the savage frown she couldn't wipe from her face.

Why wasn't he acting normal?

After a few warm-up crossovers, lunges, and spirals, Thea skated over to the bench and checked her phone.

Still no message or call from Bobby.

"What the hell, dude?" She pulled off a thin black glove and tapped out a quick message, asking him if he was heading into the arena at all that day.

She then chose the song that the Ice Chillers performed to and synced it to her small speaker which she aimed at the ice.

She ripped off her thin beanie and pushed back to center ice, assuming the position she would have when the Chill Chasers performed tomorrow before the game.

As the music notes came to her, she moved to the choreography, letting muscle memory take over. Thea's mind drifted back to the fundraiser and their final kiss before he left. Was he feeling awkward? Embarrassed?

Her muscles moved with precision, each step syncing to the beat of the music. And yet, as she spun and leaped gracefully, her mind kept wandering back to Bobby—his smile, his warmth, and the depth of their friendship that seemed to be teetering on the edge of something more.

The number of times she had relived that night over the past week...she needed a lobotomy.

The whole night had been raw, exciting, and vulnerable, revealing a side of him she'd never seen.

And damnit, she missed him! Why was he cutting her out? Was it something she did?

"Hey, Thea!" a voice called out, jolting her from her thoughts and dance movements.

She looked up to see Ian standing by her speaker, his dark hair tousled and his eyes sparkling with an unreadable expression. In his hands, he held a bouquet of lilies—her favorite flowers.

Confusion mingled with curiosity. How had he known? Bobby telling him didn't seem likely.

Thea skated over, eyeing Ian warily.

"Thought I'd stop by to apologize," Ian said, casually leaning against the dasher board. "For my behavior last week." He gave her a small, remorseful smile. "I was a douche. A *drunken* douche. And I apologize for interrupting your evening with Bobby and making you uncomfortable. And for no doubt bringing up painful memories and associations. Ilya arranged for someone to bring me home and...well, I just wanted to say I'm sorry."

Thea blinked, surprised by Ian's candid admission. A mix of emotions swirled inside her—relief, appreciation, and something else she couldn't quite pinpoint. She cleared her throat, forcing herself to speak. "Um, thank you, Ian. I appreciate your apology."

He rubbed at the back of his neck and glancing around the empty arena before looking back at her with those piercing blue eyes. "Anyways, I remembered your dad carrying a huge bouquet of lilies out of the building one day and when a bunch of guys started giving him shit, he just laughed and said that they were for his number one princess, so... here you go."

He seemed embarrassed to have remembered that.

Maybe there was a soft center under the prickly outside.

Maybe her dad wasn't as wrong as she was starting to think.

Bobby's opinion of Ian was clearly skewing her viewpoint.

It was actually kind of thoughtful...though, not sweet enough to give her butterflies.

It just made her feel more of an...impartial kudos.

"So, where's the rest of the team?" Ian asked, his eyes coasting over the ice.

"Nah, this isn't a formal practice. Just me squeezing in some last-minute solo practice before heading home for the day. I was already here for my gym workout and some photoshoots, so I booked some time. Helps me think."

His handsome face turned back to her, and she tried not to cringe at the curiosity she saw there.

She certainly didn't want to talk about her issues with *him*!

Thea almost lost her balance as the thought hit her.

Fucking hell. What was wrong with her!? She should be thrilled that he was talking to her!

Sure, it was probably spurred on by his competitive obsession with Bobby, not due to any actual interest in her, but still, it was a start...

So why wasn't she over the moon!?

Fuck, she had made a mess of things.

"Thanks for the flowers," she said, taking the flowers from his hands finally. Unable to stop herself, she took a moment to inhale their sweet fragrance, focusing on the delicate petals rather than the weight of doubts crushing her. "They're beautiful."

"You're welcome," Ian replied, a hint of warmth creeping into his smile. "It's actually nice to catch you alone for once. Seems like you and Bobby are always a package deal. Even before you were officially dating."

The mention of Bobby's name made her heart skip a beat, and she forced herself to maintain eye contact with Ian. "Yeah, we're best friends. We're together a lot," she said.

And if Ian couldn't be nice to her best friend, then maybe he wasn't worth all the effort because there was no way she was losing Bobby altogether just for a chance with her supposed 'soulmate.' Sorry, Dad.

"Yeah, I've noticed." He winced and gave her another apologetic look. "I don't set out to be an asshole around him, but I just can't seem to.... He just..." Ian rubbed at his face and groaned. "Fuck. He just reminds me so much of my older brother. All high and mighty and superior. Fucking hell, it's annoying!" Ian looked at her in supplication. "Have you ever noticed that? He has no faults. Everyone loves him. He never makes a mistake. He's even so holier than thou that he doesn't even rub it in your face when *you* make a mistake. And it's fucking exhausting to have his constant judgment reign down on you when you're basically the same fucking age!"

Thea raised her eyebrows at the biggest display of emotion she had seen from Ian.

Well.

There it was.

"I make one stupid fucking mistake!" He corrected, "Well, a couple. But I was a kid. We all were. Well, except for Pious Bobby. Nope! Not Bobby! He never makes mistakes. He never puts anyone in danger. He's about as exciting as a spaghetti noodle and still everyone loves him. Looks up to him." Ian looked at her, his eyes glassy and wide, "I just...he rubs me the exact wrong way and I just can't....not...needle him." Ian rubbed at his face again. "I sound like a total jackass, I know. But trust me, I don't try to. It's just muscle memory from dealing with my brother all my life."

Jesus.

Thea leaned against the boards and rocked forward on her toe picks, resting the lily bouquet on the empty bench next to Ian. She then turned to face him, resting her hip and elbow against the short wall.

In her best motherly impression, she gave him a stern look. "You're telling me that your beef with Bobby is just because you have brother issues you need to work out in therapy?"

"Don't mock me," he snapped back, clearly not liking her dismissive tone.

Thea checked herself. Maybe she was being a tad bit judgmental? Maybe not. But she didn't know what sort of life Ian had growing up, so maybe it was a bigger deal than she was attributing to it.

"Sorry, I didn't mean to sound so unsympathetic. I'm just trying to understand. You're telling me that you're constantly needling Bobby just because you want to get a reaction out of him?" At his noncommittal shrug and lack of eye contact, Thea pushed, not willing to let this drop. "No, seriously. I want to know. What then? You get a reaction from him, he loses his mind, punches you in your pretty face...and...then what? You just continue poking the bear? Or do you consider the game won? And then you're what—pleasant with him after that? Like, what the fuck, dude?"

Ian winced and continued staring out at the empty ice. "I didn't come down here to talk about this with you. I just wanted to apologize for being a sloppy drunk and just generally being a douche around you...and Bobby. I'm working on it."

Thea narrowed her eyes on him.

"Are you really?"

"Yes."

"Really?"

Ian rolled his eyes. "Yes." He gave her a tired eyebrow raise that had her squinting at him to assess his sincerity.

With a sniff, Thea said, "Fine. Apology accepted for being somewhat of a mess at the fundraiser. Apology not accepted for being an ass to Bobby, though." Ian's head jerked and she continued. "Prove it to me, and him, that you're sorry. Actions speak louder than words, and it's been pretty quiet."

He gave a soft chuckle and faced forward again, some lines around his eyes smoothing out.

Was he stressed about this?

Was he being honest?

"Must be nice to have someone like that in your life," Ian mused, not making eye contact again. "Someone who knows you inside and out. Someone who you'll fight tooth and nail for...and who you know will do the same for you."

"Yeah, it is," Thea admitted, a small smile tugging at her lips. That was Bobby for sure.

"I don't think I've ever had that. In a family member. Teammate. Friend. Girlfriend. Anyone. I honestly don't even know what I'd do with that kind of loyalty and trust."

Oh.

Thea stared down at the lilies on the bench, wondering what to say to that.

"Are you and Bobby the real deal or are you guys just passing time?"

"What?" Thea whipped around to face him and found him staring. The tender look he was giving her made her want to add a few extra inches of distance between them.

"Are you guys exclusive or are you guys still just trying things out? Are you guys still testing the waters to see if the friends-to-lovers thing actually works or has that already been cast in stone? Will I be seeing a marriage announcement in the company newsletter?"

Oh.

Ohhh.

Thea tried to calm her racing heart. This was it.

This was her chance to open that door for Ian...

But she didn't want to.

"Because it kind of felt like one day you were laughing about him not being your type...and then the next day you guys were dating." He was watching her carefully, and she wasn't sure what to make of his expression.

Thea laughed nervously, feeling her cheeks flush with heat. "Yeah, well, it sort of snuck up on us, I guess. We've been friends for so long, and then..." She trailed off, realizing she was about to jump into describing just how amazing Bobby was. She quickly corrected herself, remembering that her goal was to get a date with Ian, not convince him she was unattainable and hopelessly in love with Bobby. "We're still figuring things out, you know? Testing the waters. Keeping it casual and all that."

"Ah, casual and open?" Ian's eyes sparked, his lips curling into a mischievous grin.

Thea felt a small pang of guilt, but she knew this was the final period. It was now or never. She needed to set the groundwork—who knew if she'd get this opportunity again.

Bobby would understand.

She hoped.

Thea gave him a nonchalant shrug. "Yeah, we're spending all that time together anyways, and we trust each other so much, it just made sense. And I mean, as you know, we all have needs, so it's nice to...satisfy those needs, with a person you trust. Especially given your line of work."

Ian was watching her closely, an intense look on his face as he nodded. "Puck bunnies have their time and place. It's right next to paternity tests. I had to learn that the hard way." He gave her a long slow look, dragging his gaze across her face, neck, and torso, before meeting her eyes again. "So...open?" he confirmed one more time.

Everything inside her revolted at giving the shrug that she forced herself to make. "Open." She confirmed.

Her stomach rolled and she inhaled sharply through her nose to quell the nausea.

"Maybe...sometime...you want to show me what it's like to have a dependable and trustworthy person in your corner?"

No!

Her heart raced in her chest and a chill pricked at her slightly sweaty neck.

"Yeah, I think that could be really fun." Thea chuckled, the sound hollower than she'd expected. Ian's interest in her felt like a victory, but it also left her feeling conflicted.

He gave her a long look, a slow smile spreading across his face. "Good to know."

Thea's cheeks flushed under Ian's penetrating gaze, but she felt no butterflies, just satisfaction that her fake-date plan was working and that she was completing a goal her father had for her.

"Your dad had mentioned that you played college hockey," Ian segued, "but he never mentioned just how good you could dance. Maybe we could go dancing one night."

Thea's heart clenched at the mention of her father. Fond memories surfaced, and she felt compelled to thank Ian for the fundraiser he'd set up all those years ago. "I've never gotten a chance, but I've been meaning to thank you for honoring him with your fundraiser right after he died," she said, her voice soft and sincere. "According to his notes, he thought a lot of you."

Ian's eyes darted away again, his shoulders tensing as he looked down at his clasped hands in front of him. He picked at a scab on his knuckles and shifted his weight. "Yeah, uh, no problem. The least I could do."

Her gratitude turned to puzzlement as she studied Ian's face. His smile seemed genuine, but there was something off about the way he brushed aside her thanks. It felt...uncharacteristic, and she couldn't quite put her finger on why.

"Really, it wasn't any big thing," Ian insisted, his dark eyes clouding with a hint of sadness. "Your dad was one of the best in the biz. I was actually in an interview with him earlier that day before...you know." He swallowed hard. "I can remember it like it was yesterday. Bobby and your dad spent twenty fucking minutes discussing *Tale of Two Cities* before we even started."

Thea gave a soft smile, just imagining the two men geeking out. "Really? Bobby never mentioned that."

He shrugged, but the corners of his mouth lifted into a small smile. "I'm surprised. I would have thought he would have wanted to rub just how tight he was with your old man." Ian then gave a self-mocking laugh and hung his head. "Actually, I'm not surprised at all. Of course he wouldn't have mentioned it." Ian shook his head. "Dick."

Thea couldn't stop her laugh.

A mixture of nostalgia, pride, and love washed over Thea, making her chest feel tight.

"Granted, I don't know you super well, yet, but you act just like him. Your laugh is the same. And you have the same no-nonsense, no holds-barred, take no prisoners attitude."

"Some call it determined."

"Some call it stubborn."

Thea dipped her head to signal his point.

Her father had been her rock—her guiding star—and to know that she carried even a fraction of his spirit within her meant more than she could express. Even if it was the strong-minded side of him.

"Actually, speaking of: I've been meaning to ask you about that on-ice reporter job. Did you hear back yet?"

She nodded, her heart skipping a bit. "Got an email this morning that they're reviewing the final round of candidates, and that I'll hear back soon." Thea twisted a ring on her right hand and stared at the stones there. "I made it this far at least."

If Bobby answered his goddamn phone, she could be telling *him* this right now, not Ian!

"Ah, don't worry about it," Ian reassured her, his hand brushing against her arm in a fleeting moment that was too fast for her to dodge...wait...why did she want to dodge it?

Didn't she want him to touch her?

What the fuck was wrong with her?

"I'll put out a couple feelers, see what I can find. With your dad's memorial feature tomorrow night at the game, you would have thought they'd at least have an answer for you by then."

"One would think," Thea echoed lamely.

Ian studied her for a moment, his gaze intense and unwavering and her skin itched to create more space between them. Despite him opening and being more honest and vulnerable than she had ever seen him, she couldn't stop herself from comparing how she couldn't seem to get close enough to Bobby when he was near. And here she was...backing away from the man her father endorsed.

Again, she wondered what was broken in her that she couldn't find joy in honoring this part of her father's hopes and dreams for her.

"Anyway," she continued, trying to redirect the conversation back to safer ground. "I should probably get back to practicing. Thanks again for offering to help with the job situation. I really appreciate it."

"Anything for you," Ian said with a wink, sweeping a stray strand of hair from her face. His touch sent a shiver down her spine, but not the kind of shiver that set her heart racing with anticipation. It was more like the bite of a cold breeze, leaving her questioning why his advances didn't elicit the same response that Bobby's did.

Also, it was impossible to *not* compare Ian's throwaway promise to Bobby's literal actions. Would Ian fake-date her to make another man jealous? Thea had to bite her lip from chuckling. Yeah...nope. She couldn't see that happening.

As she turned and skated away, she tried to summon up a sense of victory. Instead, all she felt was confusion. She had managed to capture Ian's attention just like she'd hoped.

So why did it leave her feeling so empty inside?

Thea wanted so desperately to make her father proud, but at what cost?

Her hands clenched into fists, nails digging into her palms as she tried to make sense of it all.

As Thea made her way back to the center ice, she wondered if she preferred the version of herself that was steadfast in achieving the goals and vision that her father had for her...Or if she preferred who she was when she was in Bobby's orbit, where she was simply a 'perfectly imperfect' Thea. The way her lips twitched and her belly warmed in memory of Bobby's sweet compliment made her think that she already knew which version she preferred...

CHAPTER TWENTY-SIX

April 12, Monday
Bobby

Bobby stepped into The Five Hole, his eyes taking a minute to adjust.

He couldn't avoid Thea forever, but for now, just one more night would do.

Bobby made his way to the bar, settling onto a stool and signaling Davis, the owner and occasional bartender, for a beer.

"Long day?" Davis asked, raising an eyebrow at Bobby's tired expression, tossing his signature towel up and over his shoulder. Davis grabbed a beer and placed it on the bar in front of Bobby, his eyes taking him in.

"Long two years," Bobby muttered, snagging the beer and taking a long sip.

The sound of someone plopping down on the stool beside him caused Bobby's eyes to snap open. Davis gave him a grin and wandered back to the corner where he started pouring another drink. Bobby slowly turned to find Thea watching him closely, her green eyes filled with concern.

Fuck.

That reprieve didn't last long.

"Hey," she said softly, trying to gauge his mood. "You avoiding me?"

"Nope, just needed some space from all the couple-ness," he admitted, taking another swig of his beer. Quiet as a ninja, Davis approached and placed a Shirley Temple on the bar in front of Thea. She gave him a quick smile, reached for the drink, and took a dainty sip from the red straw.

Bobby's heart skipped a beat at the sight of her. She looked beautiful as always, with her long brown hair cascading over her shoulders and her piercing eyes. She wore a pair of form-fitting jeans that hugged her perfectly and a cozy sweater that looked incredibly soft. She smelled like citrus and something sweet that was uniquely hers. It was intoxicating.

"So, that's it? You just needed some space? That's what you're going with?"

The way her eyes narrowed didn't spell good things for the rest of this conversation.

"Sure," he said, trying to keep his voice steady. "Sounds as good as anything."

"Hmm." She arched an eyebrow.

The air between them grew heavy as they both tried to figure out how to dance around the heated kiss they shared.

Thea, ever the determined bull in a China shop, bravely pushed through the discomfort.

Bobby wouldn't have expected anything less.

"So, you don't want to talk about our kiss?"

Bobby shook his head slightly, not even bothering to stop the small lip twitch before taking another sip of his beer.

His lady was a fearless bruiser.

He swallowed and held the bottle up, inspecting the liquid in the dim light of the bar. "We had some kisses. So what? It's not like we weren't prepared for that. And as far as I know, neither one of us is a blushing virgin, so a few kisses here and there aren't a big deal. Plus, we needed to sell it to make your little plan work. And, it sure seems to be working on my end. Has he asked you out yet?" Bobby refused to look at her, now taking his time to read the words on the back of his bottle.

Did he want her to say yes?

Did he want her to say no?

Where did that leave them?

Thea shifted next to him and moved like she was going to speak. Then she pulled back and took another sip of her drink, frowning at the mirrored wall of the barback after she swallowed.

"Umm, yeah, no... I don't think it's working yet."

Bobby froze and he started hearing his heartbeat in his ears.

"I, uh, just don't think we've *really* sold it yet, you know? Like, I know he's paying attention...but I don't think it's...um...worked yet."

Bobby let out a ragged breath and sucked in another in the most discreet way possible.

He knew for a fucking *fact* that Ian had brought her flowers that afternoon. He had stood up at the mezzanine of the training facility as he watched them both talk and laugh down at the ice.

Ian didn't need to be fucking mic'd up for Bobby to know what was happening.

So why the fuck was she saying that her plan wasn't working?

His body betrayed him and forced him to turn and search hers, looking for what she wasn't saying.

Was she...into him?

Or just passing time?

Or, had he read the situation down at the ice completely wrong and he was only seeing what he wanted to see?

The weight of the situation pressed down on him, threatening to crumble him to the floor.

Why couldn't he get a read on her?

This sort of information was pretty damn important, and he needed to fucking know where her head was at before he said something...and possibly ruined their entire friendship.

"Fine. I'll tell you what I think. I think you're dodging me because things started feeling a little too real with the dating stuff." She sniffed and pursed her lips to the side, frowning at the bar top in front of her. "You don't need to go, freak out, and avoid me, or anything. It's not like I'm going to force you to fake date me." Her voice went quiet and the hair on Bobby's arms stood on end. "It's weird for me too," Thea murmured, her gaze peeping up to meet his. "What you *don't do* is run away from me. Not me. We're besties. And you shutting me out seriously sucked this week." Thea reached out, her fingers grazing the back of his hand before pulling her own back and flexing her fingers quickly before tucking that hand in between her thighs.

Her muscular, tight, dream-worthy thighs.

Bobby brought his eyes back up so he didn't get lost in imagining those puppies wrapped around him tight.

He took a deep breath and forced himself to plunge into the dangerous territory he'd been tiptoeing around since she suggested this stupid plan.

"This whole fake dating thing is just...confusing," Bobby said, trying to keep his tone light. "There's lots of...shit...that's messing with my head."

Thea's response came quickly. "Dude. Seriously. Yes. Same." She leaned in closer, lowering her voice further. "It's like this weird mix of everything—the comments from our friends, the flirting, the touching, the media attention—it's messing with my head, too."

She didn't even know the half of it.

Like his unrequited love.

"Exactly," he agreed, nodding slowly. "And it doesn't help that we have so much history together. All those memories just add to the confusion."

"Right? It's like we're caught in some kind of emotional tornado, and I can't tell what's real anymore," Thea sighed, running her fingers through her hair in frustration.

So...she was feeling...things too.

Maybe his efforts hadn't been wasted?

Bobby felt a knot of tension form in his stomach.

He watched Thea closely, searching for any sign of how she was leaning, his own emotions swirling.

Thea hesitated, fidgeting with the hem of her top before finally meeting Bobby's gaze. "All the touching, and flirting, and kissing..." she started, her voice soft and tentative before shaking her head in self-dismissal. "Never mind. That's a *me* problem. Not a *you* problem. Forget I said anything."

"Thea?"

She shook her head, rolled her lips together, and grimaced at the bottles across the way, before lifting up her drink and taking a long pull from the straw.

Bobby's brows shot up as he stared at her, trying to figure out what she was going to say.

"Thea?"

She rolled her head to the side, and he heard a small pop as she cracked her neck. Her face was still somewhat pained, and she continued her efforts of looking anywhere but at him.

"Hey. Come on. You can't chew me out for shutting you out if you're going to do the same. Honesty. That's what we got Thea-Bea. Always. Lay it on me."

Luckily, she'd never know the hypocrisy of him saying that statement.

A deep red blush climbed up her neck and face, causing Bobby to blink.

Had she ever blushed this bad before?

Before he could ask again, she murmured something, low and fast, and then went back to sipping at her drink—which was rapidly disappearing.

"What?"

She took a smaller sip this time and turned to scowl at Bobby, clearly blaming him for what she was about to say. "*I said*: combine all that swirling shit with my stupid, freaking dry spell and I'm losing my mind a bit."

Thea's growled and pouty words crashed into him like a street hockey ball through a kitchen window.

A hint of vulnerability flickered across her face as she put the straw to her lips and took a gurgly sip.

Oh.

Ohhh.

Bobby pivoted fully in his seat to take her in.

Were they talking about sex?

Really?

They were best friends and all, but sex had *never* been a topic up for discussion.

He didn't know her preference in bed. She didn't know his.

He had fucking tampons in his glove box for her, but their sex lives were *never* on the table.

Self-preservation on his part, probably. He would have possibly died of a heart attack if he had to hear about how she preferred it when a guy took her from behind or...

"So, yeah. I'm just a little... trigger-happy...on the whole *emotions* front. Clearly neither my body or brain can be trusted because it keeps spinning *this*," she waved between them, "into something that it's not. And it's fucking with me." Thea took a big breath and looked down at Bobby's knees where they were touching her chair. "So. With all that said. You're not alone. It's not a walk in the park for me either."

Bobby tried to find something to say.

Anything.

After a couple failed attempts at speaking, Bobby mimicked Thea's pose and swiveled so he was also staring straight ahead.

After a deep sigh, Bobby lifted his beer, downing the rest, and slid it forward, waving a few fingers toward Davis to catch his attention.

Without wasting a beat, Davis dropped a new straw in the drink he was mixing and approached. After substituting Thea's empty glass for a full one, Davis then swapped out Bobby's empty bottle for a new one.

Good man.

Bobby snatched the fresh bottle and took a swig, still chewing on what to say.

Quietly, so she didn't think he was teasing her, Bobby gave his own confession. "Okay, so we're both...confused. And we're both...'not alone.'"

Real fucking clever, Bobby.

Bobby swallowed and rolled his shoulders to refocus himself and loosen up the tension that caused them to creep up by his ears. "And, in the vein of being honest...a dry spell on my end is *also* clouding things."

Thea's head twisted sharply to stare at him, something in her face working, but for the life of him, he couldn't figure out what it was.

Bobby offered her a reassuring smile, hoping to ease any discomfort she might be feeling, but she was still searching his face for something. She settled on saying, "Our sexual droughts are making things a bit more complicated." She watched him, waiting for his...confirmation?

A smile cracked across Bobby's face, his tense muscles relaxing for just a moment. "Complicated," he agreed with a small nod.

'Complicated' was a fucking understatement.

As they sat side by side, their hips nearly brushing against each other, the familiar, heavy weight of desire and confusion pressed down on him.

"Too bad we can't just go out and find someone to take care of it," Thea muttered, a distant look on her face.

"Yeah, the media would *love* to catch wind of that right before playoffs."

Thea's carefully blank face broke into a small smile "We'd be all over the headlines: 'Cyclones' Star Forward and Girlfriend Caught Cheating On Each Other.'"

Bobby chuckled, his chest tight. "Could be worse."

Thea shook her head. "I'm not so sure. Management probably wouldn't be too happy with the timing."

If she would just call off the fake dating schtick, they'd be out of this issue in a heartbeat.

But *no*...

Thea wouldn't do that.

She was too convinced that her dad had this grand plan for her life that she had to fulfill: the job with the Cyclones and the hand-picked suitor that her father approved of.

The guy who *orchestrated* a huge fundraiser in honor of her beloved father.

Thea was *committed* to the idea that her father *chose Ian*.

She needed to learn who Ian was so she could decide for herself because the damn, inflexible, dramatic, *exceptional* woman who Bobby was in love with...was as stubborn as a mule.

And fuck him sideways for loving that about her.

Thea learned by experience—doing—not by being told.

And if honoring her father's preordained path for her future was what was going to bring her closure and happiness?

He'd fake date her until he fucking died.

It'd probably be a death caused by blue balls, but still.

The coroner would have fun explaining *that* to his friends and family.

Thea rubbed her face before bringing her hand around to start twirling at one of the studs in her ear. "Even if we knew someone we could be discreet with, I just wouldn't want to risk that. Even if our relationship is...fake, I still wouldn't want to even risk putting you in that position with your coaches, the team, or the media." Thea stumbled over the categorization of their relationship and Bobby turned to look at her.

She was looking at him with a caring expression that had his chest getting tight again.

As they stared at each other, he could feel the unspoken questions and desires bubbling up in his chest, thick and suffocating. The thought of acting on those desires sent a shiver down his spine, but the fear of losing Thea held him back.

There was no way she'd continue to be in his life to the extent that she was if she knew that he was hopelessly in love with her. Thea would try to 'set him free' or some other stupid nonsense.

And if she actually did end up landing Ian...there was no way he'd be cool with Thea hanging out with a man who just admitted that he loved her with every fiber of his being.

At least...Bobby sure wouldn't have been cool with that if it were him.

Thea reached for his hand, giving it a gentle squeeze. "We'll figure this out, Bobby," she reassured him. "We always do."

Her touch sent a jolt of electricity through his body, fanning the fire that had been smoldering for years. He squeezed her hand back, trying to communicate all the things he couldn't put into words but wished he could tell her.

"Promise me one thing," Bobby said, his voice low and serious. "No matter what happens between us, we'll still be friends."

"Of course," Thea replied without hesitation. "You're stuck with me, Bobbyo. Whether you like it or not."

The familiar hum of the bar faded away as Bobby stared into her beautiful eyes. He could describe every fleck, every lash, every shade and variation of color. They were eyes that he had stared into for countless hours...and eyes he could spend a lifetime re-memorizing. Again, and again.

A sudden outburst of laughter jerked Bobby out of his Thea-induced hypnosis.

Then a chair scraped across the floor as someone stood, and the sound punctured their intimate bubble.

"Look," Thea whispered, her gaze flickering to a figure watching them from a distance. She nodded discreetly, drawing Bobby's attention to a woman at a high-top table, holding a phone, pointing it in their direction.

It was a stark reminder of the world outside, of eyes always watching.

Fucking hell.

Bobby clenched his jaw, annoyance bubbling.

Becoming a professional athlete meant that his private life was no longer private.

That didn't mean it didn't still suck.

When Bobby moved to tell the girl to get lost, Thea grabbed his arm, her touch searing into his skin.

"She wants a show? Let's give her one," she said, a mischievous look on her face.

Bobby settled back on the chair and stared at her, trying to figure out what she meant.

He didn't have to wait long.

Thea threw her head back and cackled, her hand still resting casually on his arm as she roared out her signature big, belly laugh. Bobby scooted closer and draped an arm around her shoulder, drawing her in and tucking her close to his side.

Unsurprisingly, she snuggled right in.

How in the fuck could this be fake?

What kind of sick cosmic joke was it that he'd have his dream girl in every way but the way he needed her?

"Should we start planning our extravagant wedding now? I've always wanted a winter wonderland theme," Thea nonsequitured, interrupting Bobby's depressing thoughts.

"Only if I get to wear my lucky hockey jersey," he offered back, a small grin tugging at the corners of his mouth. He kept a side eye on the woman with the smartphone. Bobby's number and address had gone public a couple of years ago and he had to frantically change it all over the course of a single weekend. So, unfortunately, he knew *all* about stalkers and unhealthy 'fans.'

"Deal." Thea grinned, not noticing his distraction, and nestled closer to him. "But you'll have to promise not to let our first dance be hijacked by Tommy-Two-Step."

"Can't make any promises," Bobby replied, whispering into her sweet-smelling neck. The air near his lips crackled with electricity, and he could feel the heat radiating from her skin.

How was this fake?

It was too easy to forget that this was a performance, that they were only pretending.

The woman with the smartphone jerked when Davis appeared in front of her and held out his arm toward the door. The bartender was huge and intimidating, and though Davis never would hurt a woman, he would absolutely remove her forcibly if he felt she violated the safety and security of his patrons.

Davis prided his bar on being a safe place for the Cyclones players.

Bobby grinned as Davis followed the woman out and shared a word with the bouncer.

Bobby jerked as Thea's lips moved to his neck and started nibbling, nuzzling, and nipping in a way that made his jeans increasingly uncomfortable.

Unwilling to let her continue under a false pretense, Bobby started to tell her that the threat was gone, when Thea let out a small moan and gave a wet suck to his neck.

Bobby turned rock solid and tried to catch his breath, fighting the desire to bring her up to the apartment over the bar that Davis had for the players who needed a place to crash.

When he finally had himself under control, he tried again, only to have Thea pull away and stare up at him with a hungry, desperate look.

Without even looking for the other woman, Thea dove up and in, going straight for his mouth.

Her lips crashed against his with a ferocity that ignited every nerve in his body.

This wasn't just a show for prying eyes; it was raw, unfiltered desire manifesting in the form of a kiss.

Fuck it.

Bobby surrendered, wrapping his arms around her, pulling her closer so she slid from her chair and stood pressed tight to him, hips to hips. His hand found the back of her head, fingers weaving through her hair, deepening the kiss with a desperation he had been suffocating on for years.

If she thought his kisses from the last few weeks had been confusing, she hadn't seen anything yet.

Thea responded with equal fervor, her hands roaming over his shoulders, down his chest, as if trying to memorize the contours of his body through his shirt.

The world around them faded into nothingness, the sounds of the bar, the distant chatter, even the soft mix of music and TV playing over the speakers—all of it disappeared, leaving only the sound of their ragged breaths, near-silent moans, and wet kisses.

Bobby could feel the heat from Thea's body seeping into his, the way her breath hitched when he gently bit her lower lip, the way she clung to him as if she never wanted to let go...

Fine by him.

The kiss deepened, driven by a whirlwind of emotions that had been simmering beneath the surface for far too long.

Bobby tried to convey everything he felt, everything he wanted, but had been too afraid to say.

There was a returning hunger in the way Thea kissed him that had him almost fooled that she wanted him as much as he wanted her.

He felt his heart start to rip.

Nope.

He couldn't do this.

He couldn't let her kiss him like this under some false plan to troll some nosy fan.

He'd give anything to have her kiss him like this and mean it...

But it was all an act.

So, it needed to stay an act.

Thea...and he...deserved better than that.

Reluctantly, he pulled away, leaving her breathless and clinging to him.

Bobby rested his forehead against hers as he tried to steady his racing heart.

Bobby looked into Thea's eyes, seeing the storm of emotions reflected back at him.

Soldiering on, Bobby admitted, "Davis escorted her out. We're in the clear."

Thea cocked her head as a shadow of confusion passed over her delicate features.

Wait.

What the hell was happening?

Thea's eyebrows shot up and she leaned back, crossing an arm over her chest and rubbing at her opposite biceps. "Uh, yeah. Right. Of course."

Again, Bobby's skin started to tingle.

He'd never been accused of being an idiot.

And though he wasn't the biggest risk taker...maybe there was an opening here to get a better picture of where he was standing.

"So, I hate to say it..." *Not really.* "But about this shared drought..." Bobby wet his lips and watched her closely, looking for any hint that he needed to course correct immediately. Instead, she just stared at him with wide eyes, her cheeks flushed a rosy pink. "We know we can't go elsewhere. And we know that this celibacy is fucking with our heads. There is one other alternative..."

"Call the whole thing off?"

Well.

Okay then.

Bobby gave his head a small cock to the side in acknowledgement. "Uh, yeah, I guess there's that." He let out a weak, self-deprecating chuckle. "I was just going to say we could try getting it out of our system and see if that took the edge off and thrust us back into normalcy, but your idea works too."

Her response was immediate. "No." At Bobby's raised eyebrows and quick retreat she reached out and put a hand on his forearm, her touch searing him with heat and electricity. "No, we can't call it off. We're so close. This is...what my dad wanted for me. I have to at least see it through. He didn't raise me to quit on things when things got...complicated."

"Uh, right. Yeah, of course," Bobby mumbled back, eyebrows now drawn as he stared at the uncomfortable look on her face.

Thea was staring at him with a slightly terrified expression that had his abs clenched tight. He never had the sense for anticipating open ice hits, but he sure felt one coming now.

"So, yeah. I think you're right. Getting it out of our system is the only option."

The world once again fell quiet.

Unable to move, breathe, or even blink, Bobby sat there, staring at her, unable to respond.

Was this really happening?

Did she really just fucking agree to that?

"So, uh...just to be clear, you're saying that you think we should..."

"Go back to your place, bang each other's brains out, and hope that it fixes our broken brains."

Fucking hell, she was something else.

Bobby couldn't stop the small smile from stretching his lips as he shook his head at her.

Nope, his lady was not an overly delicate one.

She was tough as nails, as colorful as a rainbow, and as unapologetic and confident in herself as a fucking peacock.

When Thea Sharppe saw a problem, she didn't quit—she made plans to right it.

Well, okay then.

"And, uh, you want to do that..."

Thea wrinkled her nose at him. "Now. Obviously."

Obviously?

Okay, now that she was being so blasé about it, Bobby was starting to feel a weird sort of regret boiling in his gut.

Maybe this wasn't a good idea....

"I—"

"Oh, cut the choir boy act. You've had mindless sex before. So have I. It's not like we've shared stories of our various sexcapades with each other over the years, but we're both adults, trust each other, and we've had our tongues down each other's throats quite a bit the last few weeks. So, let's just go back to your place, bang it out, and see if it helps take away a ton of this confusion."

Bobby rolled his lips together and inspected her closely.

Why had her attitude completely shifted? What triggered the change?

Thea looked away, brought her thumb to her mouth, and absently started chewing on the nail there.

Before Bobby could dig deeper, Thea continued in a much less confident voice, "Things are *weird*, Bobby. They don't feel *normal*. I don't know what I'm feeling or even what I want anymore and that's fucking with me. I've never had to deal with this sort of thing before. I've always known who I am and what I want. And now, here I am, feeling things that make me want to...*throw* all of those core pieces away." She wet her lips and swallowed before continuing. "I wanted nothing more to honor his dreams for me...and now...I'm getting all confused. I'm just hoping that this...*fixes* things."

Fuck.

For a moment, they sat in silence, the weight of everything hanging heavy in the air.

Anything.

He'd do *anything* for her.

Always had, always would.

Including breaking his own heart.

He reached forward and gently pulled her abused thumb away from her nibbling teeth. He gripped it tightly and lowered their hands to the counter. Their fingers intertwined, a lifeline in the uncharted sea of this new dynamic.

"If you're sure, then what are we waiting for?" Bobby suggested tentatively, his heart pounding in his chest.

Thea whipped to face him, her eyes shining with nerves and determination.

The words hung in the air between them, heavy with possibility and promise. They stared into each other's eyes, both searching for the courage to take a leap that would change their relationship...forever.

CHAPTER TWENTY-SEVEN

April 12, Monday
Thea

Thea's shoes squelched on the sticky bar floor as they exited the bar, the cool night air wrapping around them like a sobering shawl. Typical Bobby—he offered her his jacket with a quiet smile that didn't quite meet his eyes. Despite the bizarre, crackling tension between them, he was always making sure she was taken care of.

What did she do to deserve him?

They walked side by side, their shoulders occasionally brushing in a tease of contact that sent shivers down Thea's spine. The streets were nearly deserted, the glow of streetlamps casting long shadows that danced around them like specters of their unspoken thoughts.

Thea spent the short, silent car ride to Bobby's deluxe apartment building internally debating whether she was making the biggest mistake of her life.

Or if she had already done so when she asked him to help her with this hairbrained fake dating scheme.

It had made so much sense at the time.

Ian had this weird, competitive obsession with Bobby.

Bobby was her best friend.

Two plus two equaled four!

And yet.

Here she was...

Feeling like it equaled...not four.

Ian. Her goal was Ian. Not Bobby.

Why hadn't her father chosen *Bobby?*

Thea didn't want to doubt his opinion—he knew her better than anyone—but, why *Ian*?

Bobby's building loomed ahead, its parking garage entrance dark and imposing.

Holy crap, were they really doing this?

She turned slightly and saw Bobby intently focused on pulling into a spot by the elevator. His familiar serious expression caused her racing heart to slow a little.

Thea always felt so...wild with her emotions. Like she couldn't quite manage to keep them all in her body in any given moment. She also knew that she constantly came off as a bitch due to her determination and lofty standards for not only herself, but those around her.

But Bobby *never* made her feel embarrassed for having lofty goals. He never doubted her success.

He never left her feeling apologetic for canceling a movie night because she wanted to snag some extra ice time, or impress a new brand sponsor contact. Hell, sometimes he'd even come and shoot pucks at one end of the ice while she spun around perfecting her routine. Other times, he'd sit propped up on one of the arena seats, long legs stretched out in front of him, and just spend the time reading.

As Bobby slid from the car, Thea exited quickly too, not sure how she felt about him opening the door for her. That felt too...real.

He gave her a small frown when he got to her side, but she just faced forward and continued her march to the elevator hallway. Thea's heart pounded louder with each step, her mind racing with every conceivable way this whole night could go wrong.

Inside, the elevator ride to the top floor stretched impossibly long. They stood close but not touching, that now-familiar magnetic pull simmering between them. Bobby's hand brushed against hers, a simple touch that felt like fire against her skin and she jerked away.

Damnit, Thea. Get it together, girl!

The ding of the elevator arriving at his floor felt too loud in the quiet around them. They stepped out, and Bobby led the way, his hand trembling slightly as he unlocked the door to his place.

"Do you want a drink?" Bobby's voice was rough, like he'd just woken up, revealing the nerves that matched how she was feeling.

"Sure," Thea replied, her voice barely above a whisper. They moved to the kitchen, a dance of avoidance as they each took a glass, poured wine, but drank nothing.

The silence was a living thing, swelling in the room with each passing second. Thea set her untouched wine down, her fingers trembling. "Maybe I should—should take a quick shower?" she suggested, the words tumbling out in a rush.

Bobby nodded, too quickly. "Yeah, of course. Take your time."

She fled to the bathroom, her heart a riot in her chest. She cranked on the shower faucet to let it warm up and turned to wait at the counter. The mirror greeted her with a reflection of a woman on the brink of something monumental.

'Monumentally stupid,' her unnaturally dilated eyes seemed to say.

This was *just* to get it out of their system.

One night to extinguish whatever this was so they could return to normal. It was the only way.

Heck, Bobby might be a total slouch in the slack.

Like...maybe he was a total lazy bone, and she wouldn't even get off.

Maybe...he'd be selfish.

Or maybe he'd have a nauseating odor that she just couldn't stand.

Or maybe he had a wild bush that was just...too wild. Bobby always had a well-trimmed beard but one could never tell, maybe he was an unkempt Siberian Forest down there.

Or...maybe he wouldn't find her attractive once he saw her naked and wouldn't even be able to get an erection.

She stared in horror at her reflection.

Why would she even put that *out there into the universe!*

Oh, God.

What if he couldn't get an erection!?

She fought the nausea curling in her belly.

As the mirror started to steam up, Thea flipped her head and quickly tied her hair up high on her head so it wouldn't get wet in the shower. No sense in dealing with that while also trying to deal with...whatever they were doing.

Thea then forced herself to jump in the shower and freshen up. Unapologetically, and not for the first time, Thea snagged Bobby's razor from its holder and did some last minute 'maintenance.'

He might look like a Scottish Highland Cow down there, but it didn't mean she had to.

· · · · ● · ● · · ·

When she returned to the living space, the mood had shifted.

Bobby stood pensively by the balcony door, the city lights casting his shadow across the floor. He turned as she approached, and there was a vulnerability in his eyes that she'd never seen before.

"All set," she tried saying with an offhand flair. Instead, it came out nervous and breathy.

He stared down at her, his dark brows somewhat drawn together.

"You used my razor?"

Thea couldn't stop her cheeky grin. "Naturally."

He shook his head, his own lips tipping up.

"Guess I owe myself five bucks."

She laughed and shoved at his shoulder. A move she had done a million times over, but this time...this time it was...flirty.

Oh.

The air became heavy as they stood there staring into each other's eyes. Bobby didn't look nearly as worried as Thea felt and that helped calm some of the residual worries. But one worry hadn't gone away, no matter how long she stood in the shower and tried to internally debate it away.

"You find me attractive right? This isn't going to be some pity fuck where you're limp the whole time because you see me as a cousin or a charity fuck or something?"

Bobby's eyebrows shot high. "Are you joking?"

Thea rubbed the toe of her foot into the floor and tried not to wince. "Well... I don't know. We've been friends for so long and nothing has ever happened and... I don't know. I guess I just want to make sure this is not another time that you're doing something for me and you're getting nothing from it."

His eyebrows had lowered as she was nervously rambling but now his expression paused and he slowly—masterfully—raised one eyebrow and gave her a serious look that ceased her foot fidgeting. "I'm getting nothing out of it? You're *that* bad in bed? Jesus, you're tough on a guy. Here I was, thinking I'd get to enjoy a night with the sexiest woman I know—the Queen of the Chill Chasers and all ice girls everywhere—and instead, I'm being told that all my efforts will just be about satisfying her insatiable—"

Thea leaped forward and put a hand over his mouth, laughing despite the nerves that threatened to make her hands shake.

"I don't mean it like that, you dork. I just meant...you're going to enjoy it at least. Right?"

Fuck, she hated feeling this...vulnerable.

Bobby moved his head just enough that her fingers shifted on his mouth. Slowly—deliciously—he opened his mouth and *bit* the end of her pointer finger.

Fire shot straight through her.

If she thought he was toe-curling-tempting before?

He increased the pressure.

Holy fuck, she felt like she was going to spontaneously orgasm from his nibble.

Unable to take her eyes from him, she let out a ragged exhale when he released her finger just to kiss the tip to ease any sting.

No.

Bobby wouldn't be a slouch in bed.

No fucking way.

He was going to be a fucking caveman and she was going to love every fucking second.

Fuck.

His eyes had taken on a dark, heavy look that had her questioning how much wetness her panties could hold before it started saturating the crease of her jeans.

Neither spoke. They didn't need to. This moment had been building since the day they'd started this charade, perhaps even before then.

Thea's breath caught as Bobby's fingers gently cupped her face, his touch reverent but...claiming.

Their eyes locked and a thousand emotions flitted over his face.

No. Bobby would enjoy this just as much as she did.

She'd make sure of it.

CHAPTER TWENTY-EIGHT
April 12, Monday
Bobby

He didn't know who moved first, but their lips crashed in a passionate kiss that sent shockwaves coursing through his body. They were like two magnets, drawn together by a force that neither could fully comprehend or resist.

Thea's hands were tangled in his hair, pulling him tight. The heat of their kiss grew more intense, like a fire fueled by years of suppressed emotions. Thea gave a small moan, begging him for more.

There was a desperation there that he didn't understand.

But fuck, if he was going to question it.

"God, Thea," Bobby murmured against her lips, his hand finding the small of her back and pulling her closer. Their bodies pressed together, with not an inch of space left between them. He felt her shiver beneath his touch, her hands still wildly roaming him.

Thea responded by bringing a hand around and into the dark hair of his beard, anchoring her hand against his cheek. She hungrily pulled him back to her mouth, her tongue dancing with his in a heated exchange that had Bobby questioning if he could just bend her over right there.

He held Thea close, his hands grasping at her waist as if he were afraid she'd slip away forever if he let go. But as she ground her hips against his, Bobby lost his restraint and started letting his own hands wander.

Down over her lower back, cupping her ass, and thrusting her harder into his erection.

Judging by her sharp inhale and resulting shimmy-grind on his cock, she was very much okay with that. Emboldened, he spread his fingers wide, squeezing her tight ass in a punishing grip and once again rocked her against him.

Another breathy exhale left her as she sucked on his lip.

Bobby shifted so he could reach and slide his index finger down the back crease of her jeans, then down between her legs from behind.

Thea arched her back just enough that it brought his finger in contact with her heat through her jeans and she pushed down into his hand, silently asking for more pressure.

The only thing wrong with that was that it meant that she wasn't grinding up on his cock anymore.

And that wasn't going to fly.

Chapter Twenty-Nine
April 12, Monday
Thea

Bobby's hands roamed over her body, his mouth leaving a trail of searing kisses along her neck.

Thea's hands trembled, her heart pounding wildly in her chest. Bobby started walking her backwards, pushing her up against the wall by the balcony door. Thea widened her stance and pushed her hips against his again, missing his heat.

"How could you *ever* think that someone *wouldn't* find you irresistible?" he murmured against her lips, his voice rough and filled with need.

God.

The pure, open reverence in which he said it caused lightning to rip through her body.

Thea felt as if she was on fire, every nerve ending screaming for more of his touch. She brought her fingers back up into his soft hair, tugging gently and eliciting a low groan from him.

Mmm. She'd be coming back to *that* later.

"Decide, Bea. Here? Couch? Balcony? Kitchen table, so I can eat? Where do you want this?"

Oh, fuck. Thea felt arousal flooding through her at the idea of him devouring her at the dark wooden table. She squirmed and tried to blink away the lust so she could *think*.

"Bed, I think. First. Then table while you recover. Then balcony. Then against your bookshelves in the library."

Bobby had been staring at her hungrily, devouring every inch of her while she decided, his strong chest heaving with the arousal he was trying to control. But even so, when she mentioned having him fuck her in his favorite room of the house, he shut his eyes tight and leaned his forehead hard against hers.

As his hands started roaming closer to her breasts, Thea was hit with the realization that if she didn't get into his bed right now, they'd end up doing it against the wall.

With a burst of determination, Thea broke free from their heated embrace, her skin blazing from his touch. Grabbing Bobby's hand, she tugged him through the dimly lit apartment.

Bobby allowed himself to be dragged, his hands tight in hers as she quickly brought them down the short hallway.

She knew that crossing this threshold would change everything between them…which now somehow seemed to heighten the anticipation thrumming through her.

Once inside the softly lit sanctuary of his bedroom, Thea turned to face Bobby, her chest heaving with each ragged breath she took.

Their eyes locked for a moment, and Thea tried hard to block out what he might be seeing on her face.

Then, without another word, Bobby closed the distance between them, capturing her lips in a hard kiss that sent shivers racing down her spine. His strong hands roamed the curves of her body, tracing the outline of her hips and waist. Cupping her. Teasing her. "You have no idea how long I've wanted to touch you like this."

Oh, *God*.

Yes.

Even if he didn't mean it. *Yes.*

Thea's response was a low moan, her fingers digging into his shoulders as she pulled him closer. "Show me," she whispered, her voice thick with desire. "Show me how much you want me."

Spurred on by her words, Bobby's kisses became more urgent, his tongue dancing with hers in a sensual tango that left her reeling. His hands continued their exploration, alternating between dipping up under her shirt and into the back of her jeans to cup her ass beneath her panties.

Walking her backward again, he paused at the edge of his bed, where he pulled off her shirt. At some point, he had already flicked her bra apart in the back. Reverently, he slipped his fingers up under the straps and slowly dragged it down her arms. The fabric rubbing against her nipples as it was pulled away had her closing her eyes and squeezing her thighs together in pleasure. She jerked when she felt a gentle finger at the base of her throat.

"Your skin is so soft," Bobby marveled, his fingertips now trailing over her collarbone and down the curve of her breast, stopping before touching her tight nipple. "I could spend hours just touching you."

Fuck, yes.

"Maybe you should," Thea replied breathlessly, her back arching into his touch and causing her breast to shift enough that his finger was now barely touching her nipple. She moved again, moving her body under his stationary finger, and giving her a taste of the contact that her body craved so much. Thea couldn't stop her pant of pleasure at the small contact. As she prepared to move again, Bobby's hand quickly moved, and he latched onto her nipple with a tight grip that had her moaning loud and long.

A wicked glint came in his eyes as he watched her. He took in every reaction from her as he slowly twisted and tweaked his fingers. They were the only part of his body touching her and though she wanted him on her—or in her—there was something exquisite about being at his mercy, led around by a lone nipple.

Fuck, she should get them pierced.

Bobby could tug and tug and tug.

Oh, the things he could do with a piercing and a chain…

Riptides of pleasures rolled through her at the thought. Thea panted, staring into Bobby's face as he watched her reactions to his playing.

He raised his other hand and hovered his finger over her other perked nipple, so close she could almost feel it on her skin.

"More?"

"God, yes," she moaned, but she remained still, not pushing herself into his finger this time. The torture of his play was the sweetest kind.

She jumped a little as she felt the slight stroke of his fingertip.

Her hips flexed involuntarily, and he smiled in victory.

"I'm going to have fun with these."

"Yes, please," she gasped out again, eyes fixed on where his left hand was still just barely stroking the tippiest tip of her nipple.

Thea panted as he increased the pressure and squeezed it firmly, before letting go and flicking it sharply.

She let out a rough noise that had Bobby smiling as he continued to stare down at her breasts.

"Do they like to be tasted? Bit? Sucked?"

Holy fuck, Bobby could *talk*.

She shouldn't have been surprised but still, somehow, knowing that her quiet, respectful Bobby was a complete Daddy in the bedroom? Another wave of heat rocketed through her.

Bobby released her nipples and started tracing small circles around them. Still, only touching her with those long, strong fingers. She was hypnotized as she watched him shrink the circle sizes more and more around her nipple until she was sure he would soothe the ache that had started there...only to increase the circle size and move up her breast again.

Frantically, she undid her jeans and unzipped them. Seeking a second of relief, she dove her hand down the front and rubbed a finger down her sopping wet slit.

Oh, fuck, yes.

Her eyes had closed at the contact, but Bobby let out a growl that had her eyes shooting open.

"You gonna come on me if you do that, Bea?"

Yes.

"No."

He scowled at her and narrowed his eyes. "Liar."

Yes.

"No," she protested.

Surprisingly, he lowered his hands from her breasts and looked down at her open jeans. "You gonna finish taking them off or what?"

Thea had never removed a pair of pants so fast in her life.

Panties included.

He grinned at her. "Good girl."

Mmm.

She stepped forward and slid her hands beneath the hem of his shirt to caress the hard planes of his chest and abdomen. She felt the muscles there tense and ripple beneath her fingertips.

God, he was jacked.

"Take this off," she ordered, tugging at the fabric still separating them. "I want to see you too."

Without hesitating, Bobby stripped off his shirt, revealing the chiseled physique that she had reluctantly admired all these years.

"No cheating. Pants too."

Bobby grinned and followed her orders, removing his pants and tossing them in the corner.

This was it.

Naked Thea.

Naked Bobby.

Thea allowed her gaze to roam over him, taking in the broad shoulders, the lean torso, and the defined muscles that spoke of hours spent honing his body for the sport they both loved.

And his fucking gorgeous—and well-groomed—dick.

"Beautiful," she whispered, reaching out to just barely touch the tip—like he had done to her.

The word seemed inadequate to describe the vision before her, but it was the best she could manage with her brain short-circuited by lust.

The tension between them was all-consuming, a wildfire that threatened to burn them both alive. And yet, both of them couldn't seem to stop their teasing touches which just served to stoke the flames even higher.

Thea's heart pounded wildly in her chest. She felt alive, more so than she had in years, and all because of the man who now held her tightly in his arms.

Bobby's hands moved lower, cupping her bare ass. Thea's breath hitched in her throat as Bobby's lips pecked a trail of soft kisses and nibbles in their wake that made her shiver with pleasure.

What if this changed everything between them? What if, in their quest for release, they ended up losing the friendship that had meant so much to both of them?

But as Bobby's eyes roamed over her body, filled with a mixture of awe and desire that made her feel powerful and cherished all at once, Thea knew that she couldn't turn back. This was a risk she was willing to take despite the consequences.

"Beautiful," he murmured, his voice thick with emotion as he leaned in to capture her lips once more. And as their bodies melded together, their passion reaching new heights with every touch and caress, Thea found that she didn't care about the uncertainty that lay ahead.

All that mattered was the here and now, the exquisite pleasure that only Bobby seemed to be able to elicit from her, and the knowledge that, for one brief, shining moment, they belonged to each other completely.

Her father's expectations for her be damned.

They collapsed onto the bed as a heated flurry of frantic limbs, unable to get enough of one another. As Bobby expertly rolled on a condom, he whispered into her ear, his voice husky with desire. "Tell me what you want."

"Everything," Thea breathed out, unable to articulate anything beyond that simple word. "Just... everything."

A wicked smile playing on his lips as he continued to explore her body, giving her everything she craved and more. As the night wore on and they shared climax after shattering climax; their movements were urgent, desperate, and filled with raw intensity. Thea's mind was consumed by the sensations coursing through her body, her emotions a whirlwind of pleasure and confusion. It was like being caught in a storm, with each touch, each caress, sending lightning bolts through her veins.

Whatever the future held, this night was one she would *never* forget.

And with the way her body remained unsatiated, even after a handful of exhausting, mind-bending orgasms, Thea lay gasping in his arms, back in his bed, wondering how many more times it would take before he was out of her system.

She closed her eyes, allowing herself to be enveloped by the comfort and warmth of Bobby's arms and chest, hoping against hope that this didn't ruin everything between them. Part of her wished it could be the beginning of something beautiful—but the rational part of her knew that she'd never be able to live with herself if she didn't try to understand what her father saw in Ian.

Why couldn't he have chosen Bobby?

Thea blinked and a single tear dripped down her cheek, absorbing into Bobby's soft, clean pillowcase.

Chapter Thirty
April 13, Tuesday
Thea

The first rays of morning light filtered through the sheer curtains, casting a warm glow over the disheveled bed where Thea woke, entangled in Bobby's embrace.

Holy fucking shit.

That was....

Well...

She prayed that her racing heart wasn't even half as loud as it sounded in her own ears because she had no idea what she'd say to Bobby when he finally woke up.

A friendship...*changed*...once you knew what their cum tasted like.

And fuck, he was *delicious*.

When she jumped on his offer to fuck the arousal out of them last night, she certainly hadn't expected that she'd go *feral* for his touch. One night of release was clearly not enough, but what the hell did that mean for their friendship and her attempt at honoring her father's last wish for her?

But there she was, still hungry for him, even eight orgasms later—a PR for her *by far*. Her skin was pricking with little thunderbolts where his body was touching her.

Thea literally woke up moments ago, and she could already feel herself getting wet again at the idea of Bobby sliding into her from behind.

The way one strong hand would claim her breast, and the other going down to—

Thea's phone rang, shattering their morning tranquility like glass.

Bobby jerked from his sleep and reflexively his arms pulled her closer to him, pulling her ass right into the crook of his hips.

She groaned, reluctantly extracting herself from in front of Bobby's hot, chiseled form. The cool air brushed against her flushed skin as she slid out of the bed.

"I'm going to kill them. Whoever it is, tell them I'm going to fucking kill them," Bobby grumbled from where he had tipped over face-first into the gap she left behind.

Thea chuckled and swatted a pillow, so it flipped over and landed on his messy-haired head, covering him up.

"I'm not joking," was his muffled reply. "You're next on the list."

Thea chuckled under her breath, and looked around, her eyes still heavy with sleep as she tried to track the sound. After a few more rings—damn, it took a while to get to voicemail—she bent over to retrieve her phone under her bra on the floor.

How'd that get there?

"I must say, Sharppe, that's one sight I could never get tired of." Bobby had removed the pillow from his face and had shifted it under him, so he was propped up as he stared at her ass.

Rolling her eyes, Thea grabbed a sock and threw it at him, hitting him squarely in the forehead. Unable to suppress a smile of her own, she winked as she answered the phone and raised it to her ear.

Bobby didn't notice the wink though. His eyes were concentrated on tracing every single square inch of her exposed skin.

Damnit, Bobby! It could be her mom on the phone and here she was, getting visually...debased!

Even so, she couldn't stop her smile.

Oh shit! The phone!

"Oh, sorry! Hello?"

Oh jeeze, had the person hung up?

There was a small pause until a manly chuckle hit her ear.

Thea froze.

"I was wondering if I got the wrong number with all the silence."

Ian's raspy voice came through the line and Thea's eyes shot to Bobby again. He had shifted so he was more upright, his dark hair tousled, and his mischievous eyes locked onto hers. As he took in her expression, a small crease formed between his brows and his forehead wrinkled. Concerned, he moved the pillows so his back was against the padded headboard and watched her with a serious expression.

"Oh, uh, yeah, no. This is me. You just...caught me off guard."

Another small chuckle that felt...wrong. "Don't tell me you like to sleep in?" She did. "I thought you were a go-getter. Early bird gets the worm, you know?"

"Yeah, but the second mouse gets the cheese."

Thea watched the corner of Bobby's mouth tip up just the smallest amount before straightening out.

God, that beard was deliciously abrasive.

Even now her skin felt raw from—

"So, I was thinking a lot about what you said yesterday. So, I'm putting myself out there. I know we have a big game tonight and everything, but I think I'd regret it for the rest of my life if I didn't try...here I am...calling you on the morning of a big playoff game...after pestering three different people to get your number...asking you to go out with me tonight after we win the game."

Oh.

Ohhh.

Oh, shit.

Thea's face must have showed some sort of reaction, because Bobby swung his legs around to the edge of the bed. Before he could say something to her and really stir the pot, she whipped around and started frantically shuffling through the items on the floor, careful to bend at her knees so she didn't put her ass on display again.

Doing that while talking to another man who was asking her out felt like poor form.

This whole thing felt like poor form.

Shit on a shitter.

Okay.... Um...

"Thea?"

Oh, shit. Yeah. She needed to answer.

"Um, yeah, um, that sounds good, I think. But, um, you said after you win...does that mean that you don't want to do something if you guys lose? Or..."

She could feel Bobby freeze from where she was in the corner, slipping on her clothes. Thea didn't have to see him to know that he was staring at her and listening to every word she said.

And even those she didn't.

Bobby knew her better than anyone—there was no way he was misreading what was happening.

She wished he was though.

God, this was fucking awful.

But she wasn't raised to be a coward.

Taking a steadying breath that did nothing to quell the nausea, Thea tried to fix her expression into a neutral blankness. She needed to know what Bobby's reaction was to the phone call without him being influenced by what he thought *she* was feeling.

Would he be happy for her?

Would he be pissed that Ian finally took the bait? After last night, of all nights?

Would he be...jealous?

Would he grab her phone, tell Ian to fuck off, and then kiss her back into oblivion?

And why did she *really* want that?

As Ian droned on about his post-loss ritual in detail, she turned and assessed Bobby's expression. He was watching her intently, now fully dressed, his expression unreadable.

"I mean, you did say that you guys weren't exclusive right? Did I get that wrong?" Ian's voice had turned cautious, hesitant, and Thea winced.

No. She was pretty clear about that. He understood perfectly. That was just...before.

Before Bobby turned her world upside down.

Thea's heart raced as she looked at Bobby, who seemed to have frozen in place, his expression still unreadable. Thea didn't know how to answer; their relationship had become more complicated than ever, and asking him right then wasn't an option obviously.

"Uh," she stammered, trying to come up with a response. "Yes, I did say that..."

"Wow. You really aren't a morning person." He laughed a little too loud and she pulled the phone away from her ear as she wrinkled her nose in response. "I'll fix that." He gave a weighty pause, "Or, are you just processing that I'm asking you out?"

"What?"

Ian chuckled again and said in a cajoling voice. "Not that I'm blaming you. I'm not known for dating during the last leg of the season, but I figure that if Bobby manages it with minimal fuck ups, I can probably take the time to stop and smell the roses too, you know?"

Ah, right.

Anything Bobby could do, Ian could do better.

It felt like she was back in preschool.

Did he even *like* her? Or was this just a continuation of the one-up-manship contest that was between them?

Naively she thought that he'd grow out of that once he started paying attention to her as a person.

Maybe not.

"So, what do you think? Tonight, after the game? We can celebrate and see where the night takes us."

She would have had to have been deaf to miss the implied message there.

As she was currently still aching from another man's ministrations, this whole thing felt...wrong.

Thea cracked her neck and looked over at Bobby who was giving her a gentle look, his eyes on the small compass tattoo that she had gotten on the inside of her wrist after her father died.

At one point during the night, Bobby had asked the meaning behind the tattoo. Thea explained how she had gotten the tattoo to honor her father; and the fact that he was always guiding her through life. Throughout her childhood, she was headstrong and while her parents always let her forge her own path, her father always insisted on at least sharing his thoughts before she made any big decisions. She wasn't the brightest bulb in the box, but she eventually learned—after many mistakes—that Dad was *always* right.

She wanted to take figure skating lessons when she was six? Sure, she *could*, but really, her dad said that she would enjoy learning to play ice hockey instead. Thea wanted to model for a name brand clothing store after a guy chased her down at the mall and gave her his card? Sure, she *could*, but really, Dad thought she would probably enjoy the fitness modeling that came with sponsored athletic apparel and other fitness equipment. She wanted to major in athletic training? Sure, she *could*, but her dad was confident that she would enjoy communication and broadcasting more. He had a perfect score.

Her father was her lighthouse. Her guiding star. Her compass. He knew exactly which way to point her when the seas got rough, and she didn't know which way to go.

If her father believed that Ian was her match, then it was hard for Thea to deny that.

Her father had always been right, but...now looking at Bobby, she began to doubt that. The look in Bobby's eyes as he met her own was unreadable—a mix of pain, resignation, and something else she couldn't quite put her finger on.

Fuck.

Thea's heart ached at the raw vulnerability in his face. She wanted to reach out and touch him, to bridge the gap that seemed to be widening between them, but she hesitated, unsure of her own feelings and choices.

Bobby's dark eyes danced over her and his face cleared. He offered a small smile and a low thumb-up.

"It's all good," he mouthed, taking a few steps forward and chucking her gently on the corner of her chin and jaw. His smile was warm and comforting, but did little to soothe the turmoil raging within her. He tapped her gently on the nose, a playful gesture that seemed out of place in the midst of their unspoken tension.

As Bobby got dressed and left the room, Thea's mind raced with conflicting thoughts—could she tell Ian that she needed to call him back and chase after Bobby before something was irreparably broken between them? Was last night special for him, too, or was it just sex—as they'd planned it to be? Assuming her father was right, and Ian really was her soulmate...would he be comfortable with Bobby and Thea's relationship after...everything?

Panic bubbled up inside her, tightening its grip on her throat. What if this changed everything? Did she just lose the most important person in her life?

Again?

Thea's chest felt like it was cleaved wide open, exposed and raw, as she swallowed back the urge to cry.

"Hey, are you still there?" Ian's voice came through the phone, pulling her back to reality. Thea took a deep breath, trying to steady herself as she prepared to answer. She wanted to be excited about the possibility of a new chapter in her life, but instead, all she felt was sadness and uncertainty.

"Sorry, still waking up. Um, yeah, I'd love to go on a date with you tonight."

"It won't cause problems with you and Robert will it?"

Robert? What was he? Bobby's grandfather?

"No, Bobby won't mind."

He most definitely would.

"Yeah, I figured as much. I heard him chatting it up with Rachel from the Ice Crew yesterday at the rink, so I figured he wouldn't have that double standard for you."

What?

Thea's hair stood on end, and she arched her neck to see if she could see Bobby from her spot in his bedroom.

Was he giving Rachel a call right now? Telling her that he was free from his fake-date scheme from hell?

What about *Lucy*?!

Was there *even* a Lucy or was it *Rachel* the whole time and he knew how she'd react, so he lied?

Thea jut out her chin as she thought of all the ways she was going to rip him a new one once she got off the phone with Chatty Cathy.

Ian was saying he liked to do X, Y, Z after a big win to celebrate and unwind.

"So, bring your bikini...or don't. I'm obviously very okay with either...though definitely more okay with one over the other."

Uck.

She switched hands and put the phone to her other ear.

Thea clearly was just grouchy and unprepared for this phone call, otherwise, she wouldn't be finding him quite this...exhausting. She looked at the tattoo reminder on her wrist and gave a small sigh. She had to be missing something; she just didn't know what.

"Bikini. Check. Anything else?"

"I'll shoot you a list." A list?! "It's going to be the best night of your life. I promise."

That was highly doubtful. Bobby had just set the bar impossibly high.

Obviously, she didn't tell Ian that though.

"Okay," she hesitated, her voice wavering. "That sounds awesome. I...can't wait." Her enthusiasm for securing this final goal of hers was forced and...dry.

She *should b*e jumping up and down, squealing like a banshee.

She *should be* over the moon that she achieved her goal, that he noticed her, that she was fulfilling her father's dream for her.

Instead, she just felt...tired. And eager to track down Bobby to make sure he wasn't starting something with 'Rachel.' Or anyone who wasn't her.

"Absolutely. It's going to be incredible," Ian replied, his voice light and hopeful. "Trust me. It will change your life. I gotta go, but I'll catch you at the arena later."

"Yeah, see you then."

Thea's thoughts spiraled with confusion and uncertainty. Her heart ached at the thought of losing her new connection with Bobby, but Ian's offer was everything she had been working toward.

Her father knew best. Always.

She just had to keep reminding herself of that.

Because right now, it *really* fucking felt like he didn't.

She made her way down the short hall to Bobby's main living space and silence met her. As she called out and waited for his reply, Thea's throat felt tighter and tighter.

So, this was it; it was over.

Bobby was off the hook.

They could call off their charade and move on.

They'd figure out how to resume their friendship without all those confusing feelings...provided that the sex marathon last night didn't make things worse.

Given how she had felt this morning when she woke up...there was a good chance that it only stoked the fire, not put it out.

They clearly needed to see each other in the bright light of day, without the smell of each other on their skin, and while fully dressed. Then all their attraction would just...disappear.

Probably.

Maybe.

After realizing that Bobby was gone, Thea finished getting dressed, grabbed her purse and made her way to the front door. With a sinking feeling in her gut, she turned and looked back at the apartment that felt like a second home. Her eyes landed on a framed photograph she had given Bobby last Christmas of the two of them together at the Arena. Both were in their work gear and their smiles were huge. Thea had wrapped her arms around him in a side bear hug. Lila had snapped the picture.

Thea remembered how terrible his gear had smelled after that game and a sad smile tugged at her lips.

She looked one more time at the entryway and imprinted everything about it into her memory banks. Even the way it smelled. Embracing the burn that ripped through her sinuses and caused her eyes to tear up, Thea cast one last look at the framed picture of a simpler time and opened the door to leave.

Somehow, she got the feeling that she wouldn't be coming back.

At the very least, not in the same capacity that she had before.

Thea sighed, caught between the past and the future. Why did this have to happen today of all days? She glanced at her compass tattoo and squeezed her eyes shut. Of course, it had to be today. Gah, the universe—it was a fickle, confusing bitch.

She tried to focus on the promise of her date with Ian—to feel excitement for honoring her father's wish for her—but her heart ached for something—someone–else.

Fuck.

Was this truly what she wanted, or had she let something far more precious slip through her fingers?

CHAPTER THIRTY-ONE

April 13, Tuesday
Thea

After Thea got back to her apartment, she found herself pacing and checking her phone with an urgent enough consistency that made her want to throw up.

Okay...so Bobby wasn't texting her...

Or calling her back.

No big deal.

He had a big game that night, after all.

He was probably just...getting ready for it—trying to stay focused.

But the thought of not touching base with him, of seeing him, of not knowing how he felt about everything...

The Cyclone's six o'clock game was a long way away.

What the hell was she supposed to do for the entire day?

Lila was missing from their apartment...again. So, it wasn't like she could have girl time to talk it out.

Though, Lila might not be the best person to talk to about Thea's confusing feelings for Bobby given Lila's schoolyard crush...

Thea could call her mom...if her mom wasn't already half a bottle deep into a vodka bottle. They both handled the loss in their own ways.

Her mom didn't normally drink...but on this day? *This day*, every year, her mom *drank*.

Which was ironic...given that drinking was what took him away from them in the first place.

Slowly, Thea raised her eyes to the framed picture of her and her dad standing by the ice at one of the Cyclones first games in Springfield.

She was just a kid, but even then, she had known it was the place for her.

Her dad had worked with a lot of teams over the years, and at her declaration that she was going to die a part of the Cyclones family, he told her that he felt the same.

The irony made her chest ache.

Three years. It had been *three* years since her heart had been ripped to shreds.

There was something poetic about her heart feeling extra awful today, not only because of the grief of missing her dad, but because her *rock*, who she found shortly after, was also missing today.

Unable to process the emotions choking her, Thea fell back on her father's favorite trick: drowning in work rather than feelings.

Like a woman possessed, Thea caught up on everything she had let fall by the wayside. She churned out several blogs and articles, organized all of her brand videos and content into pretty graphics, added all of her content to her social media calendar software, and scheduled the next months' worth of content.

It was an eclectic group of side hustles, but they fed into each other, and it paid the bills with extra for retirement. She recognized how chaotic it could be to manage all of the irons in her fire, her ADHD loved the variety and diversification of risk. The Chill Chasers didn't pay a livable wage as it was part time, but the fans she amassed...they translated and converted in the other areas of her business. Her brand was solid.

She hadn't given much headspace to the on-ice reporter job because honestly, there wasn't much reason for her *not* to get it.

Not from a nepotism standpoint, given her father's past relationship with management, but Thea regularly was asked to fill in and write content for the Cyclones' internal sports network. Not all teams managed their own marketing, advertising, photographers, videographers, reporters, and broadcasting internally, but the Cyclones did. Thea had done everything from writing articles for their emails, blogs for their website, and done one-on-one featurettes with the players, and more. She'd even done a few games as the color commentator for their premier network.

The Cyclones would be nuts to not want her full-time.

So, why hadn't they called her...?

Frustrated, she thrust back from the computer and checked the time. It was still pretty early for Chill Chaser duties but it's not like she wouldn't find something to do if she got to the arena early on game day.

Plus, maybe she'd run into Bobby.

With a huff, she packed everything she would need and headed toward the arena. If nothing else, she'd grab a quick workout to release some tension before the game.

· • • ●•● ● •• ·

Thea strode into the gym, her body tight with determination. She adjusted her ponytail and flexed her fingers trying to release the tension that had magnified when she heard that Bobby hadn't reported into the arena yet.

He was always here hours before a game.

Where was he?

The gym hummed with activity—the rhythmic whir of the various air bikes and treadmills, the clang of weights being lifted, and the buzz of conversation filled the air. As Thea entered, her gaze swept across the familiar faces, hoping that she'd miraculously spot Bobby. No dice.

But she did see Lila.

It felt like it was the first time in weeks that Thea had seen her outside of practice and game nights.

Thea's brow furrowed.

Where had Lila been lately?

Oh, God...was she another...'Rachel', or 'Lucy'?! The thought made her want to drop a weight on her roommate's unsuspecting toe.

No. That couldn't be it.

Bobby wouldn't date her Lila...

And Lila wouldn't date Thea's Bobby...

Right?

Lila stood near the free weights, her blue eyes fixed on her reflection in the mirror as she executed a flawless bicep curl.

Feeling snakes curl in her belly, Thea walked over and greeted Lila with a smile that felt tight.

"Hey, stranger. Long time no see."

Instead of her signature peppy response, Lila barely glanced at her, offering a curt nod before returning her focus to the mirror.

Alarm bells rang.

"Everything okay?" Thea asked tentatively. Her words hung in the air, unanswered.

The silence between them grew ever more uncomfortable.

Shit.

"Seriously, Lila," Thea pressed, concern tightening her stomach and neck. "What's going on?"

"Nothing," Lila muttered, not meeting Thea's eyes. She set the weight down on the waiting rack with a loud clank before turning away, signaling an end to their conversation.

Was it something she had done? Thea went through her mental checklist of chores and responsibilities, hoping she didn't miss a payment for something. After a quick tally, Thea then moved on to mentally picturing their shared calendar in the kitchen; did she forget to go to an event of Lila's at school?

The more she tried to remember, the more her concern for Lila intensified.

"Okay, Lila," Thea said firmly, crossing the gym to stand in front of her friend, who was now lifting free weights on the bench press. "I can't figure it out. What did I do? What did I miss? I admit I've been distracted and distant lately, and I'm so sorry if I dropped the ball on something. Will you please just talk to me?"

Lila set down the dumbbell with a thud, finally meeting Thea's gaze. Her eyes were narrowed, lips pressed into a thin line. "Are you kidding?" Lila asked, her voice cold and uncharacteristically sharp.

"What?" Thea jerked back at the ice in Lila's voice.

"Are you seriously asking me what's wrong like you don't have a clue?"

"What are you talking about," Thea replied, taken aback by her friend's anger. "What the hell is wrong?"

"Fine," Lila spat, pushing herself off the bench and stepping closer to Thea. "Since apparently you have no idea what could be wrong...let's talk about your little *relationship* with Bobby. Or should I say '*fake*' relationship with Bobby?"

Thea blinked, momentarily stunned.

"Yeah, that's what I thought," Lila sneered, her pretty face looking devastated before she fixed an angry expression on and turned away.

"Why do you say it's fake?" Thea moved around to stand in front of Lila to stop her from walking away. "Why don't you think that Bobby would want to date me?"

Lila looked thunderstruck. Quietly, she hissed, "Are you fucking kidding me right now? What, you want me to pump your tires for you?"

Thea felt her spine snap straight and she glared down at the demon who had possessed her friend. "No," she ground out between clenched teeth. "I want to know why you think it's so outlandish that someone like Bobby would like someone like me."

Lila shot her head back and laughed without humor, looking up at the ceiling. She then lowered her gaze and stared hard at Thea, her sneer still present on her normally friendly face.

"Are you really that blind?" Lila snapped, frustration evident in the way she squeezed her hands into tight fists. "He looks at you like you're the only woman in the *world*, Thea. The world! He's *always* there for you and you've never even given him the time of day. And what? We're all supposed to believe that you woke up one morning and just decided that you loved him back? After years of him pining after you? Fuck off with that horseshit."

Thea stared at her friend, her mind racing as she tried to process the information.

Was that true?

Had Bobby really looked at her like that all along?

He would have told her if he had feelings for her...right?

He wouldn't have agreed to fake dating if...

"So, we're supposed to believe you guys are all in love, when two days before all you could talk about was getting Ian to ask you out. Clever idea, though. Using his jealousy of Bobby. Looks like it worked. Congrats." Lila's sweet face looked disgusted. "Ian couldn't get here fast enough today to tell everyone that he had a date with you tonight."

Fuck.

"Was Bobby here?"

Lila's face scrunched up and Thea regretted her question immediately.

"Oh, does that bother you? That the guy you spent the night with found out you literally accepted a date with another guy while you still had his beard-burn?"

Thea winced and started to chew on her thumbnail. "Who told you we spent the night together?" She tried to keep her voice quiet but at this point, there was no hiding that she and Lila were having it out in public for everyone to listen.

"I'm your roommate—"

"Yeah, but you haven't been around—"

"—because my supposed-best friend decided to start *fucking* the guy that I'm in love with!"

The gym fell quiet.

Shit.

Thea took a small step closer, "Lila, if we could just—"

"Oh, no." Lila shook her head and retreated a step. "You don't get to want privacy now. Not when you've been all about publicizing this whole fucking disaster this whole time." Lila shook her head, tears welling up in her bright eyes. "You knew how much I liked him. And you did it anyways..."

"Lila, I just thought it was a *crush*. I didn't think it was—"

"Would it have mattered?"

Thea jerked. "What?"

"Would it have mattered if you knew that I loved him? Would you have cared? Or would you still have asked him for his help?"

"Well, I might have still asked him for his help...he's my best friend..."

Lila's face broke even more.

"But I wouldn't have allowed it to go as far as it did..."

"Wouldn't you?"

Thea felt like she just received a punch to the chest.

"If Bobby was given that chance—that one small window—to show you how it could be with him...do you honestly believe for one minute that he wouldn't have at least *tried*?" Lila's voice broke. "And you expect me to believe that if Bobby made that move and you started to see how amazing he really was...that you wouldn't have responded to that? All because you knew my feelings were 'real'?" Lila shook her head. "No. You would have ended up right in bed with him anyways."

Thea's world felt as though it had tilted off its axis.

There was no way that Bobby felt that way about her.

They both admitted to just reacting to their circumstances...

Well...actually...he had said some incriminating things last night...

Thea's stomach cramped and her breath was coming in short, unsatisfying gasps.

Fuck.

"And because he loves you. I bet he's never once complained about your little arrangement. Even though it's probably fucking torture for him to see you prostituting yourself out to get the attention of the team's resident jackass." Lila angrily wiped at her eyes. "You're taking advantage of him, Thea, and it's not right."

The gym suddenly felt stifling and oppressive, the sound of weights crashing down echoing like a judge's gavel in her ears.

Was she hurting Bobby by asking him to go along with this?

Sure, he had reservations in the beginning.

Thea just thought they were because he didn't like Ian...

Not that he was contemplating how much pain he could withstand just to see her smile...

"Listen," Thea said, forcing herself to meet Lila's accusing gaze. "I didn't mean for things to get so...complicated. It wasn't my intention to hurt anyone. Bobby knows what this is. He doesn't have feelings for me. He would have told me...or made a move...or something."

Lila was several inches shorter than Thea but the way her lip curled had Thea feeling as big as a mouse. "Yeah, right. Because being honest with your best friend that you're in love with them is always a super easy conversation to have. Especially when you're worried how they will react and if it will ruin your friendship forever. Spare me the Utopia of perfect, honest, and transparent relationships."

"Hey!"

Lila's condescending laughter echoed through the gym, a harsh sound that seemed to reverberate in Thea's chest.

Thea shot back defensively, her eyes narrowing at the dismissal. "Right. I forgot you don't believe in being honest about your feelings. If so, you would have asked out Bobby years ago. And you *say* you love him, but really, you hardly even know him! So how would you know how he feels?"

Lila scoffed and met Thea's gaze with an intensity that made her feel exposed. "You probably know less about Ian than I do about Bobby. And I haven't ever asked out Bobby out of respect for *your* relationship with him!"

"Bullshit. You never asked him out because you're shy as shit whenever he looks at you and aren't brave enough to put yourself out there!" Thea stiffened, her hands curling into tight fists at her sides. She could feel the hot surge of anger coursing through her veins, mixed with a confusing cocktail of guilt and hurt.

Lila reared back like Thea slapped her. She then leaned forward; her face flushed. "I get shy and embarrassed when I talk to him because even when he's talking to me, he's looking at *you*! There's not a *second* that you're in a room with him where he isn't counting your every *breath*! How can he even see me when I'm standing in your enormous shadow! You're manipulating and playing with people's emotions like it's some kind of game!" she exclaimed, her bright blue eyes blazing with anger. "Bobby isn't just some pawn you can use to get Ian's attention, Thea. He was supposed to be your *best friend*, and he deserves better than that."

Her heart pounded in her chest as she struggled to process Lila's words, her mind racing to find a defense.

As she stood there, her breath coming in shallow gasps, Thea couldn't help but wonder if Lila was right. Was she a terrible friend and person?

Had she missed Bobby's feelings for her?

Thea's mind raced, images of Bobby flashing through her thoughts. His dark hair, disheveled from hours of practice; his easy smile that seemed to light up the room; and most of all, those deep brown eyes that always seemed to see right through her.

Had she really missed—

Her thoughts were interrupted by the sound of weights clanging together nearby, jolting her back to the present. She glanced around at the other gym-goers, all of them absorbed in their workouts, blissfully unaware of the emotional turmoil she was experiencing. Thank God for headphones.

"Look, Thea," Lila said more gently, her expression softening *barely*. "I'm not saying you're a bad person. I know you have a good heart, that's why you're my friend and my roommate. But, you *can* be selfish. Just think about what you're doing to Bobby."

Thea swallowed hard, blinking back the tears that threatened to spill from her eyes.

Lila shook her head. "This whole fake dating thing is probably ripping his heart out."

The gym around them seemed to fade away as Thea's world narrowed down to Lila's words.

The thought of hurting Bobby like that made Thea feel sick to her stomach.

"Okay," Thea whispered, her voice barely audible above the hum of the gym equipment. "I hear you. I'll...I'll fix this."

"Yeah, good luck with that," Lila said non-convincingly, her expression not quite as harsh as moments before but definitely still pissed.

Without another word, Lila turned and walked away, leaving Thea standing alone in the gym.

Thea felt as if she were drowning, her chest tightening with the weight of Lila's words. She barely noticed the gym around her, the whir of treadmills and clanking of weights fading away as her mind raced.

Was Lila right? Did Bobby really have feelings for her?

Her heart was beating too fast, and she felt faint.

It would...make sense.

It would make total sense...

And if it were true...

Oh, Jesus.

The torture he must have been through during all of this...

And this morning when Ian called...

Fucking hell!

She couldn't shake the image of Bobby's heart being torn apart by their fake relationship.

And worse, she couldn't deny the flicker of something deeper within herself—growing feelings for him that she had been too self-absorbed and goal-oriented to see before.

Sucking in a harsh breath, Thea leaned over and gripped the upright of the weight bench for support. Her hands were clammy, and her heart pounded in her chest like a wild drumbeat.

Time was running out.

Did Bobby have real feelings for her?

Did she have real feelings for Bobby?

And where did that leave Ian?

She needed to decide—and soon—before she made the biggest mistake of her life.

CHAPTER THIRTY-TWO

April 13, Tuesday
Thea

After Thea tucked tail and retreated to the Chill Chaser's locker room to get ready for their pre-game photo ops with the fans, she couldn't stop the highlight reel from playing her the Bobby-highlights of her life.

His quiet smile when she was being ridiculous.

The way he didn't get frazzled by her drama.

The way he always made sure to have her favorite ice cream.

The way his forehead scrunched up when he got to an intense part in a book.

The way he always smelled like soap and fresh ice on an early winter's morning.

Fuck.

Thea angrily wiped away the makeup on her eye that she messed up...again.

Holding her breath and trying not to let her hands shake, she started the process all over again.

"Thea?"

She jumped and her hand smeared the eyeliner that she had just so carefully reapplied.

Jesus Christ!

She gritted her teeth and whirled to face the intruder when her breath caught in her throat and her better judgment prevailed.

"Ah! Mrs. Perry. What are you doing back here?" Thea looked around at the small locker room, hilariously wondering if she was in the wrong room.

The older woman gave her a bemused smile and slid into the small stool at the mirrored cubicle next to Thea. "I'm here to talk about the rinkside reporter job. Jeb was supposed to reach out to you two weeks ago but..." Mrs. Perry sighed and shook her head. "There was a...mix-up."

Thea's heart started thumping loud in her chest and she felt every cell in her body start to vibrate with excitement.

"You've held a lot of different roles with us: host, reporter, Chill Chaser Captain, and digital content product—we're hoping you'll take on a new one."

Thea's hands started shaking and she lowered them to her lap, pinching them between her thighs so Mrs. Perry couldn't see them tremble.

"You're passionate, knowledgeable, and incredibly well-spoken. The fans, players, and management all adore you and we can't think of a better person for the job. Again, I apologize for—"

"Not a problem at all," Thea blurted out, unable to stop the smile from lighting up her face.

God, she couldn't wait to tell Bobby.

The HR manager smiled and shook her head. "We should have gotten this all straightened out weeks ago, that's our fault. I have an offer packet for you here." Mrs. Perry pulled a thick large envelope out of her tote purse. "You can take a week or two to review it and let us know what you think. The contract doesn't start until next season when Frank's contract is over, naturally, but we'd like an answer sooner rather than later so we can make alternate arrangements, if necessary. A digital copy has also been uploaded to your employee portal." Mrs. Perry shrugged and gave her a small smile. "I remember hiring your dad all those years ago. He was a spitfire. I've never met a more enthusiastic and astute hockey analyst."

Mrs. Perry's eyes started to shimmer, and Thea felt her own start to well up.

"You remind me a lot of him," she said softly.

Thea sucked in a choking gasp to try to prevent her imminent meltdown.

"He'd be *so happy* to see you considering this job—he always spoke so highly of you. You could do no wrong, and in his eyes, there was nothing his little girl couldn't do," Mrs. Perry reached forward and patted Thea's forearms.

"We've been fighting internally about it for the last few years, but I finally won. I want to show some snippets of your father's various interviews from over the years. I've been working with our media team and videographers to pull up all the tape they have of your father during his time with us. For the last few months, I've been having them pull various clips that truly capture the essence of your father's impact with us. Everything's in place but I wanted to ask if you were okay with us playing some of those tonight when there was downtime before, during, or after the game." Mrs. Perry's mouth pinched into a tight line. "*Another* thing Jeb was supposed to clear with you *long* before now so you could prepare and not be blindsided..."

Thea was already shaking her head and leaning forward eagerly. "Absolutely. I would love that. *He* would love that." Her voice was thick and clogged, but if Mrs. Perry noticed, she didn't comment on it.

Instead, the other woman cleared her throat and looked at her feet. She then glanced back at Thea. "If you're up for it, the rinkside post-game tonight is yours. Frank already let me know that he's on board...given the date." Mrs. Perry swallowed. "The mic is yours after the game if you want it."

Her heartbeat roared in her ears and alternating waves of ice and fire washed down her.

Thea tried to wet her lips, but her mouth was too dry.

"I'd...I'd...love that," she croaked out.

Mrs. Perry stood, and Thea rushed to follow suit. After giving a firm handshake, Mrs. Perry's face softened even further as she stared into Thea's eyes.

"If only he could see you now. You haven't just met his grand expectations; you've exceeded them."

With a small, proud smile, Mrs. Perry left the small locker room and disappeared into the underbelly of the arena.

Thea collapsed back onto her hard stool and stared frozenly at the closing door.

She wished she could tell her dad.

Her heart squeezed and her chest and stomach tightened painfully.

Thea sniffed and wiped at her eyes.

She wished she could tell *Bobby*.

CHAPTER THIRTY-THREE
April 13, Tuesday
Bobby

The scent of sweat, disinfectant, and topical muscle rubs filled the air as Bobby laced up his skates. The locker room was buzzing with conversation and excitement. His teammates' voices bounced off the walls, but his thoughts kept drifting back to Thea...and her *fucking* date with Ian.

He'd never wanted to purposefully lose a game before, but fuck if he didn't want to now.

Fucking hell, he was an idiot.

"Hey, Bobby, you good?" Ty asked quietly, plopping next to him on the long wooden bench and casting a concerned glance at him.

Nope, not even close.

"Yeah," Bobby lied, forcing his fingers to keep tying the laces on his skate.

He had to focus on the *game*, not on Thea's plans tonight.

"You sure?" Tommy and Jason ambled over. "You looked like shit during warmups, and we can't afford any distractions tonight. You tend to get a little...punch-happy when unfocused. You know what coach said abo—"

"I said, I'm good," Bobby growled at Tommy, trying to push the image of Thea and Ian out of his mind, but it clung there, stubborn and persistent.

Like Thea, in general.

Fuck.

"Look, bro," Jason said, clapping a hand on Bobby's shoulder while taking a seat on the side opposite Ty. "You're one of our leaders out there. We wouldn't be here without you. So, whatever's going on in that head of yours, leave it in the locker room, all right?"

He *couldn't* leave it in the locker room.

Bobby saw Ian talking animatedly with some guys on the other side of the room.

No...his issue was going to follow him right onto the fucking ice.

Bobby jerked his neck sharply, eliciting a loud crack, and gave a grunt to Jason before standing up and taking two steps closer to his locker nook. Taking the hint, Tommy and Jason dispersed, but not before he heard them whisper quietly behind his back.

Ty stood, balancing on his skates, and took a few steps so he was level with Bobby. Matching Bobby's pose, Ty kept his eyes on the masculine wooden cubbies, his gaze coasting over the various pictures tacked to the alcove walls. His eyes paused on a picture of Bobby and Thea lounging by a pool with some friends. Then Ty's eyes moved to an unfolded thank you card with a picture taped on the side that didn't have any writing. A picture from the fundraiser Bobby has so painstakingly planned to honor a great man taken far too soon.

"You organizing that again this year?"

Bobby grunted and bent over to grab some tape and wax.

"I bet Peyton would love to cover it. Get the event some extra publicity."

"Not happening." Bobby stiffly sat back down and yanked his stick into his lap.

"Hey, she's already written about it once; it wouldn't be that hard to do it again from a new angle." Ty scratched at the back of his neck. "Why you handed off the credit to Asshat over there..." Ty's voice faded as he turned to look at said asshat.

"You *know* why. He was going to be traded and he was our best shot at the Cup that year. So, I did what was best for the team. So just...shut up already." Bobby's entire body was so tight, it almost felt like it was vibrating.

"Bobby—"

"Just shut up!" Bobby flew to his feet and got in Ty's face, scant inches separated them. "I never got in your face about your *many* relationship shitstorms, have I? No. I *fucking* haven't. Now, back the fuck off," Bobby bit out between clenched teeth, his hands folded into fists at his side.

The locker room fell silent as the best friends stared at each other.

Quietly, Ty kept at him. "I heard Ian talking earl—"

Bobby bent down, grabbed his stick, his tape, and wax, and stalked toward the door.

Ty followed him.

The room resumed a quiet conversation as they all went back to whatever they were doing...or they at least pretended to.

"Bobby. Wait up." Ty choppily jogged after him, his body swaying as he balanced on the thin blades of his own skates.

After they were far enough away from any prying ears, Bobby whipped around to face Ty, his chest on fire. "What, Ty? What do you want to say? That I was an idiot? I already know. That it was stupid to try? To hope? I already know that too. So, what else do you want to say?"

Ty's somber eyes scanned Bobby's face and his shoulders lowered in defeat. "Are you okay?"

"No."

Ty's lips pulled to the side in a painful grimace. "Anything I can do to help?"

"If you could stop me from getting into a fight so I'm not dropped or traded in the off-season...that would be great. I never had a set home growing up and Springfield is...home to me. I don't want to leave it. If Coach decides I'm not worth the hassle...I'm out. I've managed to get away without needing to muscle anyone out there the last few weeks, but..." Bobby swallowed what felt like glass shards in his throat. "But if you could just keep an eye on me tonight and help me remember that, when things get tense."

"A bit bloodthirsty tonight?"

"You can only imagine."

Ty gave him a slow nod. "I'll scoot in, calm you down. No way you're going anywhere, brother. This team needs you, even if Coach is bemoaning the minutes in the box, we revolve around you. You're our rock. I've got you."

Bobby lunged forward and pulled Ty into a tight hug. After a moment, he thumped Ty on the back and pulled away. "Gotta grab some ibuprofen; I've had an insane headache all day and I can't shake it." Bobby looked over at Ty. "Sorry about before."

Ty grinned and punched him solidly on the arm. "Don't even worry about it."

They turned and headed back toward the locker room, spending the short walk idly joking about Fido's latest food preferences and what the snobby dog refused to eat. When they got back to the doors, both gave friendly nods to the security team and pushed back in. Inside, Coach was getting ready to start a speech, so the men gathered around and fell silent as they waited for the inspiring words to fall.

As Bobby looked up across the uneven circle of men, he saw Ian's smirking face staring back at him. After a heartbeat of Bobby wondering how he could manage to pulverize him on the ice and make it look like an accident, Ian's cocky grin grew and, in a move that screamed that he wanted to be put into the hospital, Ian winked.

Fucking *asshole*.

CHAPTER THIRTY-FOUR
April 13, Tuesday
Bobby

As they filed out of the locker room and onto the ice, Bobby's heart raced with more than just an adrenaline for the game. The chilly air of the rink nipped at Bobby's exposed skin as he glided onto the ice for a quick warm-up. He took a deep breath, trying to focus on the familiar chill and the feel of his skates cutting through the ice. His hands felt unsteady on his hockey stick, and his movements lacked their usual grace.

His mind was still clouded with thoughts of Thea and her date with Ian, and though he knew it was selfish, he hoped the team lost so miserably tonight that Ian was convinced that it was Thea that had brought the team bad luck, and never called her again.

Bobby looked toward the corner where he knew he'd see Thea waiting to clear the ice with the rest of the Ice Crew and his chest tightened when he saw her.

No.

No, he didn't hope that they would lose.

Thea wanted this—wanted to feel like she honored her dad's wish—and wanted Ian—almost more than anything else.

So, if being with Ian was what made Thea happy, then Bobby hoped they would win and that her night was every bit as magical as she was hoping it would be.

After a clumsy and distracted warmup, Bobby made his way to the line for the national anthem and shifted on his skates, unable to keep his body still with how fast his mind was racing. The whole pre-game process was muffled and passed by in a blur. The only thing that broke him out of his stupor was a familiar voice being played through the arena speakers.

His heart pounded in his chest as he looked up to the jumbotron and saw Thea's father, Dick, sitting there on the screen, talking to the cameraman. A series of short clips later and the arena announcer read a small tribute to the work that Dick had done for the Cyclones, the community, and the other teams he had helped. On an ending note, when the announcer mentioned how much Dick treasured his family before tragically dying at the hands of a drunk driver, Bobby couldn't stop himself from looking over in Thea's direction.

There was no spotlight on her, but even so, Bobby found her in an instant.

Like always.

His chest squeezed as he saw the pride and grief on her face as she gazed up at the big screen like it was the most amazing thing she'd ever seen.

What he wouldn't give to take away that pain.

He'd give anything.

Even if that meant giving *Thea* away.

As the announcer asked everyone for a moment of silence, Bobby quieted his feet and mind to pay respects to the man who shared with Bobby his love of hockey, books, and *Thea*.

Shortly after, the first period began, and Bobby pushed himself to concentrate, but it was a struggle. He'd never dealt with this self-doubt before but each time he contacted the puck, he could feel the weight of comparison to Ian.

And how he was coming up short.

Again.

"Davidson, get back on defense!" Coach Montgomery yelled from the bench as Bobby's focus wavered, causing him to miss an important check. His internal battle raged on, and despite his best efforts to keep it under control, he found himself in the penalty box twice in the first period alone.

Luckily, it was only for boarding, then hooking. Ty had been true to his word and interrupted whatever might have escalated into a full blow fight.

"Hey, man, you all right?" Ilya asked, falling in line with him as they made their way down the tunnel back into the locker room after the whistle blew for the end of the period. "You seem...off."

"It's just taking a minute to work through," Bobby replied, forcing a grin. "I'll be fine next period."

"All right," Ilya said, still looking concerned. "But remember, we're here for you if you need us."

"Thanks, Cap," Bobby said, appreciating his friend's support.

Before Bobby could make his way into the locker room though, his coach grabbed him and pulled him down the hall.

Shit.

Coach Montgomery's stern blue eyes bore into him, searching for answers.

Bobby refused to look away.

"Listen," Coach said, lowering his voice. "I don't know what's going on with you right now, but you need to put it aside. Stay in the moment, Bobby. Personal matters have no place on the ice, especially when Sven Larsson is playing lights out."

Bobby snapped his jaw shut so he didn't say anything he'd regret. The Boston Grizzlies were definitely outplaying them, and he needed to get his shit together.

He gave his coach a stiff nod before shifting as if he were going to head back to the locker room. Coach Montgomery reached out and grabbed his arm. "One more thing. You've kept the temper under wraps the last few weeks, and the team is grateful, but you're sloppy out there tonight—and don't think we haven't noticed Ty playing interference for you. He's not your babysitter. You can either control your own damn temper and assume the role the team needs you to have, or you can't. If you don't enforce, then one of our enforcers will step up—so let them do their damn jobs! And if they don't...well,

I need to know that too. Stop trying to do it all—that's not what you're here for. And let your babysitter off the hook. He shouldn't have to worry about keeping an eye on you. Stop being selfish."

And with that well-placed barb, his coach left him in the hall.

The urge to punch the brick wall next to him was fierce but the risk of injury wasn't worth it.

Nothing was worth it.

Bobby felt his body droop as he leaned forward and rested his helmeted forehead on the wall.

Why was he even still here?

There were plenty of other teams that would take him.

Teams that didn't have Ian buzzing around and acting like a gnat.

Bobby sighed and leaned harder into the wall.

Yeah, but those teams didn't have *Thea*.

They weren't *Springfield*.

And they didn't have his *boys*.

His boys—who needed him to step up.

He needed to accept Thea's decision and move forward. So, she didn't love him. So, what?

She never had. He was stupid to think sex would tip the scales so much that he went from friend to a love interest worth besmirching her father's last wish for her.

The act of trying to fulfill her father's wish for her was an important piece of her closure...if his last therapy session with Kayla was to be believed. Thea needed to feel like she achieved the life that he wanted for her in order for her to heal and move on.

So...to do that, she needed Ian, not Bobby.

But his teammates—his city—they needed *him*.

• • • • • • • • • •

When the second period began, Bobby was a new man.

Right from the start, Bobby found—or made—moments of brilliance. His skates sliced through the ice with renewed energy, and he navigated the rink with the skill that had earned him his first line spot. Beneath the surface, the internal turmoil persisted, gnawing at him like a relentless ache, but he embraced the pain and let it fuel him, as he battled on the ice.

A fierce competitiveness surged within him, propelling him to take risks he would usually avoid.

During a line change, Bobby spotted an opportunity. One of the other team's superstars was momentarily vulnerable, and without thinking, Bobby lunged forward, landing a massive hit that sent the opposing player crashing to the ice. He then zipped to the bench and let his replacement shoot out.

"Damn, Davidson." Ian whistled from the bench next to him. "You finally grew a pair out there."

"Get your hand off me," Bobby snapped, shoving Ian's arm away with more force than necessary. He could feel his pulse thundering in his ears, adrenaline and anger threatening to get the better of him.

He couldn't afford to let his emotions consume him, not now. As he took a deep, steadying breath, he resolved to channel all of his energy into helping his team secure a victory.

A victory for the team...meant a victory for Ian...which meant a victory for Thea.

It was his loss, but Thea's win.

And that's all that mattered.

Once it was his line's turn again, Bobby's breath fogged up the visor of his helmet as he leaped back onto the ice, his muscles tensing. As his teammates battled for possession of the puck, he cycled and took his position by the net, waiting for an opportunity to strike.

The puck ricocheted off the boards, and Bobby's gaze locked onto its trajectory. For a fleeting moment, his thoughts cleared, and all that mattered was the black disc hurtling toward him.

Despite the close distance to the goal, Bobby took a risk. He wound up and unleashed a powerful one-time. The puck soared through the air, narrowly slipping past the opposing goalie's glove and into the net. A deafening roar erupted from the crowd as the red light flashed behind the goal.

Bobby felt a brief smile flickering across his face. But even as he reveled in the momentary euphoria of his success, his happiness flatlined.

Normally, he'd be looking forward to Thea's analysis of that play after the game.

Now...he'd be going home to nothing but silence.

As the second period horn sounded, the team marched as one back to the locker room, buzzed by the dominant period they had just shared. The score was now tied 3-3, and they were heading into the final period.

It was anyone's game.

CHAPTER THIRTY-FIVE

April 13, Tuesday
Thea

In the corner by the Zamboni gate, the deafening roar of the crowd filled Thea's ears as she sat on the edge of her seat, eyes glued to the ice. Her heart raced and anxiety gnawed at her. It was the final period of the game, and the score was deadlocked at an agonizing 3-3.

"Come on, guys! You can do it!" she yelled, her voice barely audible over the thunderous applause that surrounded her.

Her Chill Chaser duties kept her busy for most of the first two periods, but she got lucky with the rotation that night. Usually, she was clearing ice shavings, working three times per period to clean the ice, or frantically walking up and down the stairs selling beers and merchandise. But tonight, she got the third period off to enjoy the rest of the game. It would be such a change of pace to be paid to actually watch the game and comment on it.

If.

"If" she took the reporter job.

She still needed to open the envelope and see what they offered her.

But...did it really matter?

It was the job she was qualified for. The job her father had wanted for her. There wasn't even a question.

Unlike the doubt about what to do about Bobby.

When she had told her Ice Crew about the job offer, everyone was excited for her... especially Rachel who had Chill Chaser Captainship in her sights.

Even Lila's freeze out had thawed for a moment as she offered her congratulations.

Only for a moment though.

Then Lila was back to treating her like The Worst Friend Ever.

Which, Thea totally was.

The revelations of the day had left her exhausted and emotionally fragile. Not only was it the anniversary of her father's death and they kept playing bittersweet tributes to him on the Jumbotron, she was also trying to process the fact that *maybe* she didn't care that her father chose Ian...

She wanted to choose *Bobby*.

And that betrayal of emotions felt like *such* a huge disrespect to her father's memory that she wanted to sob. Or punch someone.

Her Chill Chaser duties had done little to offer suitable distraction...but sitting here and watching the game? It was a bit better.

For the first period, Ian had controlled the pace of the Cyclones' offense. With two goals to his name, he skated with unmatched speed and precision, slicing through the opposing team's defenses like a hot knife through butter. His dark hair under his helmet was plastered to his forehead, his eyes laser-focused on the game. Every play he orchestrated turned to gold only to be foiled by the other team's goalie, who was having the game of his life.

But Bobby...

He had an uncharacteristically rough start to the game. He was sluggish, awkward, and clumsy. Every time Thea saw him skate up close to the glass in front of them, she could see the distraction and exhaustion in his eyes. Add that to the fact that he didn't look over and give her his signature smile and wink at the start of the game...Thea once again fought back the urge to vomit.

Earlier in the game, she was making her way up and down the stairs with a large tray of beers for sale and some fans were talking about whether Bobby was playing with an injury. Maybe they weren't wrong.

A broken heart—if Lila was to be believed.

Thankfully, when he came out for the second period, a switch had flipped, and he righted the ship.

He slid right back to his quick and clever style of play, and the fans went wild. Even so, he was playing *different* than usual. Usually known for his quick but conservative demeanor on the ice, Bobby was playing more aggressively than she had ever seen.

His face on the jumbotron was a mask of intense concentration, his every movement fueled by a ferocity that left Thea feeling both awed and concerned.

And then when the third period hit and all that zest had faded, he just looked...defeated.

"Wow, Bobby's having a weird night," Peyton Knowles murmured, scribbling something in her notepad. The sports reporter tended to hang out near Thea when Thea wasn't busy with Ice Crew responsibilities. Peyton and Thea would analyze the games, breaking down the progressions and player dynamics. They'd formed a semi-friendship over the years and Thea wondered, not for the first time, if she should extend an invitation to do something with Peyton *outside* of the arena.

When Thea had told her about her rinkside opportunity post-game, and the job offer, Peyton squealed in excitement.

Now, the woman frowned in concern as she watched Bobby skate to the bench—no trace of happiness to be found.

Thea started chewing on her nail again and she tried to focus on the game. If she was going to have to give a report post-game...she needed to be able to say something about the other players...not just obsess over everything *Bobby Davidson*.

Distantly, on Peyton's other side, Thea heard Lila giggling with Brian and Rachel about whose stick was bigger.

Ugh. Why couldn't they have been on-ice duty for this period?

As Thea continued to stare at Bobby sitting on the bench, his shoulders curled in and his face serious, she fought off another wave of unease.

Was their recent 'breakup' the reason for his performance?

Seeing him *off* like this, after always being so fierce and unbridled, lent strength to Lila's assessment.

Which was *really* fucking terrifying.

After a series of plays, Bobby's line was leaping back onto the ice, charging across to the puck.

"Seriously, Thea, I've never seen him play like this before," Peyton continued commenting. "This is so *not* Bobby."

Thea's green eyes narrowed as she watched Bobby shove an opposing player out of his way with surprising force. "Umm—"

"Actually, Thea and Bobby broke up. She didn't tell you?"

Thea leaned forward and shot Lila a dark look which she pettishly ignored.

"Yeah, apparently, she got a better offer in Ian Novak." Like a total bitter harpy, Lila then turned and said loudly, "Oh, Brian, I just realized she'll be able to give you your stick answer tomorrow morning."

Thea clenched her jaw, fighting the urge to reach over and show Lila how hockey players responded to insults and teach the peppy, bitchy figure skater a lesson she wouldn't forget.

Don't resort to violence. Don't resort to violence. Don't resort to violence.

Peyton's disappointed voice distracted her enough that Lila wasn't going to be going on the post-game ice with a busted lip and a black eye. "Oh. I had no idea." Peyton paused, "That's too bad. Guess we know why Bobby's playing like he is. Poor guy."

Thea stiffened and turned to face her. "What?"

Peyton just shrugged, looking uncomfortable and confused. "She just said you broke up...I was saying that sucks..."

"Yeah, but why do you assume he's broken-hearted and wounded and shit? He's *fine*. We weren't serious or anything."

Peyton's eyebrows climbed high as she stared at Thea, open mouthed. "I think I'm missing some—"

"We left it on good terms. He's fine. I'm fine. He's not a story."

This time Peyton's back shot straight. "If you think for one minute that I'd write a story about Bobby's heartbreak, then you don't know me at all. One, because I would be laughed out of the newsroom for focusing on a player's *relationship* drama, but two, he's my friend—I know exactly how publicity-averse he is. Not every guy spends every free moment organizing a record-setting inaugural fundraiser event and then hands it off to a teammate who needs good publicity, so he doesn't get axed. You don't do that shit to friends."

Thea felt like a Cyclones beanie had been pulled down over her ears. The roar of the crowd faded into brown noise as she took in Peyton's insulted expression.

"What?"

Peyton curled her lip just enough to let Thea know that she made a big misstep with her.

"Nothing. I'm outta here. I want a different angle to finish the game." Peyton stood, walked in front of Thea to the stairs, and then started the long walk back up to the mezzanine.

Fuck.

Thea turned to look back at the ice, the unease in her stomach starting to bubble its way up and into her throat.

Everything was just...

It was all just too much...

Her dad. The job offer. Bobby. Ian. Lila. Now Peyton.

It was too much.

Sucking in a deep breath so she wouldn't cry, Thea centered herself and channeled her father. He'd redirect and focus on the game—so that's what she would do too.

Chapter Thirty-Six
April 13, Tuesday
Bobby

The third period was brutal. Though Bobby's unexpected and unpredictable play style had thrown the other team off during the second period, they had strategized during their intermission and had adjusted accordingly.

But what they shifted to account for Bobby's countermeasure left an opening that Ian took complete advantage of. He was back to controlling the game with an intensity that Bobby wished Ian had all the time.

There were no sloppy passes, no offside calls, no intentional fuck-arounds done only to irritate Bobby.

Ian wanted to *win*.

And he was doing everything in his power to make it so.

Bobby fought back the shadow of a grin. If Ian could play with this sort of camaraderie with him all the time, he'd probably hate the guy less—you know, if he wasn't about to steal away the love of his life.

Bobby knew there was no way that Ian would feel comfortable with Bobby and Thea resuming their original friendship. Not after...everything.

That was, if they even could. Last night might have irrevocably shifted things forever.

The play was fast and violent, and the refs were missing calls left and right, which caused things to deteriorate...fast.

Ilya and Tommy were having incredible nights on defense and the rest of the team was stepping up and dominating when they were out there. With minutes to go in the third period, frustrations were mounting.

Ian, who was normally invisible in his taunts on other players, made one comment too many. The retreating player after the icing call slammed to a stop and spun around, charging back toward Ian with a vengeance.

The teammates on the ice were able to intercept the feuding players but after that, the tension only escalated.

If Ian didn't have the skills to back it up, the guy would have gotten the piss kicked out of him years ago. More than he already had, that is.

Ian's shot clock counter was defying the odds at this point, and it was only a matter of time before one of his snipes slipped past the Grizzlies' goalie. Comparatively, Bobby's opportunities had stalled out. Any momentum he had manifested in the second period was dissipating with every additional second he was on the ice.

Combined with the fury he felt every time he saw another punishing hit on his teammates go unanswered...and he wanted to roar.

In a rare moment where Bobby found himself on the bench next to Tommy, he turned to the man, ready to chew him out for not exacting punishment when he saw Tommy lower his head and grimace in pain, doing his best to block his reaction from the televised cameras.

Bending low, Bobby asked, "What's going on? What hurts? How bad?"

Tommy winced, his face still pinched in pain and his breathing short and fast. "I think a couple of ribs broke during that last hit. Definitely have a broken finger on my left hand, and..." Tommy swallowed hard and kept his face below the top of the boards as he gasped out, "And I'm gonna need someone to look at my knee."

Fuck.

Tommy had a not-so-great history with pain meds, so he was in for a long recovery if his status report was correct.

That also meant that Cyclones were left shorthanded for an enforcer on the ice. Jason could fight pretty damn well, but he was the centerpiece of his line. They had a couple of other guys that could hold their own, but they wouldn't do much damage besides earning themselves a five-minute major.

Shit.

As one of their coaches barked out Bobby's line, he adjusted his grip on his stick and prepared to fly onto the ice. They just had to last until one of Ian's rockets found its way into the back of the net. They just had to hold the Grizzlies off long enough for Ian to do what Ian did best—win.

The Grizzlies landed hit after damaging hit.

After tangling with one of them in front of the net while their goalie made another save, one of them chuckled and gave Bobby a taunting look.

"They got you pussy-whipped now, don't they? They took your balls and sliced those things right off. You're neutered, man. Useless. How does it feel?"

Bobby clenched his jaw but faced forward.

Ian...was not so even tempered.

"Feeling pretty confident for a man who's got in a total of one fight so far this season. Pretty easy to have a big mouth when other people do the fighting for you, isn't it?"

Quickly, all the teammates moved to pull the two men apart as they started chirping in each other's faces.

Luckily, no punches were thrown, and the face-off resumed as planned.

But that's where luck ran out.

Uncharacteristically, Ian lost the face-off and the play turned toward the Cyclones' end of the ice. As they shifted into defensive mode, Bobby felt a shift in the arena. With a quick look at the time remaining, Bobby cursed.

With four minutes remaining, they either had to win it now, or keep the Grizzlies from scoring a buzzer-beating goal.

Either way, stressful as fuck.

The Grizzly players started cycling through their passes, trying to find that perfect opening. The play was quick enough that Bobby's line didn't get an opportunity to sub off.

Just then, the player by the blue line saw his opening when Ian slipped a little too far out of position.

Rifling off a slapshot at over one hundred miles per hour, the puck was fired at their goalie, Teemu.

And...without thinking...Bobby shifted and slid into the projected shot path.

The pain was almost unbearable.

His outstretched leg had blocked the shot and the snap of his bone felt like it drowned out the entire arena.

A whooshing buffeted his ears as he fought to stay on his feet, to continue to provide a modicum of defense while he waited for his team to take control of the puck. Trying his best not to stumble and appear overly injured, Bobby used every ounce of willpower he had to hide the severity of the fracture.

But there was no hiding it completely.

After Ty shot the puck down to the other end and earned them an icing call, he circled around with Bobby to assess the damage, his face grim and worried.

Bobby refused to open his mouth to speak...if he did, he'd vomit everywhere.

Ignoring his teammate's concerned looks, he took his place outside of the face-off and watched in detached surprise as Ian nodded over to Ty to take the puck-drop.

Ian's intentions became clear when the Grizzly player he was matched up with started to get a little physical with each other.

One of the primary refs shouted out a stern warning to the men, "Enough is enough. I've had it. Just play the damn game. Next fight is an ejection. Period."

Ian and the opposing player backed off long enough for the ref to turn back to the players in the face-off.

The reprieve didn't last long though. Ian and the other man were right at it, swearing in each other's faces. The ref turned around, the fury clear in his face.

Bobby looked up at the clock: two minutes left.

Fuck.

The two men started shoving at each other and the crowd went wild for the promise of a fight.

Double fuck.

No way could the team afford to lose Ian on a fighting major.

But Bobby…

He was a liability out there now…and had already lost…

So…what would it hurt?

CHAPTER THIRTY-SEVEN
April 13, Tuesday
Thea

Oh, sweet baby Jesus.

Oh, holy fuck.

It was like the whole arena paused as they waited for Bobby to get back up.

It wasn't more than two seconds, but for Thea, it was a lifetime.

Her heart thumped in an even pattern that left breathless and lightheaded.

The Grizzlies still hadn't shot the puck, instead they recovered it after it deflected from Bobby's leg, and now they were playing a taunting game of keep-away while they brought out their second line change.

Fuck.

Bobby was clearly injured as he did his best to put most of his weight on his right leg. Playing to their advantage, the other team would deke to pull him to his left, and then go right again, trusting that his recovery would be shot.

For the most part, they were right, but they didn't account for the pain he was willing to put himself in.

He managed to prevent any shots from being delivered from his area and when the player passed the puck off, Ty managed to win it and send it flying down the ice.

Icing.

Fuck.

The fans were still on their feet, and all eyes were still on Bobby as he skated away from a small huddle of his teammates.

Was he okay?

Thea absently tasted blood and looked down. Little river of red dripped down her thumb and she winced, wiping her chin to get rid of any evidence and looked up to the Jumbotron to inspect Bobby's zoomed in face.

Oh, God, he was in *pain*.

His eyes were *haunted*.

They needed to get him off the ice and to the x-ray machine. Playing on a broken bone...

He was only making it worse!

As Ty skated into the face-off circle to take the drop, the crowd erupted.

Confused, Thea looked around until she saw Ian and a Grizzly defenseman getting in each other's faces.

After some sharp remarks from the refs and some teammates keeping their heads, the players were separated, and the linesperson prepared to drop the puck again.

Only for the arena to erupt once more and Ian and the opposing player started shoving each other. Their yells could be heard even over the din of the crowd.

Just as Ian dropped his gloves and raised his fists—

Bobby skated between them and got in the defenseman's face.

Time stalled and Thea watched in horror as it played out in slow motion.

In another uncharacteristic move, Bobby got into the man's face, but didn't touch him at all.

Instead, his face twisted into a mocking taunt that would send anyone over the edge. The jumbotron was zoomed in on his face and Thea gripped the top edge of the dasher boards in front of her, her knuckles turning white.

As the players and refs tried to pull the two men away from each other, Bobby continued mouthing off at the guy but allowed himself to be led away.

But the other guy wasn't having it.

Breaking free from the men restraining him, the player practically flew across the ice.

Pushing Ty out of the way, Bobby shielded his friend from an uncontrolled, open hit to the back.

Rather than circling Bobby and engaging in a normal ice hockey fight, the crowd collectively gasped as the man speared Bobby with his shoulder and tackled him down onto his back.

Thea's chest compressed with the thwack of contact made between the ice and the back of Bobby's head.

Thank God for helmets, but even so...

As the referee and a linesman moved to pull the man off Bobby, Thea could still see Bobby chirping something up at the man.

"God, what's gotten into him?" she muttered, unable to tear her eyes away.

"Something not good," Rachel muttered back from seats away.

With a sharp gasp, Thea watched as the player ripped free from the officials' holds and back onto Bobby.

Thea let out a cry as the man's right fist pummeled into Bobby's face.

Again.

And again.

And again.

Oh, God.

A fight was supposed to be over once a player was down on the ice!

Thea had tears streaming down her cheeks and she got as close to the glass as possible, trying to get a better view. Frantically, her eyes darted up to the jumbotron to see if they were showing Bobby's face, but they had panned away and showed the officials practically dragging the rabid player to the bench.

Just as Thea was about to find a way to see if Bobby was okay, Ian and Ty managed to scoop Bobby up and position his arms around their shoulders. Slowly, to roaring cheers and sharp whistles, the men brought Bobby to the bench where he slowly, so slowly, stepped through the open door.

Thea's heart stuttered painfully when his step looked rocky and uncoordinated.

Oh, *fuck*.

She placed a hand to her heart and pushed hard, trying to slow it down.

Bobby wasn't jerky coming off the ice. He was liquid. He was water. He was fluid and superhuman.

Thea held her breath as she watched him gingerly wobble and out of sight.

Just then, the referee skated to the center of the ice, and announced that both men were ejected from the game for misconduct.

The fans *lost their minds*.

Thea bit her lip and recoiled as the crowd jeered and booed the refs. Items and trash were tossed onto the ice and the refs skated over to the officials' crease. After chatting with the timekeeper there for a moment, two of the officials split off and started talking with the coaches of the respective teams. A few seconds were added to the clock...like it mattered with Bobby's unknown injuries.

In an attempt to distract the furious fans, the media team started playing more clips from her father's interviews, featuring one where Bobby was sitting with Ian and Ilya. The sounds of the arena, the cheers and jeers of the fans, faded into the background as she focused solely on Bobby's young face. It wasn't more than three years ago, but he looked so...different. Young and cocky. It was cute.

As the spectators flipped their attention to the large screens around the arena, it gave the referees time to signal for a quick, impromptu, Ice Crew cleanup.

Thea clenched her fists, wishing she could check in on Bobby and see if he was okay.

She hadn't gotten any further details on Bobby's ultimatum from the coach, but Thea did know there *was* one. Bobby refused to talk about it, so she was in the dark on the fine print but...did that count as a fight? He had thrown off his gloves as the man speared him to the ice.

But he hadn't punched back, even though he had gotten ejected for fighting.

Stupid interpretation of the rules.

So...even though the refs considered this a fight...did his coach?

Why did he take the fight for Ian!? What was he thinking!?

Thea dropped her eyes to her feet and then collapsed into her chair, her heart aching.

She knew why...she didn't have to wonder.

Ian was playing better that night. Bobby was off. He wanted a win for his team...and for Thea.

And he was already injured so it was no big loss...

Because it was so inherently Bobby to let himself get hurt for the benefit of others.

Thea rubbed at her eyes and sucked in another shaky breath. She needed to go to him.

Now.

She needed to check on him, but she also needed to tell him that she loved him and that she was stupid and that she was sorry.

Maybe not all in that order.

But she needed to get to him *now*.

She couldn't let him spend another minute thinking she was going to go on a date with Ian. Sure, he might have a broken leg, jaw, and lost his job, so her relationship status might not rank on his priorities, but...

She needed to tell Frank that she didn't want the rinkside post-game tonight; she needed to check on her man.

If he'd have her.

Before leaving, Thea bent down to grab her water bottle and froze when she heard Lila's question to Rachel and Brian behind them.

"Do either of you have Bobby's number? I want to shoot him a text."

Thea couldn't stop herself from sitting up straight and turning to face her.

"What?"

Lila turned her head slightly and faced Thea, a worried look on her face. "You have his number. Can I have it please, I want to shoot him a text."

Thea's face felt frozen as she stared at Lila.

She *had* to be joking.

Lila waited expectantly, her face turning more and more confused as Thea sat there unmoving.

"Okay, so *you* don't want him, but you don't want anyone else to have him either. Good to know..." Lila muttered as she rolled her eyes and turned back to Rachel and Brian.

Brian chuckled and ran his finger over his phone's screen as he searched. "Nope. Don't have it. I'm surprised you don't, given how close he is with Thea."

Lila wrinkled her nose and looked at Thea for a frustrated heartbeat before turning back to him. "He was *her* friend, not *mine*. I'm not even sure he knows I exist. But, if she's moved on with Ian, then I'm sick of waiting. So, I need his—"

"I have it." Rachel was running her finger over her own screen, her eyebrows bunched as she scrolled. "Here. 413-555-0110."

On instinct, her brain hummed along: oh, one, one, oh.

As the realization hit her, Thea's breath caught in her throat, a surge of adrenaline coursing through her veins. The room seemed to tilt as she turned to face Rachel, her heart pounding with shock and disbelief.

Everything around her blurred, the air thick with an unsettling realization.

CHAPTER THIRTY-EIGHT

April 13, Tuesday
Thea

"Oh, one, one, oh," Lila repeated distractedly, typing it into her phone and then turning forward as her fingers flew over the screen.

Thea's heart stuttered, a hollow thud that seemed to echo through her entire body. Her ears rang faintly, as if the world had suddenly turned to white noise, drowning out everything except those numbers—413-555-0110. A chill swept down her spine, crawling over her skin like the first touch of winter, cold and unbidden.

Oh, one, one, oh.

Oh, one, one, oh.

Oh, one, one, oh.

The tune she had made up played mockingly in her head. The number from her father's notebook. The notebook where he had penned countless details about his job, interviews, and players. And now, in the cruel clarity of hindsight, a number not associated with Ian, but with Bobby.

Bobby.

He had interviewed Bobby *and* Ian that day. As well as Ilya and others.

Ian had mentioned how the pair had talked about books and had essentially forgotten he existed.

Her father's new TBR pile...

Oh, one, one, oh.

How many nights had she spent, her stomach tight with confusion, wondering what her father saw in Ian that made him so perfect for her? All this time, she was focused on Ian when she should have been paying attention to someone else.

Wait...how was Lila texting that number?

When Thea called it years ago, it was—

"Huh. That's weird. It bounced back as undeliverable. Are you sure you gave me the right number?" Lila turned around to face Rachel, her forehead wrinkled.

The arena spun slightly, the world tilting as a vertigo of confusion and grief for her massive mistakes hit her.

With a blush blooming on her cheeks, Rachel shot Thea an apologetic look before turning back to Lila. "Bobby and I had a short...thing...a few years ago." She turned to Thea and spoke fast, "like, *ages*, ago. Like, before you even joined the Chill Chasers..."

Thea's eyes focused on Rachel's lips, moving slowly as if underwater. Everything was disjointed and Thea couldn't feel her face.

She had been chasing a mirage, one crafted by her own hand, while the oasis had been beside her all along, unnoticed, unappreciated.

"—the number is from a few years ago, though, so he might have changed it since then..." Rachel had turned back to Lila. She shot a concerned frown at Thea before looking down at her phone again. "Let me see if I have anything else..."

Thea slowly faced forward, her movements stiff and painful.

Okay. Okay. Breathe.

The realization of her colossal fuckup hit her like a sucker punch to the gut, knocking the wind out of her lungs.

Bobby. It had been *Bobby* who her father had envisioned by her side, not Ian.

The weight of it all crashed down on her, threatening to swallow her whole.

All that wasted time...

Thea had spent years chasing after a phantom, suffocating her own desires, all in a futile attempt to fulfill her father's last wish. A wish that she had totally, monumentally misinterpreted.

And, in the process, confused and hurt a lot of fucking people.

How could she have been so blind?

Not only that, but why did she let some random note on her dad's disorganized notebook dictate so much of her life?

It was like coming up for air after being under the surface for too long.

The magnitude of her actions and mistakes hit her like a freight train.

Why had she allowed herself to be ensnared by the notions of a hastily scribbled note, letting it dictate the course of her life? Why had she granted it such power, clinging to it as her final tether to her father's memory? He was gone, and she had countless other memories and mementos to stay connected to him. Yet, she had clung to that note with a desperation bordering on obsession, never questioning its true meaning.

She always told Bobby that her dad thought Ian was her soulmate—like it was an ironclad fact—but she never shared the pages with him, offering him the full picture of why she thought that. She had dreaded his scrutiny and pity. Thea had feared that he'd dismiss the note as nothing more than a vague whisper of intention or maybe even say that she grossly misinterpreted it in her grief.

Well, he would have been right.

Her heart had yearned for the illusion of a final connection to her father—one final way to make him happy—and it blinded her to the truth.

To honor that misinterpreted note, she had betrayed herself, Bobby, Ian, and even Lila, all in the name of a fantasy that had never existed.

Thea's chest tightened, her breaths coming in shallow gasps as panic clawed at her throat. She felt dizzy and disoriented, as if the arena was in the middle of an earthquake.

The game was continuing around her, but she was in a daze. She could see the fans standing and cheering as the final minute ticked down. Absently, she registered that the Cyclones were on offense, and they were setting up an opportunity for a game-winning shot.

Drunk like, she stumbled away from her seat and onto the rubber flooring behind the Zamboni gate. The Ice Crew members standing there exchanged concerned glances as she leaned against the boards for support. With each step, guilt and self-hate weighed heavy on her shoulders, threatening to suffocate her.

Ignoring the sudden siren blast behind her, she pressed on, her mind consumed by how selfish she had been. The cheers of victory felt distant and hollow, drowned out by the numbness of the guilt she was grappling with. As she disappeared into the dimly lit tunnel leading back to the locker rooms, the floor vibrated with the celebrations from the arena above, a painful contrast to her own feelings of defeat.

CHAPTER THIRTY-NINE
April 13, Tuesday
Thea

With trembling hands, Thea made her way to the locker room so she could find Bobby.

Lila's words from earlier in the afternoon echoed in her head, each syllable stabbing at her heart like tiny daggers.

Looking back at the adoring, tender, and teasing way that Bobby acted with her...

Yeah...

Thea hung her head and sighed.

How could she have missed Bobby's feelings for her all this time?

Ian wasn't going to lose any sleep over her canceled pursuit of him, but Lila...

That was a tough one.

Thea knew Lila had a crush on Bobby. Just as she knew Bobby made it very clear he wasn't interested.

Now she knew *why*.

But that still didn't excuse the fact that she'd rubbed her 'relationship', no matter how fake, in everyone's faces—including Lila's—without giving her the courtesy of explaining it first.

On the flip side, though...it's not like friends couldn't crush on the same guy.

What if Thea woke up one day and randomly realized that she was in love with Bobby?

Was she just supposed to never date Bobby ever because her friend announced that she had a crush on him first?

Girl code was confusing.

But so were hearts.

And as much as she loved Lila...she loved Bobby more.

Hell, if Thea was willing to spurn the man her beloved father chose for her and still prepare to choose Bobby, then the girl code played no part here.

Did that make her a terrible friend?

Maybe. Probably.

Tears pricked at the corners of her eyes as she grappled with the weight of it all. She had spent so long chasing a fantasy, so long trying to live up to a vision that was never truly hers. And in the process, she had lost sight of herself, of her own dreams and desires.

And worse, she had been selfish, blind to the pain she was causing in those dearest to her.

Looking down at the compass tattoo, a newfound determination stirred within her. She couldn't change the past; couldn't undo the mistakes she had made. But she could choose how to move forward. She could choose to let go of the guilt and the regret, to forge a new path for herself—one that was guided not by her father's note, but by her own heart.

And yet, amidst the chaos and guilt of her thoughts, one nugget saved her from totally spiraling: she *had* made a choice. Before Rachel had even uttered the phone number, Thea was prepared to cast aside her misguided attempts to date Ian. She had chosen Bobby, despite the cloud it cast over her heart and her father's memory. This wasn't a fallback. This wasn't a safety blanket. Bobby wasn't her choice now that she knew she had 'Daddy's approval.'

Even so, the relief she felt that her dad would be happy for her...it felt like standing under a tropical waterfall. Thea felt a strange sense of peace wash over her.

She had chosen herself. She had chosen love, real love, over duty and obligation.

She couldn't change the past, but she could make amends for her mistakes.

And the first step in that journey was finding Bobby.

· · · ● · ● · ● · · ·

Her jogging footfalls echoed in the empty corridors as she made her way to the locker room.

Her favorite security guard, Kevin, stood at the entrance, his usually stern expression softening when he caught sight of her.

"You fixin' to get me in trouble, Miz Sharppe?"

"I'll do my best not to, Kevin."

He gave her a somber inspection. "He's not too happy, right now."

No, he wouldn't be.

Kevin shifted and nodded toward the door. "Try to help our boy, will ya?"

Thea started to push the door but paused when she heard, "Try not to be here when Coach gets back. I can't handle another lecture."

She shot him a small, grateful smile and entered the room, wincing as the residual smells of the players hit her.

Didn't matter how long she had played hockey; the smell would always be a punch to the nose.

The locker room was eerily quiet compared to the chaos outside.

Thea's pulse quickened as she spotted Bobby sitting on a bench, his head buried in his hands, elbows resting on his thighs, his hastily splinted and ice-applied leg stretched out before him, and his hockey gear was piled in a heap in front of his stall. His dark hair was damp with sweat, plastered to his forehead, while his body moved with the force of his deep breaths.

"Bobby...are you okay?" Thea's voice cracked as she approached him cautiously, her heart constricting at the sight of him.

Bobby jerked and stiffly turned to face her, his face red, bloody, and sweaty. The weight of his gaze bore into hers, and she could see the uncertainty flickering behind his already-swollen eyes. Pain wrinkled his forehead and the bruised skin by his eyes.

"Dude. Did they give you anything for the pain?" Thea approached and sat next to him on the long, dark wooden bench.

"They did. Want to bring me to the hospital for more tests and shit too, but I insisted they let me grab my stuff." His lips were barely moving.

And if that didn't indicate his pain level, she didn't know what would.

"Good, I'll grab your stuff." She slid off the bench, trying not to breathe, and sorted through his belongings to figure out what needed to be brought home with him. "You shouldn't have scared them off, they could be doing this right now, not me."

Bobby chuffed out a weak but strained laugh and Thea turned to give him a tentative smile.

At his confused expression, she tried to hide her wince and went back to grabbing handfuls of stuff.

"Bea...why are you here?" Bobby asked, attempting a casual tone that didn't quite hide the exhaustion and agony in his words.

She tried not to freeze and die on the spot when presented with his transparent pain.

This pain had nothing to do with his injury.

"Where else would I be?"

"Celebrating with everyone else? Doing Chill Chaser shit? Kissing Ian on the ice at the spot where he completed his hat trick?" Bobby's suggestions increased in sharpness and Thea felt her shoulders tense.

Trying not to let each question pulverize her already pretty-well-tenderized heart, she blithely asked without turning, "Ah, so it was Ian that scored then. That's good. He played well tonight." She paused and scooped her collection of Bobby's belongings into her arms and turned. "You, on the other hand, Jesus. Total nightmare. We'll dissect it on the way to the hospital. And tomorrow. And the day after that. And maybe at Christmas too."

He gave her a steady, level look that had her false bravado blowing away like a leaf in the breeze.

Fuck.

"Bea..."

"Fine! I just...I made a mistake, okay?" Thea's voice wavered as she admitted it, her eyes locking onto Bobby's with a mix of desperation and regret. "I screwed up, Bobby. Big time. I let my own stupid obsession with living out my dad's dream, and I hurt you in the process." The words tumbled out of her like a dam breaking free. She blinked back tears, suddenly feeling more exposed than she ever had in her skimpiest Chill Chaser uniform.

There was a vulnerability in his eyes that she had never seen before, as if he were bracing himself for a blow that would shatter him completely. Softly, he asked, "How'd you hurt me?"

Well. Here went nothing.

"Do you love me?"

"Of course."

"No." Thea shook her head. "Not like that. Like..." God, she felt like she was in middle school again. "Like...do you *love-me* love me?"

Bobby sat back and his lips twisted to the side as he scrutinized her.

"Who's asking?"

Thea rubbed the toe of her sneaker into the rubber flooring, looking up and over his head.

"*I* can't be asking?"

"No."

Damn, that answer was fast.

Somewhat insulted, Thea narrowed her eyes on him and stuck out a hip—Ice Queen Attitude.

"And why not?"

"Because you tend to be somewhat self-concentrated. Not in a mean way...you have too much going on in your own head and you get stuck there sometimes." He paused and gave her a soft look to let her know he meant no offense. "So...what happened?"

Thea wrinkled her nose at him and almost imperceptibly, his body loosened.

She hid her tidal wave of relief.

"Lila might have said something…"

"Of course she did," Bobby said with a sigh and a shake of his head. He dropped his gaze to his feet and then back up to hers. "And?"

Was he serious? Talk about playing dense and making her work for it!

Then again…it was nothing less than what she deserved.

But…

Thea stared hard at him, scrutinizing his unusually bland expression. Then she noticed the corner of his lip twitch.

The bastard!

He was totally doing this on purpose.

She snarled at him, and his grin burst through.

"Okay, so you want to know if I *love-you* love you." Bobby then twisted, grabbed his abandoned crutches that were leaning on the bench next to him, and threw them under his armpits before letting out a soft grunt as he stood. "Of course, I *love-you* love you. Always have. How many guys make sure they store tampons in their car for their friends? Or bring them Tums at four am when they've drank too much?"

"One time." Thea protested with false indignation, trying hard not to throw herself in his arms and make a total fool of herself.

"One time too many," he corrected. He gave her a small, tender smile that had Thea's heart racing. "So, Lila ran her mouth and, I'm assuming bitched you right-the-fuck out because she has a crush on me and thought that you broke my heart when you used me to get Ian's attention."

Thea's throat felt taut, and her heart was pumping in an irregular rhythm that had her fearing she was going to pass out and crash into Bobby, further breaking his leg…they still needed to get to the hospital.

"Didn't I?" Thea's voice felt small and tight as she stared up beseechingly into Bobby's beautiful brown eyes. "Didn't I break your heart?"

He stared at her, not saying a word, his bruised face studying her.

When Thea thought she would explode from the silence, he reached a hand up and chucked her jaw with a gentle fist. "Yeah, but you're here now, right?"

Thea sucked in a ragged breath. Feeling the tears collect in her eyes and her throat completely catch fire, she could only nod at him, otherwise, she'd open the floodgates.

Affectionately, he brought the same hand back to her cheek and stroked a thumb over it, his eyes staring at her in wonder. Thea couldn't resist briefly closing her eyes at the loving touch.

"Looks like I owe Lila some flowers."

Thea's lips trembled as she fought back an emotionally deranged laugh.

Bobby grinned, his white teeth flashing under his dark beard, and his lip split at the movement.

Knowing their time was almost up—and really wanting to get him to the hospital—Thea let out her frantic confession. "I hate that I hurt you, Bobby. I hurt you with my stupid fake dating scheme, and I hurt you by not seeing what was right in front of me. I was so caught up in this fantasy of what I thought I was supposed to want that I didn't stop to consider what I actually wanted, or who I actually wanted it with." She reached up and put her hands on either side of his face, framing it and being careful of the bruises forming there. "I love you, Bobby. I love you more than I've ever loved anyone, and I'm so sorry for everything I put you through. I know I can't take back the heartache I caused, but I want to make it right. I want to be *with you*, Bobby. I want to be your girlfriend...for real this time."

A slow, peaceful smile spread across his face, lighting up his features in a way that made her heart skip a beat.

"And your dad's opinion about Ian being the one for you?" he asked, his voice hoarse.

"I decided it was irrelevant. I was on my way to you—I would have found you sooner, but something came up and...well, I can tell you that part while we wait for the slowpokes at the hospital to triage you."

"Regular citizens get triaged by slowpokes. *Bobby Davidson* doesn't get triaged slowly." He gave her a teasing look. "But you're more than welcome to tell me the story there anyways." Bobby looked toward the door and frowned. "We really should make our way out of here."

When Bobby moved as if he was going to start crutching away from her, Thea snatched his arm and held him still. "Wait. That's it? No groveling? No explanation? No reunion kiss that curls my toes and sets my heart at ease? Just...'We should make our way out of here?'" Her voice was shrill, and incredulity filled her every pore.

Bobby stared at her, his eyebrows shooting high, before looking back to the door. "Are you seriously getting upset that I didn't make you grovel or demand an explanation of everything right here, right now?"

Well...when he put it like that...

"Bea, you make my head spin." Bobby shook his head and dipped his face so it was only inches away. "You're lucky I love you and your dramas." Then with a sigh that did nothing to detract from just how happy it made him, Bobby leaned all the way in and gave Thea the sweetest, tenderest, most loving kiss of her life.

Thea's toes curled, her hands went up to his face, and she couldn't stop her lips from forming a smile while they shared their heartwarming kiss. She pulled away just enough to breathe out, "Does that mean you'll marry me?"

He chuckled, his eyes combing her face, his own expression filled with wonder. "Let's not get too hasty here. You're talking to a very injured, and very *unemployed* man. Let's see if you like where my next team is…if there is a next team, and then we'll talk. I know you're a 'Cyclones girl' through and through. I don't want to put you in a position where you have to leave."

Thea pulled him in for another firm kiss, closing her eyes and putting every fiber of love possible into the kiss. Then she pulled away again and said, "Nah, I'm a 'Bobby girl' through and through. There's not a place on this planet where I won't follow you." She gave him another quick peck, "But we do need to get going, I want the doctors to check you out." Gingerly, she pressed at the biggest cut on his lip and tried to hide her scowl as she thought of the douche who fought unfairly.

"Can't even feel it," he mumbled, his voice low and comforting.

Didn't matter. The guy was getting his tires slashed the next time Thea was in Boston.

Thea grabbed the items she had dropped unceremoniously earlier, and she followed Bobby into the hall, away from where the team could be heard charging down the tunnel with their raucous celebration.

As they turned the corner to get her own stuff from the Chill Chaser locker room, Bobby let out a soft chuckle and shook his head, navigating on the crutches like a man who had spent a lot of time in them.

"What's funny?" Thea asked, smiling at him.

God, she was so…happy.

This was right.

This was…everything.

Bobby shook his head and kept crutching along, a lighthearted smile on his face and he looked at her briefly before glancing back where he was placing his crutches.

"Just thinking how awkward it would be to be picked up by the Grizzlies."

Thea stumbled and tightened her hold on the things in her arms.

Bobby just chuckled and shook his head again, the hilariousness of the idea clearly speaking to him.

His head *had* hit the ice pretty hard...

"Is the team transporting you to the hospital or am I driving?"

Bobby frowned for a moment, trying to remember.

"Actually...not sure. If you're driving me though, we gotta grab some food for Fido before we leave the parking garage."

Okay...maybe he did have a concussion.

Concerned, Thea stopped walking and waited for Bobby to pause as well. Then she walked up to him and assessed his pupils. She started asking concussion protocol questions and he gave her a confused look.

"What are you doing?"

"Bobby. I'm serious. Answer the questions. Did they check your head?" She lowered her hands to his wrist and tried to search for his pulse.

Did his pulse even matter? She had no idea, but it seemed like a good data point to have in case he collapsed at any minute.

"Why do you..." Understanding flooded his expression and he stared at her with an affectionate and resigned smile. "We're not taking him home. He doesn't like people touching him. We all bring him food. Ilya even made him a small doghouse that he left in the back corner where no one parks. We can't seem to catch him, not even with food-baited traps. Pup's a genius. So, we have a vet come by and check on him from afar. He got a round of shots a few months ago and we haven't been able to get near him since. I wanted to drop off some food while I was thinking about it. No concussion. Just a team dog that we try to keep as safe as we can."

Thea stood frozen staring up into Bobby's patient expression. "We have a dog, and you didn't tell me!" Her loud question echoed off the wall and Bobby winced, a big smile on his face.

As he turned to continue toward her locker room, Thea jogged a few steps to pull even with him. "Bobby! We have a dog, and you didn't tell me? I could have been leaving treats! Or snacks. Or blankets. Or something! Bobby Davidson, so help me—"

Abruptly, Bobby stopped, pivoted and pulled her into an intense kiss that had her leaning into him, her armful of stuff clenched tight and pushing into their chests.

He pulled away and gazed down at her.

Silently, she met his gaze, her heart and mind still racing.

Bobby gave a satisfied nod and started crutching away again, muttering, "I like that new perk. Stops a drama right in its tracks."

Distractedly, Thea bustled after him, trying to wrap her head around what just happened.

As it caught up to her, she gasped and whirled to face him. "You said you like my dramas!"

He briefly turned to inspect her before facing forward again, his handsome face utterly happy and at peace.

"Yeah, I do. But I like your kisses more."

Basking in his familiar teasing, forgiveness, and love, Thea sighed a happy sigh—confident that she had finally found her true north.

CHAPTER FORTY

Epilogue: September 25, Saturday
Thea

The dimly lit parking garage of the hockey arena seemed to take on a life of its own, the fluorescent lights casting eerie shadows against the concrete walls as Thea, Bobby, Ty, and Ilya huddled in the back of Ilya's pickup truck. Their breathing was the only sound as they waited for a sighting of the stray dog that had adopted the garage as its home.

"It's been an hour," whispered Thea. "How much longer are we supposed to wait?"

Disappointment flooded her. There was a small part of her that hoped that they'd be able to see the pooch and offer it some food.

Every time they called a dog rescue agency, they were met with the same results: a triggered cage, missing food, no dog, and the promise that they'd keep trying.

The trail cams that the different agencies had left, all showed the same thing: one *clever* fucking dog who needed a bath and a good meal.

"Shh," Bobby cautioned softly.

The group peeked over their sides of the pickup bed, their eyes scanning the area with hopeful longing, each eager to glimpse the elusive creature.

Unable to stand the silence, Thea ventured again, "Ty, are you ready for your debut into polite society next weekend?"

Ty groaned and thunked his forehead against the edge of the pickup bed.

Not because she broke the silence and possibly scared the dog.

"Don't remind me. Tommy already has me convinced that I'm going to get up there and be bid on by a bunch of pervy old ladies."

"Better than not being bid on at all?" Bobby added with a soft chuckle.

Ty groaned again, his forehead thunks echoing within the concrete hardscape of the parking garage. "Great. Now I have *another* thing to worry about."

Thea laughed and smiled at him, "I promise I won't let there be crickets. Bobby has already given me strict orders to swoop in when he's about to be sold so I can snatch him at the last minute. If it looks like you need saving, I'll just write a second check."

"And if he doesn't need saving?" Ilya asked, his question quiet and calm.

Thea waved dismissively, "I'm not worried. I've heard Lexie Galloway will be there with her girlies, so I'm sure Ty will be perfectly fine."

"For the love of God, don't let her win me. I can't take that kind of drama in my life." Ty whipped around to face Thea, his bright blue eyes huge and flighty.

Bobby clapped him on the shoulder and gave him a brotherly shake. "Bea's right. A little bit of drama might do you some good. Get you out of the funk you're in."

"I'm *not* in a funk," Ty said.

"You're totally in a funk." Bobby argued as he raised an eyebrow in challenge.

"I'm *not* in a funk," Ty was quick to deny it.

"You're in a funk," Thea and Ilya said in unison.

As Ty opened his mouth to protest again, Ilya interrupted him. "I think I see something!"

Ilya pointed toward a parked car where a shadow was moving. His eyes narrowed as he tried to pinpoint the dirty dog in the darkness.

Thea tried to be quiet as she copied the others and scrambled to Ilya's side.

If the dog learned to trust them, then they could help it.

Thea's breath caught in her chest as she watched the shadows play tricks on the concrete walls, her heart pounding with anticipation. Her eyes darted from one corner of the dimly lit parking garage to another, searching for any sign of the elusive stray dog they had all come to care for.

"There!"

Her voice echoed off the cold, concrete walls and she winced as they all swiveled to stare at her.

"Sorry," she mumbled, raising her shoulders up by her ears and shrinking down into her sweatshirt.

Bobby chuckled softly and kissed her hair. "Always with the dramatics." He then turned his eyes and kept scanning the garage, shifting his weight slightly so his freshly cleared leg didn't start to ache.

Turns out, he was right—the hospital did *not* make *Bobby Davidson* wait. Instead, the Cyclones' alternate captain received surgery to repair his broken fibula the very next day. A plate and four screws later and home he went. And because Lila was still pissed at her, Thea went home with him. Within a month, all of her stuff was moved out of Lila's apartment, and she was settled in with Bobby. At first she was worried that she was moving in just to move out as soon as Bobby got the news that he was traded in the off season...

Fortunately, Cyclones' management and coaching staff liked Bobby right where he was—occasional brawler and all—and didn't actually exact any punishment for his foolish 'fight' in that last game.

Despite the iciness on Thea's friendship front, Bobby's had faced an entirely different shift.

Ian was actually pleasant to him now. Some of the players had returned back to the practice facilities to prepare for training camp and apparently Ian was committed to making amends for his past behavior.

Ian was driving Bobby nuts in a totally different way now—it was adorable.

"He just kept talking to me when we were on the bikes next to each other! It's like he didn't even care that I was trying to finish the book."

Thea had just patted his hand sympathetically and gave him a supporting, understanding smile that caused him to scowl at her and storm off to the library.

Bobby shifted again and Thea frowned at him. "Is your leg okay?"

He smiled distractedly and kept his eyes on the jungle of parked cars around them. "Yeah, why?"

"You just keep fidgeting."

He stopped his scanning and looked at her. "Do you see my thighs?"

Thea looked down at them. Big, muscular, juicy, delectable. "Yes?"

"You told us we were going to grab a bite to eat. Not eat take out in Ilya's truck bed. Nice jeans and thick thighs don't mix. You know this."

Thea looked down at her own jegging-clad thighs and then grinned up at him. "Ooops."

He gave her an adorable glower that had her leaning forward and stealing a quick kiss.

"I wanted the smell of fast food to tempt him. Forgive me?"

He wrinkled his nose but grumbled back, "Always," and then turned back to their search.

"I still can't believe you guys have been hiding this dog from me for so long," Thea added, unable to stand the silence. "What else are you keeping secret?"

"Hey, it wasn't just me," Bobby protested quietly, his dark eyes twinkling as they continued to scan. "But we just didn't want to bring attention to it and have management interfere."

"Got 'im," Ilya's whispered voice whipped through the air. They turned to see him nodding toward a nearby SUV. "Let's get out, grab your food bags."

Quietly, they all hurried to the tailgate to quietly lower themselves down.

It was almost eerie watching these three professional athletes move so slow and controlled.

Following Ilya's gaze, Thea caught sight of the dog cautiously peeking out from behind the vehicle. Its eyes were uncertain, but curious. The group collectively held their breath, not wanting to scare the timid creature away.

"Maybe he recognizes our scent from everything we've been leaving for him," Ilya suggested, his voice barely audible in the hushed atmosphere of the garage.

"Let's spread out," Ty suggested, already moving to one side a bit. "We don't want to scare him off by crowding too close together and looking too imposing."

Ilya nodded his agreement, his normally stoic expression softened by the hint of a smile, but still...the light didn't reach his eyes. It never seemed to.

As they positioned themselves around the dim garage and squatted down to seem less scary, Thea held her breath, hoping the movement didn't scare their furry friend away.

"Let's put down some food," Ilya suggested, his voice gentle.

As the group cautiously extended their hands, placing food on the ground far in front of them, the dog finally crept out from its hiding place only to pause and study them, his body vibrating.

The faint sound of a car engine echoed in the distance, casting an eerie sense of anticipation over the dimly lit parking garage.

"Let him come to us," Ilya added, his expression softening as he looked toward the dog. "Trust takes time."

"Hey there, buddy," Ty whispered softly, his calloused fingers lightly brushing against the cold concrete floor as he extended his hand toward the dog.

The dog took a tentative step forward, its eyes darting between the outstretched hands filled with treats. It sniffed at the air cautiously, its movements betraying an innate wariness born from a life spent on the fringes of human society.

Surprisingly, the animal inched closer to the hockey team captain—the largest of the men—its ears perking up ever so slightly as it took its halting steps.

"That's it," Ilya murmured, his deep accent vibrating through the air like a soothing balm. The dog hesitated, its eyes flickering between the group of friends and the tempting morsels by them as it weighed its options.

"Keep coming," Ilya crooned, his face softening as the dog took another tentative step forward.

Thea's heart pounded in her chest; her body tensed with anticipation.

It was just a stray dog...but even so, it felt *important* to help him.

Thea felt Bobby waddle up next to her, keeping low and slow so it didn't frighten the dog.

Besides a small ear twitch in their direction, the dog kept his eyes on Ilya.

Bobby wrapped a warm arm around Thea's shoulders, and she leaned into him, taking a deep breath of his wintery smell.

They all held their breath as the medium-sized mutt got within five feet of Ilya, at this point slunk so close to the ground that his belly was nearly touching it. It was covered in so much dirt and mud that it was impossible to tell its true coloring or even its age.

The abrupt slam of a car door shattered the fragile moment, startling the dog and sending it darting away into the shadows.

Frustrated, they all stood up and watched the dog zip between cars and disappear altogether.

"Where the hell does he manage to hide?" Ty asked, arching his neck and looking around with a frown.

Bobby released Thea and started scooping up the food on the ground. "We've combed this place a hundred times. There's got to be a hole somewhere that we don't know about."

"Closest we've ever got to him though," Ilya remarked absently, his voice still soft and thoughtful.

Ty finished scooping up the rest of the food that they had placed down and let out a weary sigh as he stood up. Grinning, he asked, "Okay, okay. I'll break the seal. What are we naming him?"

Thea eagerly shot out her idea. "Storm?"

"Rusev?" Ilya cracked a grin.

"Prince?" Ty asked, eyes still watching where the medium-sized dog disappeared.

"Compass?" Bobby asked, throwing Thea a happy wink.

"Funk?" Thea gave Bobby's best friend a saucy smirk.

Ty narrowed his eyes on her before turning to Bobby. "She's exhausting."

Bobby pulled her in for a tight hug and pressed a firm kiss to her hair. "I know. It's awesome, isn't it?"

The men all laughed at Thea's pouty snort and eye roll. They shot out more names as they walked back to Ilya's truck.

Ilya stood apart from them, his gaze fixed on the spot where the dog had disappeared. His brow furrowed in concern, and the light that had briefly filled his eyes seemed to have faded once more.

"Are you okay, Ilya?" Thea asked softly, her voice laced with genuine concern as she broke away from the group and approached him.

"I'm fine," he replied, forcing a small smile onto his face. "I just...worry for the dog. It's not safe down here."

"We'll try again," she promised.

"And what then? We get it to trust us...just to betray it?"

Thea hesitated, not quite viewing it that way. "We're not trying to betray it by trapping it. We're trying to give it a better life."

"But what if it's happy here?"

Thea followed Ilya's gaze and started nibbling at her thumbnail. "Ignore me. It's the right thing to do. It's just funny how sometimes, the thing we want most, always seems to be impossible to have." Ilya's eyes met hers for a brief moment before flickering away again. There was a lingering sadness in his gaze—a deep-rooted pain that seemed to have taken up permanent residence in his soul.

As they made their way back to their cars, Thea wondered what had happened to Ilya in his past to cause such sorrow.

Bobby waited for her and gave her a curious look as she walked straight into his chest and hugged him tight, savoring the feel of his arms around her.

Once Ilya was on the other side of the truck, Thea felt comfortable enough to whisper in Bobby's ear, "I know my matchmaking and love-orchestrating skills leave a lot to be desired but you're Mr. Romance and your friend needs your help." Thea paused and then leaned back in, "Actually, both your friends need your help."

Bobby pulled back slightly and gave her an inquisitive look, one eyebrow climbing high.

"I'm still learning how to turn my attention outward but...your friends are hurting. Ty...he deserves to find someone who will treat him right. Someone who won't lie and hurt him like the ones you told me about. And Ilya....the look I just saw in his eyes...was the same one I used to see in yours..." She gently stroked Bobby's beard and gazed up at him, her heart full and warm, despite her worry for their friends. "That: I'm-in-love-with-someone-I-can-never-have, look."

Bobby smiled a sweet, gentle smile that had her toes curling. He placed a tender kiss on her forehead. "That's a non-starter, Bea. She's taken. I've read my share of romances and classics, sure, but I have a strict policy against cheating and homewreckers. Neither one we want to be."

Thea narrowed her eyes and challenged his assessment. "Is she carrying another couple's baby and keeping it secret? Is she an ex who dumped him on live television and then wrote a tell-all about their relationship?

Bobby smiled and shook his head. "Well, that's oddly specific."

"Is she a girl so self-centered that she can't see what's right in front of her and refuses to deviate from her plan, even if her plan is stupid?"

Bobby was outright chuckling now, his arms tight around her, holding her close.

The friction of their bodies rubbing while he chuckled? *Very nice.*

"No, Bea. She's none of those."

"Then we have work to do, my love. For Ilya and Ty. Get out your best matchmaker books when we get home. I have to study."

With that, she opened up the back door to the truck and climbed up into the back seat, sliding until she was behind the driver seat behind Ilya.

But before she closed the door and buckled her seatbelt, she heard Bobby exclaim from where he was still standing, a look of frozen shock on his face. "*That's all it will take to get you to read!?*"

The men turned to her, and she grinned. "Don't mind him. You know Bobby and his *dramatics.*"

· · · • • • • • · ·

A hidden princess, a star on ice, and a romance built on lies. Can their love outplay a royal decree and a ticking clock?

Go here now to dive into a romantic world of romance, rebellion, and rediscovery—Hooking: A Steamy Bachelor Auction, Secretly-Royal Hockey Romance – https://mybook.to/SCh

Discover More From Ella Haines

Springfield Spartans Standalone Professional Football Romances:

Crystal Clear: A Steamy Springfield Stripper *Novella*
Offensive Holding: A Forbidden Friends-To-Lovers Stripper Romance *Novella*
Illegal Substitutions: A Friends-To-Lovers Steamy Football Romance
Illegal Contact: A Steamy Workplace Football Romance
Unsportsmanlike Conduct: A Steamy Single Mother Football Romance
Intentional Grounding: A Steamy Opposites Attract Football Romance
False Start: A Steamy Second Chance Football Romance

Springfield Cyclones Standalone Professional Hockey Romances:

Boarding: A Hockey Romance *Novelette*
Embellishment: A Steamy Fake-Dating Best Friends Hockey Romance
Hooking: A Steamy Bachelor Auction Hockey Romance
Interference: A Steamy Best Friend's Ex, Hockey Romance
Misconduct: A Steamy Forbidden Psychologist-Patient Hockey Romance

Tripping: A Steamy Captain's Forbidden Little Sister Hockey
  Romance

Social Media Information - Ella Haines

Did you enjoy this book?

If so, please visit **www.EllaHaines.com** and sign up for the newsletter to receive additional scenes, freebies, and updates on future releases.

Newsletter signup here:
http://ellahaines.com/newsletter-for-freebies/

Also, if you have an eagle eye and caught any typos that slipped through the rounds and rounds of edits, take a moment and think if you'd like to be an ARC or beta reader for any future releases! If so, drop me an email! I'd love to have you on the team.

If you find any typos, you can let me know here: EllaHaines.author@gmail.com

About Author - Ella Haines

Ella Haines is a lover of all things love. Raised to know that she could be anything in the world, she made the wild and crazy decision to become a neurotic accountant. Balancing trial balances and filing taxes didn't quite fill her bucket, so she started dabbling in short stories. Those short stories evolved into complex storylines with empowered women, their families and friends, and the hunky men who adore them.

Request For Review

If this book brought you a smile and you think others might enjoy
it, please review it on your purchasing platform
(and copy it to Goodreads if you're willing and able).

This helps to spread the word about the book. Social proof to other
readers is important and helps them find their next favorite read.

It also brings me joy and keeps me writing <3

Content/Trigger Warnings

Warning:

This book will contain explicit language, a deceased father due to drunk driving, a resulting PTSD-like relationship with alcohol, and <u>**steamy**</u> **sexy times**. The narrative includes a flawed heroine who gradually learns to become more aware of and considerate towards others. If these are triggering for you – here is your warning to maybe avoid this book. Regardless, I promise there will be an HEA.

This book is a work of my imagination, and any mistakes are entirely my own.

Though I have experienced and witnessed the impact of alcoholism within my own family growing up, I owe a huge thank you to my beta reader who courageously shared her own experiences and trauma with me. Her insights were invaluable in helping to craft a story that is both realistic and complex.

As always, a big thank you to my editor and proofreader.

Made in the USA
Middletown, DE
13 August 2024